"Hello, Adam. Welcome back."

"Hello, Mrs. Morgan," he replied, and Lacy wondered whether anyone else could hear the slow, scathing emphasis on her name. "You're looking particularly… prosperous. Marriage seems to have agreed with you."

"And traveling has obviously agreed with you, Adam," she observed pointedly, scanning his well-cut tuxedo in deliberate replication of his earlier perusal of her. "You're polished to a rather high gloss yourself."

"Apparently, we've both learned the value of wearing the right uniform."

She narrowed her eyes. "Uniform?"

"Yes. After all, if you don't suit up, they won't let you play, will they?"

She took a moment to breathe past her anger. Perhaps *his* clothing was just a costume to disguise the irreverent rebel he'd always been, but her transformation was deeper, more fundamental. She hadn't "suited up" to play a poised young widow. She had changed far more than her gown. She was no longer naive, desperate or foolish.

"I really wouldn't know," she said coolly. "Unfortunately, I have very little time to play. Which reminds me, I should be getting back to the other guests. Perhaps you'd like to see some of our more expensive paintings. After all, now that you've gone to the trouble of suiting up as a rich philanthropist, we wouldn't want to deny *you* the chance to get in the game."

Dear Reader,

We've all made more mistakes than we can count. We've stumbled and grumbled. We've misjudged, misbehaved and just generally messed up. The road not taken haunts us, and the road we did take is littered with our mistakes.

But sometimes we get lucky—sometimes life offers us a second chance. And, if we've learned anything, we try to do better, to be kinder, wiser, stronger. We use our new chance to fight our way to happiness.

When Adam Kendall, the hero of A *Self-Made Man*, comes back to Pringle Island, the home he left ten years ago, he isn't looking for a second chance. He's looking for revenge. Lacy Morgan, the childhood sweetheart he abandoned, doesn't want to start over, either. She just wants to be left alone.

But somehow these two wounded people, who thought it was too late for happiness, discover that they learned something very special during those lonely years apart.

They learned how to forgive. And they learned how to love.

I hope you enjoy their story. And I hope that your days, too, will be filled with love and happiness...and all the second chances you need!

Warmly,

Kathleen O'Brien

A Self-Made Man
Kathleen O'Brien

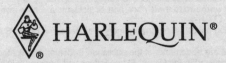

HARLEQUIN®

TORONTO • NEW YORK • LONDON
AMSTERDAM • PARIS • SYDNEY • HAMBURG
STOCKHOLM • ATHENS • TOKYO • MILAN • MADRID
PRAGUE • WARSAW • BUDAPEST • AUCKLAND

ISBN 0-373-70967-6

A SELF-MADE MAN

Copyright © 2001 by Kathleen O'Brien.

This edition published by arrangement with Harlequin Books S.A.

® and TM are trademarks of the publisher. Trademarks indicated with
® are registered in the United States Patent and Trademark Office, the
Canadian Trade Marks Office and in other countries.

Visit us at www.eHarlequin.com

Printed in U.S.A.

To Manning, who proves daily that "happily ever after" isn't just something you read about in books.

CHAPTER ONE

"OH, MY LORD, WHAT'S THE matter with the baby?"
The horrified bellow could be heard fifty yards away.
"Lacy! Where are you? The baby is upside down!"

The chatter in the crowded riding arena skipped a
heartbeat. More than a hundred guests had gathered
in the cleverly converted Barnhardt stables, expecting
to be lavishly feted in return for their financial support
of the new Pringle Island General Hospital Neonatal
Unit. This development—an upside-down baby—was
clearly quite a surprise.

"Lacy! Come here!"

Under the soft light from overhead fixtures, two
dozen faces turned toward Lacy Morgan with expres-
sions of well-bred curiosity. Down along the main
aisle, which had once housed the eight Barnhardt
horses, other guests poked their heads inquisitively
out from the individual stalls, where they had been
viewing the items placed for auction.

"Lacy, come quick!" The call grew shrill. "Lacy,
for heaven's sake, come look at this baby!"

Lacy sighed internally, recognizing Tilly Barnhardt's voice immediately. No one but Tilly could hit
that particular note and hold it quite that long. And
no one but that eccentric elderly matron would have

dreamed of interrupting this glittering event, the kick-off fund-raiser for the neonatal wing, with such a dreadful caterwauling.

"Excuse me. I believe I'm being paged." Lacy bestowed an apologetic smile on her companion, a gentleman who, for the past half an hour, had been telling her everything any human could want to know about corn options—and perhaps, if she were truthful, just a little more. Murmuring reassuring noises at the other guests, she plucked a champagne flute deftly from a passing waiter's tray and, lifting her long blue silk skirt slightly with one hand, she glided across the softly polished hardwood floors toward the echoing wail.

She found her elderly friend just inside the tack room, standing in front of a huge oil painting, scowling fiercely.

"Tilly, my love, do hush." Lacy held the champagne flute out with a smile. "Half the guests think someone is being murdered in here."

"But look! Look what some fool has done!" Tilly extended one long forefinger toward the painting dramatically. "It's the Verengetti! It was our coup! The highlight of the entire show, and it's been hung *upside down!*"

Lacy patted the older woman's shoulder, her fingers encountering the familiar rough patches of worn velvet. Tilly had worn that same black velvet dress to meet two presidents, bury three husbands, and raise about five million dollars for the hospital. As the wealthy widow of Pringle Island's most beloved obstetrician, she could afford to buy a new evening gown for every night of the week. But she could also, she always said, afford not to. Her lack of pretension was one of the qualities Lacy valued most.

"It's not upside down," Lacy explained, turning her own attention to the riot of pink and blue splotches that were the Verengetti trademark. In the center the pink and blue formed a baby held in a woman's arms, and the woman was clearly standing on her head. It was probably a statement about the cosmic implications of motherhood, but Lacy knew that Tilly would find any such explanation unacceptable. "It's supposed to look like that, Tilly."

Tilly snorted. "Nonsense." She studied the painting, tilting her head at such an extreme angle Lacy began to fear that her stiff white wig might topple. "Really?" She transferred her glare to Lacy. "Like *that?*"

Lacy nodded. "I'm afraid so." She extended the champagne again, and this time Tilly took it.

"Well." The older woman drained half the flute in one swallow. "Well." She flicked a wry glance at Lacy. "I guess you'd know, with your fancy art degree and all. I guess that's the kind of stuff they teach you at graduate school nowadays."

Lacy smiled. "I'm afraid so."

It was an old joke between them. Tilly was the only woman in town who hadn't ever been impressed by Lacy's rather extensive academic credentials. Tilly's indifference had driven Lacy's late husband crazy when he'd been alive. Malcolm Morgan had wanted everyone in town to admire what a refined, intellectual trophy wife he'd created out of poor little Lacy

Mayfair—and for the most part everyone had obliged. Everyone except for Tilly. And, of course, Lacy herself.

Lacy cared less than anyone about her own transformation. After all, what did book learning have to do with appreciating art and beauty? She remembered the day ten years ago when, on a high school field trip, she had seen her first real painting. No college could teach you that sense of paralyzed awe, that sudden tingling as genius touched your soul, just as surely as a hand pressing upon your skin.

Ironically, now that Lacy gazed routinely on works of great beauty, she almost never felt that physical thrill anymore. Yes, she really was Malcolm's creation, wasn't she? Lacy Morgan, elegant in blue silk, might have learned a million facts, but she had forgotten something that scruffy little Lacy Mayfair had once known better than anyone. She had forgotten how to feel.

And it wasn't just paintings that had lost their power. After years of Malcolm's tutelage, she could identify any opera from a single musical phrase, but no aria ever sounded quite as poignant as her favorite rock and roll ballad had once sounded on an old cheap radio, while she danced with Adam Kendall in the rain....

Adam Kendall. Perhaps it was being here in these stables tonight that had conjured his name. Once, ten years ago, she and Adam had met here at midnight, searching for a place to be alone. If she let herself, she could even smell the hay again, could imagine that she saw the moonlight reflecting in the horses' dark, liquid eyes as they blinked curiously at the intruders.

But she wouldn't let herself. She shook herself mentally and took a deep breath, pressing her lips together tightly. She didn't have time to dredge any of that ancient history up right now. Not tonight.

Not ever, for that matter.

Tucking the feel of Adam's arms and the smell of freshly cut hay back into the airtight mental casket in which they'd been locked for the past ten years, Lacy borrowed a sip of Tilly's champagne and studied the Verengetti dispassionately. Did she even like the painting? She wasn't sure. But she liked the money it would bring to the hospital in tonight's silent auction. With a coldhearted objectivity that even Malcolm might have envied, she calculated how much. Fifteen thousand, perhaps? More if it weren't for the upside-down problem.

Tucking her arm through Tilly's, Lacy nudged her friend toward the central reception area. "We'd better get back," she said. "It's not going to do the neonatal unit any good if people start whispering that we're in here stringing babies upside down. And besides," she added, completely deadpan, "Howard Whitehead is eager to tell you all about corn options."

Tilly snorted. "That impossible old windbag," she said forcefully. "He knows he's going to give us ten thousand dollars tonight, but he'll insist on boring us all to death first." She glanced over at Lacy. "I swear, I don't know how you stay so calm. It's not human, damn it. Don't you ever lose your temper?"

Lacy laughed. "Not with a man who's planning to donate ten thousand dollars, I don't."

Companionably arm in arm, they wandered down the main aisle, peeking occasionally into the stalls, exchanging greetings with old friends, answering questions about the artwork. They had almost reached the arena again when Kara Karlin, one of the hospital's board of directors, came rushing toward them.

"Oh, there you are," she said breathlessly. "Lacy, you won't believe who's here tonight! And he's asking for you!"

Tilly groaned. "If it's Howard Whitehead, tell him you couldn't find us."

Kara's eyes were big brown discs glistening with excitement. "No, no. It's someone else. Someone new. Well, not really new, but—" She dragged Lacy awkwardly toward the center of the crowd while she talked. "Oh, you'll see. You just won't believe it. He's the most— I mean, talk about glamorous. I mean, he's so completely— Oh, come on, Lacy. Hurry!"

"I'm hurrying," Lacy assured her, amused and more than a little curious. Who could reduce this middle-aged matron to such babbling incoherence? She hoped it wasn't another second-rate entertainer— their quaint small-town New England streets occasionally attracted film productions. Last year a minor soap opera star had nearly brought the town to a standstill by buying condoms at the local gas station. "But, honestly, Kara, unless you want me to trip over my skirt and meet this exciting personage flat on my face, you'd better slow down."

Kara took a deep breath and squeezed Lacy's hand. "Fine. Be that way. But just look," she said excitedly, coming to a theatrical standstill and staring straight ahead, "and see for yourself!"

Lacy paused, surveying the crowd slowly, searching for the mysterious new arrival. If this were another celebrity sighting, she hoped she could muster a polite display of excitement. Sadly, she wasn't particularly impressed by actors. But that wasn't really their fault, was it? She wasn't particularly impressed by anything anymore.

She scanned the familiar faces. Howard Whitehead had snagged some other poor soul. The hospital director was lobbying the mayor. The candy stripers were bunched together, flirting with a waiter. A couple of artists whose work had been donated to the auction were happily arguing in the corner.

And then there was that group of women over by the stage, all bleached smiles and winking diamonds, all clustered around a tall, dark-haired...

The man looked up suddenly, as if he sensed her presence. He looked directly toward her, his gaze as unerring as radar. He stared at her boldly, poised, unblinking, unflinching. And her heart stood still.

Oh, dear God. It couldn't be.

But it was. Even from across the arena she could see that his eyes were blue. A deep, rich, melted-sapphire blue. As blue as her dress. And with a disturbing flash of insight she knew why she loved this dress, why she had bought it in the first place, why she wore it whenever she could. She touched her neckline, cool silk under shaking fingers, flushing instinctively, as if everyone in the room would suddenly know why, even after ten years, she still draped herself in silk the color of his eyes.

"I—" She knew Kara was waiting for a response, but she discovered that her lungs had flattened to a useless emptiness, and she couldn't speak. Her lips felt swollen, clumsy. "He—"

"Yep." Kara chuckled triumphantly, apparently interpreting the stammering as confirmation. "See what I mean?"

Yes, Lacy saw, though it hurt her. She couldn't take her gaze from him, couldn't turn away. Not one single muscle in her body seemed to be under her own control.

Her helpless shock seemed to amuse him. He watched her for a long, brazen moment, letting his own gaze wander over the elaborate French twist of her thick brown hair. *He had always preferred it loose....* Then down the low, tight bodice, the full, flowing skirt of her evening dress. *He had vowed he would buy her just such a dress someday....* And then up again, to the hand she had pressed against her breast, to the ugly square diamond she wore there. He hadn't even been able to afford a high school ring, *but...someday, Lacy. Someday.*

But someday had never come. And now she wore another man's ring. She saw his eyes harden as he stared at the diamond, and she lowered her hand nervously. She shouldn't have. It was the sign of weakness, the hint of shame he apparently had been waiting for. He watched her hide her trembling hand in the folds of her skirt. And then slowly, with an intense and private knowing, he smiled. It was a beautiful smile. A cruel and unforgiving, diabolically beautiful smile.

He hated her.

A sudden whirlpool formed in her bloodstream, pulling down, down toward a sinking, sickening vortex. Was she going to faint? She wouldn't allow it, wouldn't give him the satisfaction. How dare *he* hate *her?* She pressed her fingers against the rough wooden wall as she felt herself spinning, drowning in a maelstrom of emotion.

Had she said she no longer knew how to feel? Then what was this wild barrage of sensation? Lips, bonfires, rain, hands, music, magic, tears, pain, blood, pain, pain—the memories came hurtling at her like jagged bolts of lightning. She was almost bent double from the sheer electric power of it.

"Well, I'll be darned. If it isn't Adam Kendall!" Just behind Lacy, Tilly's voice was full of a delighted surprise, and in typical uninhibited fashion it carried across the arena easily. "Come here, young man, and give your old friend a kiss!"

Adam's expression lightened as he recognized Tilly, and, with a few polite murmurs, he obediently began to move toward them. He seemed indifferent to the bevy of disappointed beauties he left behind, but Lacy could tell, from the angle of their collective gaze, which was focused somewhere just below Adam's waist, that they were consoling themselves by admiring the geometrical perfection in the ratio of shoulders to hips.

And it was perfect. Lacy knew, much better than

these women, just how achingly perfect he was, phys-
ically. Strong muscles tapered down his long, lean
torso, ending in sexy, shadowed hollows just deep
enough to accept a kiss. Skin tanned golden from
shirtless summers at the concrete factory ran like
honey down his back, falling to the paler, tight silken
curves of his buttocks....

She heard herself make a small noise, and then she
felt Tilly's hand on her elbow, steadying her. Amazing, really, how much welcome strength could be con-
veyed through those thin, elderly fingers.

"Courage, child," Tilly whispered, and thankfully
Lacy felt her balance returning. She took a deep
breath, raised her chin and, with all the equanimity
she could summon, forced herself to watch calmly as
Adam Kendall, the most desirable, dangerous man
she had ever known, walked slowly, arrogantly back
into her life.

"Mrs. Barnhardt," he said, and this time his smile
held no sting. He accepted Tilly's outstretched hand,
then bent to kiss her cheek. "It's good to see you
again. *La he extranado.*"

Tilly made a small scoffing noise, but Lacy could
tell she was flattered by whatever Adam had said. In
the old days, Tilly had given him Spanish lessons in
exchange for odd jobs around the house, occasional
grooming of the horses. Today his accent was flawless, a testimony to her success.

"Nonsense," Tilly said tartly, covering her pleasure. "Dashing young men do not miss creaky old
ladies like me when they set off to see the world. Not
for a split second."

Adam laughed. "The world can be a pretty rough place, Mrs. Barnhardt, even for dashing young men. I remember one particularly ugly winter when I would have traded the whole damn globe for a slice of your blueberry pie."

Tilly blushed and scowled simultaneously. "Watch your language, young man. You know, I tried to mix a little etiquette into those Spanish lessons, but apparently it didn't take. You haven't even said hello to my friends." She urged Kara forward. "I don't think you know Mrs. Karlin. She's the head of our hospital volunteer board."

Kara grinned goofily, apparently struck dumb by Adam's smile, and then overcompensated by vigorously pumping his hand. He didn't protest. He merely raised one eyebrow in mild curiosity and allowed her to continue. Finally, Kara seemed to notice that she still held his hand and let go abruptly, apologizing in unintelligible mortification.

Tilly chuckled. Turning to her other side, she slipped her arm around Lacy's shoulders. "And of course," she said with just a hint of protective warning in her voice, "you must remember our little Lacy."

Lacy forced herself to meet his gaze, bracing for the pain of recognition. She had always loved Adam's eyes. Stunning blue dramatically framed by black brows and black velvet lashes. Clear, intelligent, audacious, sexy. Uptilted with a secret laughter he had reserved for her, glowing with a rogue tenderness that lay deep beneath the streetwise facade.

And the fire—oh, yes, the fire! Startled by the sight,

she realized that she had naively assumed that their decade of separation would have extinguished Adam's fire—just as it had snuffed her own. But it was still there, the fire that had warmed the coldest nights of her life....

Apparently it would take more than ten years to turn Adam Kendall to ice. She could only imagine the parade of women who had lined up to keep the flames alive after he left Pringle Island, and Lacy, behind.

She fought a shiver that skimmed across her shoulder blades and, somehow, with the help of Tilly's firm embrace, held her posture erect. She offered him a smile and held out pale, numb fingers.

"Hello, Adam," she said with extreme courtesy. "Welcome back."

He took her hand. His tanned fingers were warm, his grip so strong her bones pressed tightly together. But she hardly felt either warmth or pain. He might as well have been shaking hands with a plastic mannequin.

"Hello, Mrs. Morgan," he said, and she wondered whether anyone else could hear the slow, scathing emphasis on her name. "This is a pleasure. You're looking well."

"She's looking *well?* Nonsense!" Tilly tightened her hold. "She's looking magnificent, and you know it. *Bellisima, no crees?*"

Adam once again scanned Lacy slowly. "Yes," he agreed finally. "*Bellisima.* She's right, Mrs. Morgan. You're looking particularly...prosperous. Marriage seems to have agreed with you."

Tilly frowned. "Adam—"

But Lacy had, at long last, found her tongue. Apparently even mannequins could speak up if pushed far enough.

"And traveling has obviously agreed with *you,* Adam," she observed pointedly, scanning his crisp, sinfully well-cut tuxedo in a deliberate replication of his earlier perusal of her. "You're polished to a rather high gloss yourself."

He shrugged, smiling. "Just window dressing." He cocked his head sideways, proving his point by suddenly looking far more like a pirate than a gentleman. "Apparently, Mrs. Morgan, we've both learned the value of wearing the right uniform."

She narrowed her eyes. "Uniform?" His smile was really quite unpleasant. Why, then, did it still cause that little hitch in her heartbeat?

"Yes." His grin broadened, though it never quite reached his eyes. "After all, if you don't suit up, they won't let you play, will they?"

She took a moment to breathe past her anger. How dare he? Perhaps *his* clothing was just a costume, a veneer applied to disguise the irreverent rebel he had always been, but her transformation was deeper, more fundamental. She *wasn't* that same untamed child he had once known, painfully thin from poverty, slightly scraggy from neglect, starved for love. *His* love.

No, by God, she hadn't "suited up" to play a poised young widow. She had changed far more than her gown. She was no longer naive, desperate or foolish. And she had learned to live without love.

"I really wouldn't know," she said coolly. "Unfortunately, I have very little time to play games. Which reminds me, I should be getting back to the other guests.''

She ignored Kara's shocked inhale, not caring whether the woman thought she was rude. How could Kara understand? Kara Karlin, the mayor's daughter, knew nothing of Lacy's past. Lacy Mayfair simply hadn't existed for the Pringle Island upper crust. Socially, she had been ''born'' on the day she married Malcolm Morgan.

Lacy turned to Tilly. ''Perhaps you should take Adam and show him some of our more expensive paintings,'' she said, meeting Tilly's worried gaze with a grim implacability. ''After all, now that he's gone to the trouble of suiting up as a rich philanthropist, we certainly wouldn't want to deny him the chance to get in the game, would we?''

UP IN THE OLD HAYLOFT, right next to the hot black spotlight that had been trained on the podium below, Gwen Morgan looked down on her stepmother, who was conversing with some rich guy in a tuxedo. Lacy looked spectacular tonight, Gwen acknowledged reluctantly. That vivid blue suited her, and the choice to go without earrings or necklace was brave in this crowd, but somehow right. Every other woman looked vulgar compared to the elegant widow Morgan.

But then, when didn't Lacy Morgan look perfect? She had been making Gwen feel ugly, awkward and clumsy, either over- or underdressed, and occasionally even downright invisible, for the past ten years.

Gwen nudged the spotlight an inch, so that its light caught the crown of Lacy's head, shining on the thick, glossy knot of exquisitely dressed hair. Another flawless call. Gwen touched her own tangled mass of perverse curls, remembering the day, years ago, when she had nearly scorched it all off her head trying to iron it into some desperate approximation of Lacy's long, swinging pageboy.

Her father, telephoned by the nuns who ran the elite boarding school where Gwen had been incarcerated at the time, had been furious. What fool would bother such a busy man over such a triviality? "Just leave it alone, for God's sake," he had barked. "Your hair is problematic enough already."

Problematic. Even at thirteen, she had known the word was a euphemism for "disappointing." He'd found her problematic all around—from her messy hair to her bad grades, from her pitiful tennis serve to her intractable acne. And especially problematic had been her maddening habit of being in the way when her father wanted to be alone with Lacy.

Lacy Mayfair Morgan. Her "stepmother." Her father's new child bride. A child bride only five years older than Gwen herself. A child bride who, though she'd been born on the wrong side of the tracks, had definitely inherited what Gwen had started to sarcastically call the Sleek Gene.

As Gwen watched now, Lacy smoothly turned away from the tuxedo guy to speak to some other penguin-suited moneybags. The younger girl had a sudden, regressive urge to throw something down on her stepmother's understated French hairdo. A spit-ball, maybe, or a water balloon...

Naw. Why bother? It would just give Lacy another chance to handle herself with magnificent aplomb, showcasing the Serene Gene, which apparently was also in her DNA. Gwen watched her stepmother move safely out of range, and she wondered if this was what God felt like. Bigger, higher, above the fray, comfortably able to pass judgment anonymously.

She sighed irritably. Probably not. For one thing, she was pretty sure God didn't have pests like Teddy Kilgore fiddling insistently at her navel ring.

She captured Teddy's thumb and squeezed it hard. "Put your paw on my belly button one more time, and I'll break every one of your fingers."

It was too dark up here for her glare to have much effect, but she frowned at him anyway. At twenty-one, Teddy Kilgore was two years younger than she was, a straight-A pre-med student, the apple of his snobby mother's eye, and pretty much a roaring bore. But ever since the day Gwen had come home from boarding school wearing her first training bra, Teddy had been making passes at her every chance he got.

Sometimes she liked it. Sometimes she didn't. Right now she wished he'd have another beer. Maybe then he'd pass out and let her concentrate on watching the Stepwitch.

No one but Teddy knew Gwen was in town yet. She would have to announce herself eventually, of course. She needed someplace to stay. And, naturally, she needed an advance on her monthly check, which only Lacy could arrange. But Gwen wasn't ready. She wanted to have these few minutes of secret superiority, silently observing Lacy before the balance of power shifted, as it always did, back to her stepmother.

"Damn it, Teddy," Gwen whispered, exasperated. The young man had leaned over and begun nibbling at the small gold navel ring, pulling it between his teeth. She couldn't shove him away without losing an inch of skin, so she grabbed a handful of his silky black hair and tightened her fist warningly. "That hurts."

He lifted his head and gave her a pout that he undoubtedly thought was sexy. "Aw, c'm'on. If you don't want men to play with it, why do you wear it?"

"That's the important word," she answered, not easing her grip on his hair even fractionally. "*Men.* Unfortunately you don't qualify."

"Well, darn." Teddy took his disappointment in stride. He rolled over, lying flat on his stomach on the loft, and wiggled his fingers in front of the spotlight. "Look," he said mischievously. "I can make dirty finger shadows on the curtains down there."

Gwen looked, wondering if there might be any amusement in a game like that, but though she could see some hazy movement on the curtains behind the podium, she couldn't make out details. Teddy might have been creating a bunny or a T-rex. She squinted. Or maybe a profile of Adolph Hitler?

Teddy was chuckling, apparently more impressed by his efforts than she was. "Look. I learned this one at school. It's two people with—"

"Shhh!" Gwen put her hand over Teddy's fingers

and captured them against her pink crystal-studded T-shirt. Lacy was nearby again, this time talking to someone Gwen couldn't see. Gwen thought she had heard her own name mentioned. "I want to listen to this."

"What—?"

"Shh!"

"—and we understand she's been living in Boston," the disembodied voice was saying, the tones making *Boston* sound as decadent as Gomorrah. A Pringle Island snob, then—Gwen knew the type. Her father had been the worst. "We couldn't believe it, of course, but we were actually told that Gwen was installed in a doctor's household…acting as an au pair!"

Lacy looked unfazed. "Yes," she said. "I believe that's true."

"Oh, Lacy, my dear." The speaker, who Gwen finally recognized as Jennifer Lansing, the town's official Minister of Gossip, made a wounded little note of utterly false sympathy. "I know how you must feel. A *nanny!* After all the advantages you and Malcolm gave her, to be working as a, well, it's really just a glorified baby-sitter, isn't it? Malcolm must be turning over in his grave."

Lacy laughed. "Surely he would understand. She's quite young, after all. There's plenty of time to pick a real career."

Jennifer sniffed. "She's only a few years younger than you, Lacy dear, and… Well, really, there's no comparison, is there? Still, perhaps baby-sitting is a step up from her last job, which I hear was waitressing in Spandex tube tops at the Honeydew Café. Better babies than lewd old men with roaming hands, I suppose.''

Lacy bowed her elegant head, accepting the other woman's sympathy. "I'm sure you're right. But speaking of babies, have you seen the lovely Verengetti that was donated tonight? I can't help picturing it in your conservatory. Not everyone has a room with enough scope and style to carry off a painting like that, but you..."

Gwen watched with a barely repressed fury as Lacy led Jennifer away. The nerve of those two self-satisfied snobs! Just exactly what did they think was wrong with being a nanny? Just because neither of them had any children... And as for the Honeydew Café—well, Jennifer was so tightly wrapped, so bony and repressed that people would pay her *not* to wear Spandex.

Besides, who had appointed them Gwen's career counselors? She could spend a year laying sewers, if she wanted to. Or she could go be a rodeo clown. It wasn't anyone's business but her own.

She didn't realize she hadn't released Teddy's fingers until he protested. "Hey," he complained, tugging at them. *"Ease up!"*

She looked over at him, still half-blind with resentment. "Sorry," she mumbled, trying to hold on to her composure. She felt more like screaming. She felt like yelling down at the departing Lacy that she didn't give a flying flip what anybody thought of her choices—that her father might have turned Lacy into an obedient little robot-snob, but thank God he hadn't managed to make one out of his daughter, too.

Teddy must have misinterpreted the intensity in her expression, because his eyes widened, and he made a clumsy move toward her, his lips already pursed for a big, juicy kiss. His awkward lunge pushed them both in front of the spotlight. Suddenly Gwen was truly blinded, this time by hot, white light. She realized that their writhing shadows must be projected on the podium backdrop below, like some X-rated shadow play.

A rather conspicuous method for announcing her arrival in town. The idea definitely had merit, she realized with a rising sense of defiant glee. She stopped struggling and let Teddy wrap his arms around her waist and lower his lips to hers.

Let's see the Stepwitch handle this. Gwen had observed one indisputable fact through the years: if there was anything that made her frigid little stepmother uncomfortable, it was sex. In fact, she'd bet her trust fund that the widow Morgan, proud possessor of the Serene Gene, hadn't had a real red-hot firecracker kiss in five years.

Maybe longer.

As Gwen guided Teddy Kilgore's happily stunned face down toward her collarbone, she recalled what an icy, utterly passive, silently submissive wife Lacy Mayfair had been to Malcolm Morgan.

Heck, maybe ever.

She ran her hands up and down Teddy's back with exaggerated strokes, knowing it would take broad gestures to attract adequate attention. Teddy responded enthusiastically. "Hot damn," he murmured against her neck, and then set about taking advantage of his amazing good luck.

He wasn't a bad kisser, actually. If she hadn't had other things on her mind, she might even have enjoyed it. Her efforts were rewarded quickly. Within no more than a minute, she heard a few startled sounds from the people right below them. Slowly, as more and more people caught on, a rustle of curiosity moved through the crowd, silencing the normal hum of conversation.

Her fingers buried in Teddy's black hair, Gwen twisted him a few inches to one side and peered over his shoulder into the audience below. Most of the people were watching the shadow show on the curtains, some smiling with incredulous amusement, some holding back shock with well-manicured, bejeweled fingers.

But one person had already figured it out. One face in the crowd was turned the other way, up toward the loft, up toward the spotlight. Staring straight at the actors.

It was Lacy, of course. Her beautiful face was pale, impassive, as always, but Gwen knew she must be horrified. Echoes came to her from years past. Her father's voice. Disgusted. Cold.

Control yourself, Gwen, for God's sake. Haven't you ever noticed that Lacy never makes a spectacle of herself like that?

Gwen tilted Teddy's shoulder out of the spotlight's glare, and tossed her stepmother a broad grin and a wink.

Yeah, she thought wickedly. *But I do.*

CHAPTER TWO

TWO HOURS LATER, even though the auction was going beautifully, Lacy was done in. The band was still playing "baby" songs—a gimmick that had seemed quite amusing when they'd planned it a month ago.

"Baby, I'm Yours." "Be My Baby." "Baby, Come Back." "Walking My Baby Back Home." What had she been thinking? And all these paintings of babies—sleeping babies, nursing babies, crying babies, babies cradled lovingly in the arms of doting Madonnas. Suddenly Lacy found the whole thing completely exhausting.

Maybe it was Gwen's absurdly rebellious arrival. Lacy could only imagine the resentment that had made the young woman put on such a display. When people had begun noticing the sexy silhouettes on the curtains, they had been transfixed—as Gwen had no doubt intended. For a moment Lacy had been stumped. How was such a flagrant piece of bad manners to be handled? Finally, though, she had decided to chuckle, announce that apparently her stepdaughter had joined a theater troupe, and then begin to softly, calmly applaud the performance. Other chuckles had followed, other applause had joined hers, and finally two sheepish young faces had peered down from the loft and grinned.

And, thank heaven, the crisis was averted.

Still, it had taken a lot out of her. Gwen had avoided her the rest of the evening, but Lacy knew a confrontation was inevitable before the night was over. Gwen never came back to the island unless she wanted something, and she never asked nicely. Lacy didn't blame her. It must be galling to have to ask at all.

And yet, wasn't it unfair of fate to ask her to handle Adam's return and Gwen's bitterness all in one night? Her head was aching, and she longed to go home, crawl under the covers and sleep for a week.

However, as chairman of the fund-raising committee, she couldn't leave until the last bid was in the box, the last champagne glass drained, the final donor safely out the door. But she simply had to have a moment alone.

She looked around guiltily, like a prisoner scanning the tower watch. For once no one was bearing down on her, requiring a decision or requesting an opinion. Holding her breath, she eased into the small, remote stall at the end of the aisle, an area half hidden by a bank of lush ferns laced with small sparkling white lights. Formerly the stable's breeding chute, it was too narrow to allow an effective display, so only two or three paintings hung on its padded walls. Most of the guests probably didn't even know the space was there.

Grateful for the privacy, she pretended to study the largest painting. Ironically, it was one of her late hus-

band's, which she had donated to the auction somewhat self-consciously, aware that giving away a painting you despised hardly qualified as generosity. She
wondered if anyone would buy it. Though it was tech-
nically proficient—executed by a fairly well-known
Southern artist—she had always hated the thing.

Saturday Morning: Half Past Paradise, it was ti-
tled. It showed a sunny summer day in a rustic setting
by a river. In the foreground two young lovers lay on
a blue-checked picnic blanket, locked in an erotic embrace. In the background, on the corner of the blanket
nearest the swiftly flowing water, an infant lay sleeping, utterly forgotten.

Malcolm had bought the painting only a year into
their marriage, and had always hung it in a prominent
place. Lacy had never told him how she felt about it.
Why should she? She hadn't ever told him how she
felt about anything.

"If you want to melt into the woodwork, I'd advise
a different dress." The sheltering curtain of fern
fronds rustled, and suddenly Adam Kendall was in
the stall, standing right behind her. The white lights
crowned his dark head like a twinkling halo. He
touched her sleeve, his fingers deeply tanned against
the blue silk. "Something less conspicuous. This is
the uniform of a player, I'm afraid. Not a bench
warmer."

She looked at him, his broad shoulders effectively
blocking the entrance to the shed, and was suddenly
uncomfortably aware that these breeding chutes had
originally been designed to prevent reluctant mares
from escaping.

She fought down a moment of panic. He had caught her, and that was that. She had always known, deep inside, that this day would come. Once she had longed for it, dreamed of it, imagined it down to the clearest detail. Now she just wanted to get it over with.

"Ten years," she said musingly, half to herself. "Ten years since we've seen each other, and all we can find to talk about is clothes?"

He continued to finger the silk, a small smile playing at one corner of his mouth. "But I thought we were doing quite well. It isn't easy to find the perfect metaphor, you know. Reading between the lines is a dying art, don't you think?"

How could she pretend not to understand? And, in a way, he was right. Their clothes really were symbols, weren't they? His old white-kneed jeans and rust-speckled T-shirt had said poverty, hunger, ambition. This new designer tuxedo said luxury, triumph, complacence. *But the ratty old T-shirt had smelled so comfortingly of soap and sunshine, and of him. When she had pulled it off, over his shoulders, over his head, she had always pressed it against her face and inhaled deeply, taking him into her lungs before tossing it aside.*

Ten years ago, his unkempt black waves of silky hair had said rebellion, defiance, indifference. This new elegant, sculpted disarray said sex, power, confidence. *But those tousled waves had always tumbled toward his eyes as he lowered himself over her, dipping his head to her breast. The locks had feathered her skin as he kissed her.*

For a long moment she simply studied him, listening to everything his new persona had to tell her, from his squared shoulders to his gleaming cuff links. From his smile to his suntan. From his perfectly knotted tie to his arrogantly arched eyebrow.

But what about that scar? Just below his left eye a tiny line glistened, as if someone had traced the high curve of his cheekbone with a thin silver pencil. Or a knife blade. Where had it come from? What did it say? She stared at the scar, realizing that it was the only imperfection he retained. The only proof that the ten years without her hadn't been an unbroken string of success and laughter, of wealth and women and satisfied abundance.

"When did you get that scar?" She raised her gaze to his, wondering why, of all the questions she had stockpiled during a decade of silence, that was the only one she could bring herself to speak.

"Years ago. There was an explosion. About a hundred inch-long pieces of glass tried to carve their initials on my face." His voice was mild and expressionless, as if he were discussing the weather. "One of them did a pretty good job."

"Was it an accident at work?" She fought the urge to touch the silver scar, to test its depth, to measure with her trembling finger how close it had come to his eye. "At the refinery? I remember that the job was supposed to be dangerous...."

He smiled shallowly. "They don't ordinarily give you hazard pay unless there's some hazard involved. And that's why I took the job, wasn't it? The idea, if I recall correctly, was to make my fortune as quickly as possible so that I could get back home." He shrugged. "It seemed rather urgent at the time."

She swallowed hard, remembering all too well. "But an explosion... You could have been—"

"What? Killed? Too messy for you, Mrs. Morgan? Perhaps you think I should have *married* my fortune instead." His voice was low, his eyes speculative as he pretended to consider the idea. "I suppose that would have been simpler. But call me old-fashioned. I've always thought money you actually *work* for sits a little easier in your pocket."

She felt herself flushing. "Adam..." She couldn't meet his gaze. "Adam, don't—"

He laughed softly. "Poor Lacy. You don't care for this subject, either? All right, then, let's see... We've eliminated the topic of our clothes. The past is off-limits. The truth is forbidden." He leaned against the teasing wall and scanned the small chute. "Well, I hear you're an art expert. We could talk about this horrible painting."

"Adam." She was shaking her head, trying to take a deep, calming breath. She wanted desperately to leave the stall, but he was blocking her exit. The front of the chute had a panic clutch, but it was on the other side, where breeders could quickly release a mare that was in danger. Ironic, she thought, that an unhappy horse could escape this chute, but a trapped woman could not.

He had come up very close behind her, and was looking at the painting over her shoulder. "*Half Past Paradise*... Interesting title," he said, putting his hands on her shoulders, turning her around to face the picture as if she were a doll, his to pose at will. "Don't tell me you like it. I won't believe you."

She willed herself to go numb, to ignore his strong fingers against her bare shoulders. She was not going to make a fool of herself. And she wasn't going to let him presume to tell her what she thought, what she felt.

"It's a very good painting, actually," she heard herself say in her best art-school voice. She summoned the vocabulary of the tour guide. "It's one of Franklin's best works. The composition is sophisticated, with strong movement in the lines, the river running left to right, the bodies lined up at a forty-five-degree angle. The asymmetry suggests dissonance, confusion, danger."

"Baloney. Pure textbook baloney," he observed, calmly unimpressed. "I'm sorry, Lacy, but I know your taste too well. I know *you* too well. You hate this picture. It may have technical sophistication, but that's not what you look for in art, or in life. You want vitality, passion, heart—and this garbage has none of those things. You'd never hang it where you'd actually have to look at it."

Furious, she edged out of his grip, swiveled and met his smug gaze, lifting her chin. "Perhaps you don't know me as well as you'd like to believe, Adam. Things change a lot in ten years. People change."

He shook his head. "Not that much."

She laughed. "Oh, yes, Adam, that much and more. You see, that painting belonged to my husband. It hung in my home, over our library mantel, in a place of honor. I've looked at it every day since I was married. Every single day for ten years.''

For a moment he didn't respond, and she took advantage of his silent surprise to slip past him. She was almost free when his hand caught her wrist.

She turned and glared at him icily, willing him to release her. It was a look that had intimidated many an importunate admirer.

But of course it didn't work on him. Not on Adam.

"I'm beginning to wonder," he said quietly, studying her face, "if I might have been wrong."

"Wrong about what? That I've changed? Yes, Adam, you were quite wrong about that. Now, if you'll excuse me—"

"No," he said, a half smile curling his upper lip, and a sardonic angle high on one dark eyebrow. "I mean I may have been wrong about married money." He looked down at her huge, vulgar, square-cut diamond, tilting her hand so that it flashed in the light. "It's quite possible that you had to work much harder for your paycheck than I did."

GWEN DIDN'T SHOW UP at the house after the party, for which Lacy should have been grateful. But as the long night wore on, Lacy realized that even an argument with her stepdaughter would have been preferable to being alone with her thoughts.

Lacy pounded her pillow for hours, making an inventory of the deadly comebacks she should have used, the perfectly crafted put-downs that would have forced Adam Kendall to choke on his own effrontery. But a fat lot of good they did her now, spoken only to Hamlet, her silver Persian kitten who blinked at her angry tone, curled up in the crook of her knee, and fell asleep halfway through her best line.

Stroking Hamlet's silken fur and envying him his easy slumber, she struggled for hours with frustration, confusion and something that felt like fear. How long was Adam planning to stay? And how much damage could he do to her peace of mind before he grew tired of the game and jetted away again to parts unknown?

She buried her face in her pillow. Oh, God, what was she going to do? The question drummed against her mind relentlessly—but she found no answer in the desperate darkness.

When dawn finally crawled in through the window, Lacy unwound herself from the knotted covers with relief. She hated this feeling—and she despised the wreck she saw in her mirror, all puffy eyes and tangled hair.

Suddenly her pride came marching in belatedly to her rescue. This wasn't Lacy Morgan. This looked more like pitiful Lacy Mayfair. And she wouldn't stand for it—she had fought too hard to banish that lonely little girl. Lacy Mayfair had foolishly allowed Adam to have the final word last night. But this morning belonged to Mrs. Malcolm Morgan.

So…what was she going to do? She was going to do what she had always done. She was going to protect herself and survive. She was going to take the lessons she'd learned over the past ten years and put them to work. Lessons about courage, about compartmentalizing, about burying unwanted emotions, about squaring her shoulders and soldiering on. She was going to wrap herself in indifference so thick even Adam Kendall's blue eyes couldn't pierce it, so cold even his hot fingers couldn't melt it.

In fact, she told her reflection sternly, for the first time in ten years she was now completely free. A long-dreaded storm had finally broken. After ten years of seeing Adam only in dreams, she had been forced to talk to him, look into his eyes, feel his fingers on her skin.

It had hurt, but she had survived. Fate had fired its last bullet at her—and it had missed. There was nothing left to fear.

Two hours later, when she arrived at the hospital, a cucumber lotion had soothed her eyes, a small silver clip snugged her hair neatly into its accustomed French twist, and a crisp ice-blue suit completed the picture of a calm working professional.

No more angst. Now it was simply back to business. Raising money, putting out office brush fires, posing with happy parents who wanted to remember their friends on the staff of Pringle Island General Hospital. These were all things that the competent Lacy Morgan, director of community relations, could do in her sleep.

Lacy smiled at the family who waited in front of her now. She had just taken their picture—proud father, ecstatic mother, robustly wriggling baby girl. Yes, she thought, handing the daddy his camera. This was better. Much better.

"Take the baby, would you please, Mrs. Morgan? We want a picture of you two together. We wouldn't ever have made it though all this without you."

With pleasure, Lacy accepted the beautiful, pink-faced infant, who was finally going home after three weeks under ultraviolet lights in the nursery. It had been touch-and-go, but this little one was a fighter. Lacy whispered soft nothings and let the amazingly delicate fingers wrap around her thumb.

Soon, when the hospital had its own neonatal unit, these success stories would be commonplace. Small miracles on a daily basis, and she would be a part of that. A worthwhile life, surely. Even if none of the miracles were her own....

The father's enthusiasm knew no bounds, and he kept the flash popping even after Lacy's eyes were half-blind with red after-images, even after his tiny daughter had begun to wail in bored protest.

"Mr. Rosterman, perhaps it's time to take—"

"Lacy?" Kara Karlin's worried voice broke in. "Can I speak to you a moment?"

Lacy looked over toward the maternity ward door, and saw Kara's wrinkled brow and pursed lips. She knew that look. Something was wrong. Shifting the baby to her shoulder, where her cries subsided slightly, Lacy left the parents struggling to get a new roll of film into their camera and moved to where Kara stood wringing her hands.

"Lacy, I'm so sorry. I really hate to bother you, but the most awful thing has happened."

Lacy smiled. Though Kara was nearly fifty and the seasoned mother of four, she lived and breathed superlatives like a teenager. Everything that happened to her was the most something—most terrible, most wonderful, most horrifying, most exciting. All peaks and valleys. Lacy, who had carefully tethered her own psyche to a flat, uneventful plain for years, realized that she sometimes took a vicarious pleasure in watching Kara roller-coaster through her days.

"Surely not the *most* awful," Lacy teased, patting the baby's back softly. "The Most Awful thing happened yesterday, didn't it, when the caterer brought the wrong hors d'oeuvres to the auction? And yet somehow we survived." She swayed slightly as she talked, creating a gentle rocking motion. The baby began to suck her fingers placidly, and the quiet was blissful. "We even managed to raise a quarter of a million for the neonatal unit."

Kara scowled. "Laugh if you like, but if old Mr. Terwilligan had touched one of those seafood canapes, his throat would have swelled up like a blowfish." She brushed her damp, graying hair back from her temples. "And besides, this is worse. You won't believe it, Lacy. The birthday clown is sick. We haven't anyone to do the basket thing."

Now that *was* a problem. The entire pediatric ward was practically holding its breath, awaiting the clown visitation and the attendant shower of toys and candy from his huge green basket. To disappoint the children would be unthinkable.

And therefore Lacy simply wouldn't let it happen. "We'll have to find a replacement," she said calmly, her mind scanning the possibilities like a computer. "Is Leo working today?" Kara shook her head mournfully. "Bart?" Another negative. "Roger?"

"We don't have a single man in the community relations department today. Oh, what are we going to do? The kids are so excited. Ronny Harbaugh was up all night.''

"Now, Kara, don't panic.'' Lacy concentrated on slowing her breath, lowering her voice, communicating serenity both to the suddenly restless baby and to the older woman, who seemed about to burst into tears.

Rotating the baby to her other shoulder, she studied the possibilities. "No men at all. What about a woman, then?''

Kara looked blank. "But we always use a man. The costume is huge. The eyes are so high—''

"Then we need a tall woman.'' Lacy scanned Kara's trim five-feet-ten inches. "What about you?''

Kara looked stunned, confused by this departure from tradition, terrified at the sudden responsibility. "Oh, I couldn't. I've never... We've never... I just couldn't.'' But she wanted to. Lacy could see a tremulous hope in her eyes. "Could I?''

"Of course you can,'' Lacy said steadily, putting her free hand on the other woman's shoulder. "The kids all love you. You'll be wonderful.''

"But I can't.'' Kara braided her fingers anxiously. "Oh, my goodness, the newsletter! And I was just about to—''

"It doesn't matter. I'll help you get the newsletter sent out. Whatever else there is can wait.''

"No, really, this can't.'' Groaning softly, Kara gnawed on one already-tortured fingernail. "Oh, this is the *worst* luck! I was just about to give a tour—''

"I'll take the tour.'' Lacy put a little steel in her voice, though she still smiled encouragingly. "Now for heaven's sake, Kara, stop worrying and start dispensing birthday presents before Ronny Harbaugh starts a riot in the pediatric ward.''

Kara's answering smile was equal parts gratitude and anxiety. ''Oh… All right, I will, then!'' She bustled toward the hallway, turning back at the last minute, her face lit with a new inspiration. ''You know, you probably should conduct this tour, anyhow, since you're the director. He's not just any investor. He's the type who'd expect the red carpet treatment, isn't he?''

Lacy's stomach went suddenly cold. She gripped the infant more carefully as she felt the room take a quick, violent tilt and right itself in the blink of an eye. Aware of the baby's parents watching her with a sudden, instinctive anxiety, she fought the urge to follow Kara down the hall.

''He?'' She spoke loudly enough to reach the bank of elevators where Kara waited. Her voice sounded normal, thank God. ''Who?''

But she knew. She knew even before Kara stepped into the waiting elevator and turned with the name on her lips. ''Only the most gorgeous man on Pringle Island, you lucky thing,'' Kara called back. ''Only that hunky Adam Kendall.''

HE HAD TO GIVE HER CREDIT. The lady had guts.

Adam raised one eyebrow as he watched Lacy coming toward him, her posture erect, her chin high and set. Even though Kara Karlin had popped in about half an hour ago to promise that Lacy would be arriving soon, still Adam would have bet his left cuff link that she'd never show. The tour would be quietly foisted off onto some underling.

He had assumed, in fact, that it was Lacy's search for a suitable underling that had kept him cooling his heels here in the waiting room of the community relations department. Not that he'd minded—the room was designed for comfort. The chairs opened roomy, inviting arms to visitors. Peach pillows as soft as upholstered clouds tumbled across the sofa. Cheerful apricot artwork smiled from behind the desk. Gentle, indirect lighting spread a buttery glow over every wall.

The room positively oozed warmth. Lacy Morgan, however, stopping now in the doorway to take a deep breath, did not.

Dressed in a knife-slim, glacial-blue suit, her long, thick hair pulled back into a cruel, shining knot at the nape of her pale neck, she affected the room like a blast of refrigeration. She didn't hurry, even after she saw him sitting there. She smoothed her sleeve carefully, then touched the top button of her collar, which was high, slightly Oriental, and clearly in no danger of slipping open—now or ever. Then she moved to her desk, a study in graceful efficiency. Her slim heels clicked against the wood flooring with a sound that reminded him of ice falling into an empty glass.

She fingered a few papers pointlessly, then looked up, gazing at him with a cold calm. "Kara tells me she promised you a tour," she said politely. "I'm sorry to have kept you waiting."

"Really." He smiled. "Are you sure?"

She obviously hadn't expected that. A faint line

marred the snowy placidity of her forehead before she caught herself and smoothed it away. "Sure of what?"

"That you're sorry to have kept me waiting." He hitched one leg over the other and watched her from the comfortable embrace of the armchair. "After last night, I thought perhaps you might have welcomed the opportunity to…put me in my place."

"Your place, Adam?" She shook her head. "I wouldn't presume to know where *your place* might be."

"Well," he murmured. "Under your thumb, perhaps?"

She laughed, a brittle sound that once again reminded him of ice cubes tinkling against crystal. "Actually, the last time I remember thinking about where you should go, it was somewhere considerably farther south. And somewhat warmer."

"Oh?" He smiled and let his gaze travel slowly south across her body. He couldn't help himself. He knew what she meant, of course—that he belonged in the lowest level of Hell. But she wasn't very good at this game, was she? She had thrust, but the effort had left her exposed.

In the space of two hot, blinking seconds, she knew how it had sounded. Her eyes widened, and her fingers tightened on the papers they held.

He didn't speak. He didn't have to. He waited for the signature cherry-red circles to bloom in her cheeks. She had always been a blusher. She had blushed when Mrs. Bickens called on her in Calculus, when Adam's fellow construction workers whistled at her as she picked him up after the late shift, when her aunt scolded her for coming in beyond the stroke of midnight....

And, with an intoxicating innocence that had sent quakes through his entire system, she had blushed in his arms when he undressed her. Though they had been alone in the melting summer darkness, it had taken a dozen murmuring kisses to coax her fingers away from her burning cheeks.

But, to his surprise, she didn't blush now. If anything, her strangely immobile face, ivory under its weight of dark hair, grew even more pale.

She stared at him a long moment and then, slowly, she came around the desk and leaned against the corner. She adjusted her skirt with graceful hands. A wink of silver at her wrist showed beneath her cuff and a scallop of white lace retreated obediently under her hem.

The shift brought their knees together, separated by no more than a sliver of an inch. It was deliberate—he could see the challenge in her steady gaze. She was completely unaffected, she was assuring him, by both his words and his body.

"Perhaps we'd better get something straight," she said in a voice that was commendably even, if not quite natural. "Touring potential investors is part of my job. Don't flatter yourself that I would let anything you did in the past—last night or ten years ago—keep me from raising money for this hospital."

He stared back at her, realizing that suddenly, absurdly, he was angry. Angry at that marble-statue face, at that automaton voice, at those graceful hands that no longer trembled. What a waste. What a criminal waste of sweet fire and flesh and blue-moonlight blushes.

What the hell had she turned herself into? And, more to the point, why did he give a damn?

"Don't worry, Lacy," he said with another cold grin, this one curving to within an inch of rudeness. "I know you better than to believe you'd ever let anything come between you and a man's wallet."

Had he still been hoping for a reaction? If so, she had bested him again. She merely nodded and returned his smile.

"Especially a wallet as fat as yours," she agreed concisely. Without waiting for a reaction, she stood. "Shall we get started?"

From then on, it was all business. Without stumbling over a single syllable or a single threshold, she led him through gleaming sterile corridors and into crisply organized offices, delivering as they went one of the most comprehensive sales pitches he'd ever witnessed. From exotic medical terminology to infant mortality statistics, from estimated square footage to anticipated funding partners and percentages, she covered her material so thoroughly that whenever she turned to him with a politely inquisitive smile, inviting questions, he couldn't think of a single one.

Except perhaps...*when did this happen to you, Lacy? Do you remember how, back at old man Morgan's department store, you were so shy you could hardly look at the customers while you counted out their change?*

But of course he didn't ask any such thing. He already knew the answer. No. She didn't remember.

She introduced him to doctors and administrators, even a patient or two, apologizing gracefully each time for interrupting their busy schedules, though apologies clearly weren't necessary. Mrs. Malcolm Morgan was obviously welcome anywhere in this hospital. Two particularly athletic obstetricians, Adam observed wryly, nearly plowed down a maternity ward nurse in their rush to guarantee that they'd intersect Lacy's path.

Forty-five minutes later, the tour ended up in a wood-paneled conference room, hung from door to door with expensively framed blueprints. In the center of the room, an intricate maze of miniature cobalt and gray buildings sprouted like some geometric fungus across a huge mahogany table.

"The finished product," she said, waving two elegant, peach-tipped fingers at the table. "Designed by Prescher and Osteen. You may remember them— they've been the premier architects on Pringle Island for generations."

"I remember," he said, strolling casually by the little painted boxes and dollhouse shrubs. He flicked a very real dead fly from the pretend sidewalk, then tilted a half-cocked grin up at her. "How is good old Biff? Did his daddy's plastic surgeons ever sand that kink out of his nose?"

But even that didn't ruffle her. God, she was good. Or maybe, he thought, it wasn't an act. Maybe she didn't even remember why he had smashed Biff Prescher's nose after basketball practice, out behind the gym with the entire basketball team standing around, watching.

"Biff's doing well," she said smoothly. "He lives in Seattle, with his wife and four children. I haven't seen his nose in years. It's Biff's father, actually, who was the architect here. You may remember old Mr. Prescher?"

His fingers twitched slightly as he followed the curving lines of the little parking lot. "Sorry, never met him. Somehow I guess our paths just never crossed at the University Club. And I don't think he ever showed up at my office behind the gymnasium for a nose job."

She raised her eyebrows gently. To his surprise, she reached out and touched the back of his hand with the silky pad of one forefinger. More proof of how impervious she was, no doubt. He waited.

"Really, Adam," she said chidingly, hitting a sophisticated note of well-meaning detachment with her well-modulated voice. Deliberately casting herself as a distant friend, a sympathetic stranger... Anything but what she was, a old lover with burning embers strewn at her feet.

"Really what, Lacy?" His eyes met hers.

"It's just that... This bad-boy-redux act is a bit much, don't you think?" She tapped his knuckles one at a time. "See? No bruises. No torn, swollen skin. I'd say these hands haven't broken any noses in a long, long time."

He grinned. "Or maybe I'm just much better at it these days."

She shook her head. "In that suit? I doubt it. We're past that now, Ad—"

He flipped his hand over so fast she didn't have time to gasp, and he caught her wrist in his palm. She looked shocked, as if she'd been carelessly touching a branch that turned out to be a snake.

"Don't kid yourself, Lacy," he said, bending across Prescher Senior's toy-block kingdom, not caring if he crushed a tower or two. "We're not past anything. I told you—this is just a uniform. Pockets full or empty, I'm still the same man, and I still don't care much for snobs. Or hypocrites, no matter how slick and pretty they are."

She was rallying, but the effort was costing her. He watched the column of her throat adjust as she swallowed her natural reactions of both fear and anger. Her blue eyes lost their strain, rounding instead in an artificially mild enquiry.

"Dear me," she said softly. "How frighteningly macho…. Should I look into acquiring a helmet and face mask—to protect my own nose?"

He considered for a moment, studying the perfectly shaped nose in question. "No need," he said finally, letting his words stretch and grow uncomfortably warm and familiar. "If I decide to tackle you, Lacy, I'll be targeting a spot considerably father south."

She was going to slap him. He saw the spark flare like silver fire in her eyes, and he caught her free hand just as it began its flinching backswing. He stopped it midair, leeched the willful fury out of it with a slow relentless pressure, and then began to guide it in, toward the soft swell of her breast.

She resisted until the very last moment, and then she finally surrendered, letting him place her hand, palm down, against the blue silk of her blouse.

"There," he said quietly, letting his hand rest atop hers, letting her deep, irregular breathing rock both palms in unison. "If I wanted you, Lacy, this is where I'd attack. Right here, where your heart used to be."

CHAPTER THREE

AFTER ADAM'S VISIT, Lacy's workday was shot. She found it difficult to concentrate on even the simplest tasks. She summoned all her tried-and-true tricks for blocking out disturbing thoughts, but nothing worked. Over and over, even in the middle of a business lunch, even while she cuddled the babies in the nursery, even while she reviewed the auction figures with Tilly, her mind kept returning to Adam.

She kept remembering the way his hand had felt against her breast, the hard look in his eyes when he called her a hypocrite. She replayed again and again, like a broken recording, the derision in his voice when he told her she no longer possessed a heart.

Well, maybe he was right. She *hoped* he was right. Hearts hurt. Hearts broke, and the broken pieces cut you to shreds from the inside.

"Lacy! Come back from whatever planet you're on and add these figures up for me. You know I don't do numbers."

Lacy roused herself guiltily and smiled over at Tilly, who was clearly already bored with the auction accounting. Tilly hated red tape. The government, she always predicted tartly, was going to regulate charity right out of existence.

"Sorry," Lacy said, taking the computer printout from Tilly's hand. "I'll do that." She didn't guarantee accurate results—not with Adam's face popping up where columns of numbers ought to be—but she'd try.

Tilly tapped her fingers on the desk while Lacy entered figures into the calculator. After about a minute, the older woman stood up and started to prowl the room, stopping in front of the mirror to fidget with her towering white wig. She muttered something under her breath, then dropped onto the couch and began flipping through a magazine noisily.

Lacy knew it couldn't last, but she keyed in numbers doggedly, trying to get as far as she could before Tilly's patience erupted.

"I'm hungry," the older woman broke in less than five minutes later, plopping herself onto the chair in front of Lacy's desk again. "And we've got that fundraiser dinner tonight, so you know we won't eat until absurdly late." She pointed to the calculator accusingly. "Can't we do this nonsense tomorrow? Let's go to the cafeteria. Kara told me they had a sinfully delicious chocolate pie today."

Lacy didn't look up. "You can't have chocolate pie," she said firmly. "Blood sugar." She wasn't worried—they had been through this a million times. Tilly had no intention of eating the pie. She just wanted to pretend she was going to—a tiny act of pseudodefiance toward the diabetes that she'd lived with—and resented—for the past sixty years. When she'd been diagnosed, Tilly had been twenty-three, a wild young beauty who had just received her pilot's license, something that had been unheard of for young women in her social set at the time. The diabetes had grounded her for life. Typical, Tilly observed irritably whenever she talked about it. Fate hated to see anyone having too much fun.

"Well, they should make sugar-free chocolate pie," Tilly said, tapping a pencil indignantly on the edge of Lacy's desk. "They can't just act as if only you young people matter. *Lots* of people can't eat sugar! Why, do you know what the statistics are on diabetes in this country today?"

"No. And neither do you. You don't do numbers, remember?" With a tolerant sigh, Lacy flipped the rocker switch at the back of her calculator. Now that the neonatal campaign had heated up, she and Tilly rarely had quiet moments alone together, so she might as well take advantage of this one.

She watched the older woman, trying to gauge her mood. She didn't want to cause an explosion. Tilly had spent a lifetime cultivating an image as an outspoken eccentric, and she'd lost the ability to rein in her emotions—if indeed she'd ever possessed it.

"You know, Tilly," Lacy said carefully, "we're going to have to talk about the private detective sooner or later."

Tilly gave her a mulish look—the same look she'd given Lacy every time the subject had been brought up over the past three weeks. "No, we're not."

"Yes, we are. He's been waiting nearly a month to hear from me on how to proceed."

"Well, let him wait." Tilly tugged at the hairline of her wig irritably. "He has my retainer. And I haven't made up my mind yet. I might just want to let the whole thing drop.''

"Tilly." Lacy leaned forward. "You know that's not true. A month ago you said finding your daughter was the most important thing in the world to you.''

Tilly harrumphed eloquently and waved her hand in the air. "That's just because my blood sugar went up so high that day, and I thought I was going to die. I've changed my mind about that, too. I don't believe I will die after all. So there's no need to rush into airing my dirty laundry in front of any private detective, is there?''

Lacy shut her eyes briefly, praying that her patience would hold out. She hardly knew where to begin refuting an argument as illogical and convoluted as this one.

"First of all, Tilly, you don't have to be on your deathbed to want to reconnect with your daughter. It's a perfectly normal urge. I've been doing some research, and believe me, the statistics are overwhelming. Almost every woman who has given up a child for adoption someday feels the desire to find that child. And secondly, being single and pregnant may have constituted 'dirty laundry' sixty years ago, Tilly, but it doesn't today.''

"Well, society here on Pringle Is—''

"To heck with Pringle Island society," Lacy broke in emphatically. "You're the queen around here. They think what you tell them to think. And besides, since when have you given a fig what other people think?''

Tilly smiled reluctantly. "Well, now that you mention it, I figure it's been about sixty years."

Lacy nodded. "Exactly. So what do you say? Shall I tell the detective to start hunting?"

"No. Yes. I mean, I—" Tilly hesitated, her blustery defiance dissipating suddenly, leaving a strange uncertainty in its place. "Lacy, I just…"

For the first time Lacy could ever remember, Tilly seemed at a loss for words. Her eyes glimmered with the hint of tears, and her face appeared to crumple, the animated spunk that was her hallmark slowly draining away. Lacy's heart faltered, as she looked at her dear friend and saw something she had never seen before: an old woman.

"Tilly, it's all right," she said quickly. "We don't have to do anything that—"

"I'm afraid, Lacy." Tilly put one delicate, blue-veined hand to her chest as if something were hurting there. "It's as simple as that. I'm afraid of what we might find out. Maybe it's better just to have my dreams." She sighed brokenly, and her hand dropped to her lap. "But then I think…what if this damned diabetes gets me after all, and I lose my chance to say…to tell her…"

Lacy shoved her chair back from the desk and went to her friend, kneeling in front of her. "Don't," she said, taking Tilly's hands in her own. "Don't upset yourself. We can talk about this more later. There's plenty of time to decide—"

"There may not be—"

"And stop this foolish talk about dying, do you hear me?" Lacy was appalled to hear her own voice trembling. She firmed her resolve and offered Tilly a reassuring smile. "You're not going to die, because Dr. Blexrud and I have decided we simply aren't going to let you."

Tilly gazed down at her for a long moment, her eyes misty and unfocused. Then she reached out and touched the tips of her wrinkled fingers to Lacy's temple gently.

"Thank you, sweetheart." As she stroked Lacy's hair, Tilly began to smile, the slow warmth brightening her face and making it beautiful. "You're a dear girl, did you know that?"

Lacy smiled back. "I'm glad you think so. Today, anyway."

Tilly chuckled, and Lacy's heart eased as she watched the twinkling mischief return to her friend's eyes.

"Yes, a very dear girl. But if you think this means you're going to stop me from eating that chocolate pie, missy, you've got another think coming."

THE HOSPITAL CAFETERIA was crowded, as usual. Tilly and Lacy each grabbed a piece of fruit and a cup of coffee and headed for their favorite spot, a small cluster of picnic tables near the pediatric playground. Though Tilly grumbled, the balmy early summer afternoon was perfect for eating outdoors, and Lacy longed for fresh air to clear her head.

Apparently she wasn't the only one. The tables were almost as crowded as the cafeteria had been, and Lacy felt lucky to snag an empty one. Tilly saw an old friend and went over for a chat, but Lacy stayed put, shutting her eyes to bask in the warmth of the sun.

She sincerely hoped there wasn't anyone she knew among the other diners—she didn't feel up to socializing. She needed to gather her poise before tonight's dinner. It didn't look as if Adam Kendall would be contributing any money to the hospital now, so she would have to treat tonight's guests doubly well. If she could only find time for a short nap....

No such luck. She had just taken a large, sloppy bite of her pear when a shadow fell over her plate. Pressing her napkin carefully against her chin, she looked up, somehow managing a polite smile without opening her lips.

Oh, great. It *would* be Jennifer Lansing, the chairman of the Pringle Island Historical Society. Lacy didn't enjoy Jennifer's company at the best of times— Jennifer's conversation consisted mainly of snobbishly chronicling the family trees of everyone she knew, which naturally made Lacy uncomfortable. To Jennifer, Lacy's family tree barely qualified as a shrub...and a common shrub, at that.

Things were particularly tense between the two women right now. The historical society hoped to build a museum, and Jennifer was busy soliciting donations from the very same people Lacy needed for the neonatal wing. Though extremely civilized, it was the most intense rivalry in town, and Lacy knew it was providing juicy dinner-table gossip all over Pringle Island.

"Lacy, darling!" Jennifer waited for Lacy to clean up her chin, then kissed the air around her cheek.

"What wonderful good luck that I should run into you now! There's something I simply must know!"

Lacy smiled. So Jennifer wanted something. That was no surprise. She raised her brows in polite inquiry but didn't hurry her chewing. Jennifer was rather like a diesel engine. She hardly needed a push from Lacy to get where she wanted to go.

"It's about Adam Kendall," Jennifer said, lowering her voice dramatically. "He's right over there, playing basketball with Jason. Good heavens, Lacy, *don't look now!*"

But it was too late. Lacy's gaze had jerked automatically toward the central play area, where a basketball hoop had been sunk into the concrete for recovering pediatric patients—as well as visiting youngsters. Adam? Here?

She swallowed her pear half-chewed. Yes. Here. Adam, stripped to his T-shirt and slacks, had just stolen the orange ball from Jennifer's fifteen-year-old son, Jason. As she watched, he arced his torso elegantly, arms extended over his head, to toss the ball toward the basket. It sank with only a whisper of net, and even Jason whooped with delight, high-fiving Adam with genuine admiration.

For a breathless moment Lacy wondered if she'd entered a time warp. She'd spent so many hours, long, long ago, watching him play this game he loved so much. It had been cruel that the coach had kept him off the team—but at six-three Adam hadn't been quite tall enough to overcome the liability of being poor. Had he been six-ten, the coach would have happily bought his uniforms for him, overlooking the fact that he had no parents to contribute to the program.

His exclusion from the team had been a bitter pill to swallow—one of many he had been forced to endure as the only child of an out-of-work alcoholic.

No trace of that bitterness was left now, even though the golden-haired, silver-spooned Jason Lansing proudly sported the blue-and-white uniform Adam had once so longed to wear. As the two male bodies battled, fighting muscle on muscle toward the basket, both of them were laughing, jiving, obviously loving every rigorous moment.

And Adam— She felt her heart kick at the wall of her chest. Adam looked so young, so virile…so happy. His body was as lithely powerful as it had been ten years ago, his pectoral muscles straining at the cotton T-shirt, his well-defined biceps curving and flexing, his tight hips shifting neatly as he ducked and dodged with an unconscious grace. His eyes were lit with pleasure. Laughter had smoothed the harsh edges from his face.

He didn't look much older than Jason. He was almost too beautiful to bear.

Lacy swallowed again, as if the pear wouldn't quite go down, and somehow forced her gaze back to Jennifer. "Yes, I see him. What about him?"

The other woman patted her perfectly coiffed blond page-boy and took one long last look at Adam, like a nicotine addict taking one last drag of a cigarette. Narrowing her eyes, she unconsciously licked her lips. Lacy could almost hear the internal purr of appreciation.

"Well, I hear you took him on the hospital tour this morning." Jennifer eyed Lacy carefully. Though few people in their social set today had any clue that Lacy and Adam had once dated in high school, of course Jennifer knew. Jennifer was a pro—she made it her business to know everything about everyone. "So. Did the tour go well?"

Lacy chuckled, then took a slow sip of coffee. "He didn't commit to the neonatal unit, if that's what you're asking," she said comfortably. She knew how to deal with the Jennifer Lansings of the world. Let them know you're on to them, but do it with the most cordial of smiles. "You're perfectly free to approach him about the museum. The word is he's loaded these days, although I'm sure you've already heard that."

Jennifer smoothed her skirt, a stalling technique that surprised Lacy. Since when did Jennifer need to buy time in one of these elementary-level verbal duels?

"Yes. I mean, no...."

Out of the corner of her eye, Lacy could see Tilly returning to the table. Jennifer saw, too, and looked annoyed.

Taking a deep breath, the blonde smiled, obviously deciding to save time by taking the candid approach. "Look, Lacy. I've already approached Adam about the museum. That's under control—in fact, we're having dinner tonight. But it's more than that. I'm...well, I'm intrigued by Adam Kendall. But I thought you might—well, I would just hate to step on your toes, you know. I'd hate to spoil your plans without at least warning you."

Her lovely smile was loaded with false sympathy for the pitiful girl who couldn't dream of competing with the stunning Jennifer Lansing. "I guess my question is—what exactly are you after, Lacy? The money? Or the man?"

The arrogance! Lacy tasted something bitter in her throat, as if the pear had been rotten. But two could play this game. Widening her eyes as if surprised, she summoned a smile that was every bit as artificial as Jennifer's.

"Why, the money, of course," she said with syrup-covered steel in her voice. "As I'm sure you know, I've already had the man."

GWEN WAS STARTING to wonder whether it had, on second thought, been such a great idea to buy a motorcycle.

It had a few good points. She definitely liked the way she looked in black leather pants and jacket. Very James Dean. And she loved the leers she got when she took off the bad-ass black helmet and her long blond curls came pouring out. "Well," one great-looking guy had said with an appreciative smile. "If it isn't Hell's Angel."

Right then, she hadn't even minded having crazy hair. Biker chicks weren't *supposed* to possess the Sleek Gene.

But she'd owned the bike only a week, and already the honeymoon was over. She had discovered that the stupid leather outfit was *hot*. Not hot like sexy. Hot like sweaty. Hot like gross and uncomfortable. And the motorcycle made an insane amount of noise, which was kind of cool at first but eventually gave her a thumping headache.

And frankly she was having a little trouble staying balanced on the darn thing. Especially when she was taking off.

She wobbled in an irritating circle now, trying to kick the starter pedal just the right way so it would catch, but she was having a little trouble with that, too. She slammed her heel down for the tenth time, including a one-syllable, four-letter special request under her breath for good measure.

The gas caught briefly, lurching the bike forward, propelling it right toward a little red Austin Healy Sprite that had just pulled into the hotel parking lot.

Then the damn thing stalled again. She tilted sideways, barely managing to avoid bouncing her helmeted head on the sidewalk like a beach ball. But not quite managing to avoid dinging the driver's door of the Sprite with her handlebar.

"Oh, hell," she muttered. This was going to be trouble. She knew how guys were about their cars. Darian, her late, unlamented boyfriend, had polished his hubcaps with a toothbrush. Twice a day. And her father—well, once he had darn near killed a valet who had left a fingerprint on the windshield.

Bracing herself for the storm, she straddled the motorcycle defiantly and evaluated the guy who was unfolding himself from the sports car. Late twenties, maybe. Blond hair. Loose Hawaiian print shirt flapping in the summer breeze, lifting to show a pair of khakis that fit well over a neat bottom. *Wow*. It was kind of hard to see color and detail through her tinted visor, but darn, he was *cute*.

He was coming her way. To her surprise, he was smiling. "You okay?"

Was *she* okay? He asked about her before he checked the damage to his car? She tilted her head, wondering if he might be gay.

She pried off her helmet to get a better look. As her curls tumbled free, his eyes widened. She knew that expression. He wasn't gay.

"Yeah," she said. "I'm fine. Sorry about the ding."

He didn't even turn around to look. "Hey, no problem. A car without dents is like a face without laugh lines. It hasn't really lived, you know?"

She stared at him. Not gay, but maybe nuts? "I guess," she said doubtfully. "But still. I'll pay for the damage." As soon as her next trust-fund check came through, she added mentally.

He shook his head. "I wouldn't dream of having it fixed. I'll tell everybody how this gorgeous woman came roaring by one day and left her mark on me forever." He held out a tanned hand. "Travis Rourke," he said, grinning. "Nice bike."

She accepted his hand. "Gwen Morgan," she said, her mouth forming an answering grin before her brain had given it permission. "Nice car." She lifted one brow. "Except for the dent."

He liked that. He laughed, showing even white teeth. The sound was comfortable, as if he laughed often, not worrying whether it might be more sophisticated to be blasé. For a moment Gwen envied him.

It was actually kind of exhausting to have to maintain an attitude twenty-four-seven.

"Are you staying here, too?" He indicated the hotel, which was Pringle Island's pride and joy—a four-star, gray-shingled resort with a thick, green golf course that overlooked the water.

"For the time being." She really ought to go stay with the Stepwitch—she didn't have enough room on her Visa for two hours at the hotel, much less two nights. But she didn't feel up to facing Lacy just yet. Maybe tomorrow.

Travis Rourke looked pleased. "That's great. I'd love a ride on your bike—when you figure out how it works, that is."

She tilted her chin. He'd been nice about the ding, but that didn't give him the right to mock her. "I just bought it, actually. It's kind of a pain, and I may not be keeping it."

"Oh, you'll keep it," he said. "Fifty bucks says you're way too proud to let yourself be beaten by a pile of tin."

"Really." She froze him with her most supercilious eyebrow arch. "I'm not sure a five-minute acquaintance quite authorizes you to make that call, does it? In fact, I can, and *will,* dump this bike whenever I choose."

He grinned. "Yeah, that's what I used to say about cigarettes, too. But when I finally quit, they had to send in the nut squad to pry me off the ceiling."

"Well. That's where we're different, I suppose."

"Fifty bucks." He held out his hand again. "A hundred."

Someone was approaching from the other end of the parking lot—a tall man with an expensive business suit and a confident walk. He was headed their way—probably a lawyer who had smelled a fee from inside the hotel and was hurrying out to scatter his business card over the scene of the accident.

Gwen narrowed her eyes, then took Travis Rourke's hand firmly. She couldn't afford to lose a hundred dollars, but she couldn't afford to lose face, either. "You're on. I don't know how we'll prove it, but it's a bet."

The approaching man was closer now, close enough that Gwen could tell that he wasn't a lawyer. At least not the ambulance-chaser kind. He might be the marble office, Rolex and cigar-smoking kind. It didn't matter much to Gwen. She hated both kinds equally.

"God, Travis, in town less than an hour, and already harassing people in the parking lot?" The tall, dark, gorgeous man turned to Gwen with a smile. If he was a lawyer, she thought suddenly, maybe she needed to revise her opinion of the profession. What a smile. "Sorry about Travis," he went on, resting his hand on the shorter man's shoulder pleasantly. "He has six sisters who dote on him, so he thinks he's irresistible to women."

Gwen tilted her head. Mr. Corporate Heartthrob was actually a buddy of Jimmy Buffet here? She looked both men over, chewing on the edge of her lip speculatively. Travis Rourke was cute—she hadn't changed her mind about that. But cute wasn't the word for this new one. In fact, the word for this one wasn't even a word. It was just a sound. A kind of whimpering mew of animal appreciation.

She gave the newcomer her special smile, the slow one that included an eye massage. She hoped Travis Rourke noticed that it was much hotter than the one she'd given him. He needed to be put in his place a bit. A hundred dollars, indeed.

"Well, hi," she said, as if she meant it. "I'm Gwen Morgan."

"Ahh." His eyebrows went up as one side of his mouth tucked subtly into a dimple. "I thought the silhouette looked familiar."

So he had been there, last night, when she and Teddy had… Gwen hated the warmth that seeped disagreeably along her cheekbones. She wasn't ashamed of her behavior—if ever a group of bores had *needed* to have a stick of dynamite rammed into their stuffed shirts, that party had been it. But she knew that somehow, once again, Lacy had managed to make her bold whimsy appear merely foolish and immature.

She took a deep breath and stretched, putting the heels of her hands against the small of her back. It was a position that did wonders for her silhouette, and definitely put any questions of her maturity to rest. "Oh, so you were at the auction? Funny. You don't look like a guy who would be a big fan of cheesy, overpriced baby pictures."

He chuckled. "Actually, I bought three of them."

"I'm sorry," she said. "Did you have too much to drink?"

"Baby pictures?" Travis looked put out, though whether it was because he'd been upstaged by his hunky friend, or because he didn't approve of the baby pictures, Gwen couldn't really tell. "You're investing in art now, Adam? I thought you'd invited me here to buy real estate."

His friend ignored him. "I'm Adam Kendall," he said to Gwen with another one of those zinger smiles. "It's nice to meet you. Your stepmother and I are...old friends."

She heard the hesitation as he tried to decide what to call it.... *Old friends?* Oh, brother. Was there any more transparent euphemism than that one?

So the Stepwitch hadn't always been made of ice? That was an interesting little nugget of information, which she stuffed into a mental pocket, recognizing that it could have its uses someday.

In fact, it might be useful right now. She'd been waiting for a sign to help her decide which of these great-looking guys to choose as her next conquest, and perhaps this was it. She rubbed her thumbs slowly over the ribbed handlebar and moistened her lips in eager anticipation. An "old friend" of Lacy's. How lucky could a girl get?

"Well, in that case, Mr. Kendall," she said blandly, reaching around to pat the leather seat behind her. "Hop on."

CHAPTER FOUR

LACY'S DINNER GUESTS left at ten-thirty, and, though she was exhausted, she forced herself to wash the brandy glasses. She never, ever went to bed with even one dirty spoon in the sink—Malcolm wouldn't have stood for it, and after all these years it had become a rather comforting habit. A habit she wasn't going to break now, no matter how she longed for sleep. Adam Kendall, damn him, wasn't going to destroy her routine as well as her peace of mind.

She still had two glasses to go when she realized that Hamlet, who usually slept on the breakfast nook windowsill, waiting for her to go to bed, was missing. Her chest tightened as she saw the mudroom door open a crack. Evelyn, her day cleaner who had stayed late to help with the party, must have left it unlatched again.

Drying her hands on the white cotton apron she'd pulled over her evening dress, Lacy hurried out to the west portico. She didn't need this right now. Seeing Adam at the hospital—and then that tacky confrontation with Jennifer Lansing—had left her so drained that she'd hardly been able to carry on a decent conversation at dinner. Foolishly, she'd drunk three glasses of champagne, hoping for a slight lift, but it had only made her disagreeably tipsy, with a head-ache threatening.

And now this. She pinched the bridge of her nose. There ought to be a law. Surviving a showdown with an old boyfriend should give you a free pass for the rest of the day.

Luckily, Hamlet was predictable. Whenever he got loose, he always dashed gleefully up the big English oak in the side yard, and then, as if the whole esca-pade hadn't been his own idea, cried plaintively to be rescued.

She leaned over the edge of the portico's balustrade and peered up into the murky branches of the hun-dred-year-old tree. *Whoops...* Squeezing her eyes shut against the tilting dizziness, she gripped the railing carefully. She took a deep breath to steady herself. She *really* should have stopped with just one glass of champagne....

Even when she felt stable enough to open her eyes again, she couldn't see a thing up in the tree. Rain was due before morning, and clouds as thick as black velvet smothered any moonlight.

"Hamlet?" She pursed her lips and aimed small kissing sounds toward the tree. The wind sent the leaves rustling like silk, but no frightened kitten emerged.

Why wasn't he crying? Protecting her equilibrium by moving very slowly, Lacy leaned farther over the railing, ignoring splinters that might snag her expen-sive embroidered bodice. The complete silence un-nerved her. She told herself she was overreacting—if she hadn't had too much wine, she wouldn't be feeling this rising panic. Her breath was coming a little too fast, and she clutched the wood with anxious fingers.

Darn it, this was why she had always refused to own a pet. For ten years now she had resisted tumble-footed puppies, sleepy-eyed cats and operatic canaries—all offered by well-meaning friends who couldn't accept her preference for solitude. She'd even turned down a goldfish, for heaven's sake! How *could* she have let this little lost kitten slip past her defenses?

She kissed the air again, praying that he would hear her, but the murmuring of the ever-rising wind was her only answer. It lifted the sweet scent of her Lady Banks roses all the way from the east garden, but it didn't bring even a hint of Hamlet. Would he have left the yard? Please, no… The night was so ruthlessly black. It could swallow one tiny silver cat without a ripple.

"Hamlet. Hamlet." Her headache had arrived. She bent over the railing, waiting for the porch to stop listing. "Oh, where are you, Hamlet?"

"I'm no Shakespearean scholar," an amused voice said from somewhere just behind her left shoulder, "but shouldn't that be 'Romeo'?"

Lacy whirled, her hand at her bare throat. "Adam," she gasped on an intake of shallow breath that squeaked in a particularly humiliating way. Instinctively, she took refuge in anger. "What were you thinking, sneaking up on me like that? You startled me."

He raised his brows, silently questioning the extremity of her reaction. "Sorry," he said politely. "I thought you heard me. I wasn't exactly in stealth mode. In fact, I just had a rather resonant encounter with your next-door neighbor."

"Silas?" Oh, dear. Lacy's annoyance fled, replaced by a sense of dread. She uneasily scanned Adam's face for bruises or bleeding. "You ran into Silas Jared?"

"I didn't get his name. Nice fellow? Silver hair? Rather large rifle?"

She nodded nervously. Silas had his rifle out. That didn't sound good.

"He's an interesting old guy, isn't he?" Adam grinned slightly. "He thinks the world of you. Doesn't care much for strange men on your property, though."

In spite of herself, Lacy smiled, picturing Adam staring down the barrel of Silas Jared's ancient rifle. Something—perhaps the three glasses of wine—made the image particularly funny.

"It's not personal," she said apologetically, hoping she wasn't slurring her words at all. She couldn't bear for Adam to know that she was tipsy. "It's just that, well, Silas sort of appointed himself my protector when Malcolm died. Sometimes he gets a little... carried away. But don't worry. That rifle hasn't been loaded since the Civil War."

"He mentioned that." Adam chuckled. "But apparently he also has a bowie knife he's itching to use." Hitching one foot up onto the porch step, he leaned across the railing comfortably. "So. Who's Hamlet?"

"Who's—" Lacy remembered suddenly, with a sting of remorse, that she still hadn't found Hamlet. She must be even more scatter-brained than she had realized.

"He's my kitten," she said, looking up into the shadows of the oak once more. "I think he's stuck up in the tree. He's just four months old, and he can't get down—"

"Is he one of those flat-faced, spoiled-rotten, pure-breds? Fur almost as silver as Silas Jared's hair?"

Lacy didn't like the description—it completely overlooked Hamlet's elegance and charm. But she had to admit it summed up the Persian cat fairly well. "Yes," she said, too tired and worried to take offense. "Why? Have you seen a cat like that? When? Where?"

"Just now. Through your kitchen window. He had his face in a brandy snifter."

"Hamlet!" Relief and exasperation flowing equally through her system, Lacy rushed back inside. Just as Adam had said, Hamlet stood on the kitchen counter, whisker-deep in the half-empty brandy glass. "Hamlet, no!"

The kitten lifted a guilt-stricken, brandy-soaked face at the sound of Lacy's voice. Young as he was, he obviously knew trouble when he heard it. He tried to dart away, but his feet could find no traction on the marble countertop. Skidding helplessly, he churned his little legs until both he and the brandy glass tipped over in a splashing heap onto the kitchen floor. For a chaotic moment the air was filled with splintering glass, meowling cat and one human cry of anguish.

Lacy rushed forward, but Hamlet, reeking of brandy and terrified beyond endurance, streaked through her grasping hands and headed for the open door.

"Adam!" she cried.

Thank heaven, Adam was already in action, shutting the door solidly behind him and capturing the fleeing animal, seemingly all in one easy movement.

Hamlet didn't bother to struggle. Instead he hung limply, eyes all blinking innocence, as Adam held him out toward Lacy, one hand on the scruff of his neck, the other tucked under his back legs. Brandy dripped between Adam's fingers.

"Oh, Hamlet, you rascal," Lacy scolded, though a chuckle was pressing against her throat. He did look so ridiculous—like a soggy toupee. And he smelled simply horrible. Still, she took possession eagerly, gathering him up against her chest with a sense of exquisite relief. She combed her fingers through his fur, searching for any dangerous slivers of glass. Luckily there didn't seem to be any.

"Thank you, Adam," she said belatedly, finally lifting her gaze from Hamlet's pitiful coat. To her surprise, Adam was watching her closely, a curious expression on his features. "Thank you so much."

He nodded with a strange half smile, not taking his gaze from her, still apparently mesmerized by...by something.

"What?" she asked nervously, wondering if she had wet cat hair on her chin. "What is it?"

Perhaps it wasn't cat hair. Maybe it was something even worse. Now that her anxiety had begun to abate, she was becoming aware that she'd made a complete fool of herself. She'd been tearful, then flustered. And completely out of control.

She felt like cursing. *This* was why she should never have let Hamlet stay when he had materialized at her back door, all skin and bones and begging eyes. Loving anything too much made you do crazy things. Made you weak.

Of course, it was also why she should never have more than one glass of champagne at dinner.

She lifted her chin and drew herself up, knowing that the effort was probably wasted, that the purring wet tangle of hair now chewing on the beads of her bodice made any attempt at dignity futile. Sure enough, Adam was grinning.

"What?" she asked again, her voice hardening just a little.

He glanced from Lacy to the kitten, then back to Lacy. "Nothing," he said calmly. "It's just that—I prefer dogs, myself." He smiled. "They hold their liquor better."

She resisted the urge to smile back. "Adam," she said, trying to focus. "I appreciate your help, but what, exactly, are you doing here?"

"You mean, besides playing goalie in this rather fascinating game of cat-hockey? I think I'm mopping up a pile of broken glass." He sauntered into the kitchen and slid a towel from the drain rack.

"No, really," she said, following him with something that felt like desperation. How had things come so unglued? How had she ended up with her cat reeking of liquor, her kitchen a shambles...and Adam Kendall standing in it, acting as if he owned the place? "Don't bother. I can do it la—"

"Don't come in here. You're barefoot."

Good Lord, she was. She looked down at her feet as if they had betrayed her. She must look like a madwoman. A brandy-stained apron flung over an evening dress, hair tugged out of its once-pristine French twist, barefoot and covered in cat hair...

"Lacy." He had already shed his jacket, and was crouching, one knee on the kitchen floor, a paper towel in his hand. He began plucking glittering shards from the soupy mess with long, deft fingers. "Throw that cat in the bathtub." He looked up, one eyebrow raised. "God—you *can* wash cats, can't you?"

"Of course," she said defensively. Why defensively? She couldn't imagine. She didn't care whether he liked cats or not. Besides, wasn't he supposed to be with Jennifer Lansing tonight? Why was he here, criticizing her choice of pets? "Of course you can wash a cat."

"Then do it," he said, returning his attention to his mission. "And while you're at it, you might want to climb in with him. Brandy doesn't make the best perfume, especially after a few hours."

One sniff told her he was right. But still she hovered in the doorway, strangely reluctant to go, reluctant to leave him here, alone in her little kitchen. Malcolm's kitchen, actually. But still...it seemed too intimate, somehow.

Hamlet had dozed off, nestled against her breast. His purring vibrated against her skin.

"Adam," she began stiltedly. "I really do appreciate your help with Hamlet." It was easier to talk, she discovered, when she couldn't see his face. "It's just that… Well, I just wanted you to know things aren't usually this…chaotic here. I'm a little tired tonight, and I was terribly worried about Hamlet. That may seem silly to you, but he's very young, and—"

Finally Adam looked up. "Don't apologize for being human, Lacy," he said dryly. "It's actually considered desirable in some parts of the world."

"But I—" She touched her dangling hair helplessly and attempted a nonchalant laugh. "You see, I had a little too much to drink at dinner. It was an awful situation. Tilly had brought in this potential investor, but then she simply couldn't stand him, and she was arguing with everything he said, and it was so stressful, so I just kept filling everyone's champagne glass, and…" She stopped herself with effort. Why was she telling him this? "Not," she added hurriedly, "that I could conceivably be considered *drunk*…"

He smiled, turning a large, curving piece of broken crystal in his fingers. "No," he agreed. "You couldn't. You've probably had…what…two glasses of wine? No more than three."

She stared at him. "How—"

Cocking his head slightly to one side, he studied her pleasantly. "As I recall, once you get to four your left eyelid droops an eighth of an inch. At five you have trouble with words like 'conceivably,' and you can't stop yawning. By six, you're out cold."

She felt herself flushing, and she struggled to contain it. Good grief, she might have guessed he'd remember that. She'd been a teenager then, for heaven's sake, experimenting with adult sins, getting high for the first time on the forbidden thrill of cheap convenience store beer. Adam himself never drank a drop, not that night or ever. The son of an alcoholic father, he'd refused to follow in his father's footsteps, which had always been skidding downhill.

But Adam had sat with her, out in Tilly Barnhardt's stables, watching over her while she stupidly drank herself into a stupor. After the first beer, she had danced, twirling merrily from the stall gate. After three, she had sung love songs along with the radio till the horses grew restless. At five, she had pressed herself urgently against Adam like a hoyden, inhibitions banished. And then, at six, long before she could persuade him to seduce her, she had fallen asleep like a baby in his arms.

"I—" For the first time in years, she wasn't winning the battle of the blush. "I—"

He laughed softly, a deep throaty sound just under his breath that somehow seemed to take the air neatly from her lungs. Oh, how she had once loved that laugh!

"Go on, Lacy, and take your bath." His eyes glimmered. "Unless you'd like me to help?"

Cheeks flaming, she fled.

SHE DIDN'T KNOW whether he'd still be waiting when she finally came downstairs again. She didn't even know whether she wanted him to be.

Though she'd hurried, it had taken her at least twenty minutes to clean up. It was almost eleven-thirty. Quite late for... For what? Why *had* Adam come by tonight?

Perhaps he'd already given up and gone home. Half of her hoped so. However, as she pulled on a pair of gray leggings and an oversize T-shirt that would look presentable now and double as her nightshirt later, she realized that the other half of her was hoping he had stayed. She was suddenly quite curious about why he had chosen to visit her tonight. And, if she were being perfectly honest, she was also eager to know why his dinner with Jennifer Lansing had ended so early. Lacy was sure that Jennifer had expected to stretch dinner out until it ended with a cozy breakfast in bed.

Besides, Lacy told herself, piling rationalization upon rationalization, the champagne fog had finally cleared, and she would love to show him that she had pulled herself together.

Leaving Hamlet curled up in a fluffy towel to sleep off the excitement, she made her way down the curving staircase.

Adam was still there.

He sat in the library, comfortably ensconced in Malcolm's gold-upholstered Queen Anne wing chair. The sight shocked Lacy so thoroughly that she froze on the bottom step. In the five years since Malcolm's death, she'd had very few dates, but all of them had been Pringle Island men who held Malcolm Morgan in such awe that they wouldn't have dreamed of sitting in his chair.

In fact, they had treated this whole house like a shrine to his memory. Mostly they had treated Lacy that way, too.

Adam couldn't have known about that, of course. But even if he had known, Lacy suspected he would laugh out loud at the idea of sanctifying a chair. Besides, he had always resented Malcolm, the way any poor-but-proud teenage boy resented an arrogant, middle-aged millionaire. Malcolm had gone out of his way to demean Adam, and, posturing as the sympathetic employer who had Lacy's best interests at heart, had often advised her to unload the boyfriend who could only drag her down.

No... Adam had more than resented Malcolm. He had *hated* him. He might not realize that this particular chair had been Malcolm's throne, but she knew that Adam would still be quite happy to trample all over the older man's memory any way he could. The only real shock was her reaction to the sight. As she watched Adam sitting there, leafing through her latest copy of *Cuisine,* Lacy discovered that it felt surprisingly good to see the stupid taboo casually broken.

When Adam sat in that chair, it left no room for Malcolm's ghost.

She breathed deeply, letting tension flow out of her on the exhale. Smoothing her tightly banded ponytail and tugging the neckline of her T-shirt into alignment, she hurried across the front foyer, into the library.

"I'm so sorry to keep you waiting," she said brightly. "It took longer than I'd expected. Hamlet wasn't particularly cooperative."

"I'll bet." Adam looked up from the magazine. "But that's okay. I just finished 'Thirty-seven Ways To Mistake-Proof Your Kitchen.'" He raised one brow. "It didn't mention cats."

"No," she agreed politely, trying to meet his smile. "It probably wouldn't."

He closed the magazine, waiting. But she didn't know what to say. As he had pointed out last night, so many subjects were off-limits between them. And it seemed too ridiculous to try to engage this particular man, this virile, headstrong, exciting apparition from her unburied past, in a discussion about cooking.

He seemed to have decided not to help her, almost as if he preferred her mute discomfort to her smooth control. He just looked at her, smiling that smile.

Trying to escape the last of the champagne cobwebs, Lacy paused beside the large black walnut reading table on which Malcolm had always displayed his bottled-ship collection. She studied the intricate sailing ships, safe inside their glass caskets, as if she'd never seen them before. She suddenly didn't want to look at Adam, whose deepening grin managed to be so familiar and so disturbing at the same time.

"Can I get you anything?" She summoned her company voice. "Coffee?"

He shook his head. "Thanks, no."

"Brandy? Or...I think we have some fruit left from dinner—"

"No," he answered, the one-sided grin so deep

now it notched a dimple in his cheek. "Relax, Lacy. If you can. You don't have to wine and dine me. I'm already convinced that you're the consummate hostess."

She thought of her wrecked kitchen, her maudlin, tipsy crooning over the kitten who had never been lost. "You are?" she asked incredulously.

He nodded. "Apparently you're something of a legend around here. I've been hearing stories about the elegant Mrs. Malcolm Morgan ever since I hit town."

Stalling, unsettled by the strange, new tone she heard in his voice, she ran her fingers along the curved neck of one of the ship's bottles, a mistake she rarely made, aware that Malcolm despised fingerprints on the glass.

But something in the atmosphere had altered since she went upstairs to wash. Before, Adam had seemed…well, not quite *friendly*, but at least politely neutral. Now a chill lingered in his beautiful blue eyes, and his voice was subtly tight. And she instinctively understood that he called her Mrs. Morgan only when he was displeased.

"That's very flattering," she said stiltedly, "but ridiculously exaggerated—"

"Don't be modest," Adam broke in, his syllables clipped. "You should be proud of your accomplishments. Everyone I've met sings your praises. I hear you're a sophisticated chef, an impeccable housekeeper, a charming hostess. And of course, an obedient and devoted consort. In short, the perfect wife for a busy millionaire."

She felt slightly short of breath, as if each adjective had been a jab she was required to dodge. "Adam—"

"No, it's true." Adam's voice was still genial, but she heard something, something extremely hard, buried deep beneath the good-humored surface. "I've heard that very expression at least a dozen times in the past two days. Lucky Malcolm, they say. He certainly had the perfect wife."

"I—"

Adam cut off her protest. He waved a hand toward the formal portrait that Malcolm had commissioned of the two of them, which hung on the wall opposite the gold chair. "Yes. *Perfect*. And if I hadn't quite believed the rumors, I have the proof right here, don't I? What a self-satisfied man I see in that picture, Lacy. He looks like the cat who swallowed the canary, don't you think? And what a lovely canary you are."

Lacy shut her eyes briefly, her heart dragging with a sudden heaviness.

No wonder Adam's mood had soured. It was a huge, ostentatious, highly idealized portrait. The painter had understood his commission well—and had captured Malcolm's fantasy to the tiniest detail. Lacy, only about nineteen at the time, was dressed in sunshine yellow and propped on a formal chair, hands folded in her lap. Malcolm stood beside her, towering over her, his hand heavy on her shoulder, as if she were a pet trained to heel by that wordless command.

Other than the clasp on her shoulder, Malcolm didn't even seem aware of her, his smugly contented smile aimed confidently forward. But Lacy's face was seen in profile, upturned toward her husband. The expression of idiot idolatry that simpered there was one she had surely never, ever worn in reality.

Malcolm had loved the portrait. He had hung it opposite his gold chair so that he could admire it often. Miserably, Lacy realized that, sitting in that same spot, Adam had just spent twenty minutes staring at it, too.

Oh, God... Why hadn't she taken it down? So often she had almost decided to do so—only to lose her courage at the last minute. The picture had hung there for ten years. Everyone who visited the house, both before and after Malcolm's death, commented on it, told Lacy how lucky she was to have it. If she had removed the wretched thing, it would have shot a buzz of gossip straight through Pringle Island society.

Still gazing at it, Adam shook his head slowly. "The master," he said softly. "And his perfect wife."

She hated the way he said those last two words. As if they were an epithet. It was the same spiteful, condescending tone he had taken with her from their first encounter—the tone that expressed a bottomless disdain for her marriage, her last, desperate grab for security and respectability.

But damn him...what *choice* had she been given? Adam hadn't been willing to stay, hadn't been willing to marry her, hadn't even been willing to wait around long enough to see if she...

Malcolm had. And, whatever else had gone wrong between them, for that she had owed her husband a great debt.

She wouldn't apologize for it now. She gazed at Adam as calmly as she could.

"I wasn't perfect," she said softly. "But God knows I tried."

His eyes changed. She didn't see the change so much as she felt it brush along her nerves. "Yes," he said. "I'll bet you did."

He held her eyes for a moment, then turned away, letting his gaze drift idly around the room, taking in the dark, walnut paneling, the pictures of sailing ships, the terrestrial globe in the corner, the heavy inkwell and silver ashtray on the writing desk.

"While I was waiting for you to clean up, I acquainted myself fairly well with these few rooms. And you know what? Except for the kitchen, I don't think I see a single thing in this house that belongs to you." He touched the ugly brass andirons with a long, tanned index finger. "It's a man's house. Malcolm's house. Not one chair, not one candlestick, *nothing* says you live here."

She knew he was right. But he didn't understand, not really. Malcolm would have let her redecorate. Once she had completed her education, he had informed her that he was ready to trust her taste, at least in selected rooms. No, it was something else that had stopped her—a soul-deep lassitude, a penetrating indifference to her surroundings. A profound inability to consider this place *home*.

Something in her simply hadn't cared.

"So it's Malcolm's house." She acknowledged the point without even looking around. She knew that the only thing in this room that belonged to her was the cooking magazine Adam held in his hand. "So what?"

He cocked his head. "So…I was wondering. Is that what it means to be the perfect wife? Is the perfect wife a nonentity? An obedient specter? A ghost in her own home?"

"Don't romanticize the situation, Adam," she said curtly, stung by the uncanny accuracy of his perceptions. "There's no need to wax Gothic about it. I suppose you could say that the perfect wife doesn't fiddle with things that aren't broken. Malcolm's house had been decorated like this for generations, long before he married me. I simply chose to leave things untouched. "

Adam stood slowly. Moving across the heavy Oriental carpet, he joined Lacy at the reading desk, where, she suddenly realized, she was unthinkingly gripping one of the fragile ships bottles in overly tense fingers.

She let go abruptly. The ship clattered dangerously in its tight container. Adam smiled again, looking down at the collection.

"*Untouched*. Yes, that was how Malcolm liked things, wasn't it? Trapped, sealed in glass, and completely untouchable."

"Look," she said austerely, "you're making a lot of assumptions—"

"You're damn right I am." Suddenly Adam pushed past the table, moving fast and reckless, setting the pitiful ships swaying helplessly on a sea of his displeasure. He was so close to her now that she could smell the faint lime scent of his aftershave. "I'll tell you *what* I'm assuming. I'm assuming that you were just another piece in Malcolm's collection. I'm assuming that he kept you tightly under glass, and that, though he's been dead for years, you haven't found the courage to break out.''

"You're wrong—"

"Oh, no, I'm not." Adam touched her sleek ponytail, catching it between his thumb and forefinger and running his hand slowly down its heavy length. "I'm assuming he's the one who taught you to wear your hair tugged, tied, braided, knotted and contained. He wanted your skirts tailored and tight, your makeup subtle, your voice low and mellifluous, your education classic." He touched her hand, where Malcolm's square diamond weighed down her knuckle. "Only your jewelry was allowed to be vulgar."

She held her breath, unable to speak a word. He was so right. How could he know so much, be so right? Unfairly, she hated him for that.

He put his hands on her shoulders, sending a quick, violent shiver shuddering down her spine. "I'm assuming he wanted your opinions to march in lockstep with his. His friends had to be your friends, his enemies your enemies. He probably told you how to vote."

She felt tears forming behind her eyes, but she held them back with a painful iron control. She would not do this, not in front of Adam. Not ever.

His voice dropped to a low murmur as his hands began to move on her shoulders. "And I'm assuming," he said, "that he insisted that your lovemaking be silent. Your body still. Passive. Unthreatening. He probably wanted you to thank him afterward.''

She twitched under his fingers, her shoulders on fire from his touch, her heart on fire from his words. ''How dare you, Adam?'' She hardly recognized her voice. ''What makes you think you know a damn thing about how…how Malcolm and I…''

For answer, he ran the palm of his hand slowly up the column of her throat. Once he reached her chin, he gently tilted her head until she was staring toward the fireplace. For the first time, she realized that the picture she'd donated to the auction, *Saturday Morning: Half Past Paradise,* was propped on the mantel, back in its place of honor.

And then, finally, she knew why Adam had come to her house this evening. He had bought the picture at the auction last night, and he had brought it back. He knew she hated that painting, no matter how emphatically she had protested. He was calling her bluff.

''Because of this,'' he said softly against her ear. ''I'm learning quite a lot from the pictures you allowed Malcolm to hang on your walls, don't you think?''

''What? What do you think you're learning?''

''You're the art expert, Lacy—you know what I'm talking about.'' He tightened his hand on her chin. ''Look at those people. They're making love. But they're not uttering a sound—the baby sleeps right through it. And see how horribly still the woman is, how stiff and unyielding. He's touching her breast, and yet her eyes are open. Her mouth is tightly shut. Her body as taut as steel.''

"But—" She swallowed, the motion pressing against his palm. "I— She—"

She wanted to tell him to mind his own business, to get out of her house, to go to Hell…. But she couldn't think properly—and she couldn't speak at all. His hand had begun to retrace its path. He slid warm fingers across the sensitive skin at the base of her throat, where a pulse beat urgently. He skimmed her collarbone, raising a rash of hot-and-cold shivers. Then he kept sliding down, inch by scalding inch, as if he were following blindly the terrible throbbing of her heart.

The flimsy T-shirt was no protection—and she hadn't bothered with underclothes. She was nearly as accessible to him as if she had been naked. Her head swam, and she took a deep breath as he closed both hands over the unprotected swell of her breasts.

"*You* don't look like that when you make love, Lacy," he whispered, touching her with just enough pressure to bring tight heat to the aching nipples under his fingers. She closed her eyes as a rain of honey-tipped spears drove through her midsection, creating a sharp pain between her legs. "You writhe like soft fire. You twist, and you cry out for fear you'll drown in your own desires. You buckle with pleasure, and you make small, hungry noises that drive a man mad."

No, I don't, she said, the words isolated like gleaming teardrops in an unfocused mind that was quickly losing control. *Not anymore.*

"Did you think I had forgotten, Lacy?" He moved his hands expertly, tender and relentless at the same time. Her T-shirt had slipped off her shoulder, and his breath was sweet heat at her neck as he bent his lips to her skin. "Did you think I would ever forget?"

The question brought a cruel moment of clarity. Of course she believed he had forgotten. What else could explain the ten years of silence? The lost, empty abandonment that had forced her into Malcolm's protection, into Malcolm's cold bed...

She fought away the thrilling sensations Adam was creating. She mustn't delude herself. Adam had made love to her ten years ago, then abandoned her without a backward glance. He would do the same today.

This wasn't love. It wasn't really even lust. She knew what this was all about. It was just another ego game he was playing, to see if he still had the magic touch. He hated the thought that he had lost her to Malcolm Morgan, his old nemesis. This was not even about her, not really. It was a twisted, years-old testosterone competition against a dead man.

And she had almost fallen into the trap. Shame filled her, stiffening her spine, giving her the strength she needed to resist.

"You know," she said with a studied nonchalance that thankfully didn't reveal any of the superhuman effort required to produce it, "if you were looking for some easy sex tonight, you probably should have stayed with Jennifer Lansing." She forced her body into complete quiescence, a perfect numbness. "I'm sure she would have been eager to oblige."

He raised his head, obviously surprised by the blank tone of her voice. She could see the out-of-focus reflection of his face in the mirror. She watched as his lips curved in that old, familiar smile.

"Perhaps *too* eager," he said, his voice thoughtful. "Maybe I like more subtlety in my liaisons. Maybe, sweetheart, I'd rather try to thaw the ice princess than tumble comfortably with the town floozy."

"That's quite possible," she agreed matter-of-factly. "But I'm afraid you've taken on more than you can handle this time, Adam. You wouldn't be the first man to think it would be a challenge to seduce Malcolm Morgan's widow. And you won't be the last."

His smile stretched into a grin. Stepping back, he let his hands fall from her breasts.

"Maybe not," he said, touching his lips to her shoulder with one last kiss that felt like both a threat and a promise. "But I'm the best."

CHAPTER FIVE

GWEN HAD HER OWN KEY to the Morgan house—but never once in the five years since her father's death had Lacy known her to use it.

Malcolm's will had stipulated that Gwen had the right to live there if she chose to, but that clause had merely brought an insulting snort from Gwen at the reading. Since then, whenever the month had stretched longer than her trust-fund check, and she had needed a free lodging, she had rung the doorbell with exaggerated courtesy and asked Lacy's permission to enter.

Lacy had always found the subtle sarcasm irritating. But tonight, for once, she was grateful for it. Gwen rang in her usual way, her thumb holding the button down longer than necessary, giving the bell a strangely insolent drawl. And that gave Lacy time to pull away from Adam. Time to double-check her face in the mirror. Time to be sure no one could guess how affected she'd been by his touch.

"Excuse me," she said evenly. "I need to answer that."

She didn't look at his face directly—she wasn't *that* certain of her recovery—but she glimpsed it out of the corner of her eye as she walked toward the

door. He was smiling with the detached air of someone watching a moderately amusing performance.

Damn him, she thought. Damn him for continuing
to assume this was an act. Once, years ago, it had
been. Once, years ago, she had used this icy exterior
to cover over emotions that boiled with misery. But
through the years the ice had made its way deeper
and deeper, until it wasn't just how she acted. It was
who she was.

She opened the door. "Gwen," she said smoothly.
"What a pleasant surprise."

Gwen laughed out loud at that. Apparently, Lacy
thought as she stood back to let her smirking stepdaughter enter, everyone found her amusing tonight.

"Yeah, I'll bet it is." Gwen inched inside backward, dragging a heavy duffel bag across the threshold with some effort. Her small blue makeup case was
slung over her shoulder, and it bumped her rear end
with each step, letting loose a musical tinkling of expensive bottles and bracelets.

As Gwen moved into the light of the foyer chan-
delier, Lacy could see that she was dressed in one of
her wildest outfits ever—and that was saying a great
deal. She wore a pink-and-tangerine-flowered knit top
over turquoise shorts that seemed to be made of cashmere. Her disheveled curls were tied back with a
green silk scarf, and her long, fake fingernails were
painted flamingo pink to match her lipstick.

Still, Lacy knew something about clothes—Malcolm had made sure of that—and she estimated that
this orgy of color had cost Gwen at least a thousand

dollars. No wonder she'd been reduced to coming home for a free bed.

Losing patience with the slow dragging, Gwen kicked her duffel in the rest of the way. "Yeah, well, it's kind of a surprise for me, too. I was crashing at the Cartwright, but apparently my Visa blew a fuse, so they more or less invited me to leave."

Lacy managed not to wince. She interrupted efficiently, preventing her stepdaughter from launching into any more candid details. "Gwen, do leave the duffel for now. I'll help you with your bags later. Right now I'd like to introduce you to an old friend of mine—"

Gwen straightened quickly, and looked curiously across to the parlor. She didn't seem at all embarrassed to discover her financial woes had been overheard. In fact, to Lacy's surprise Gwen's smile broadened.

"Well, I'll be," she said, putting her hand on one saucily cocked hip and grinning at Adam, who was standing in the doorway holding one of Malcolm's bottled ships, as if he'd been studying it. "If it's not the hunky ambulance chaser."

Lacy was lost. Ambulance chaser? "No, Gwen, this is Adam Ken—"

"Oh, Mr. Kendall and I have already met," Gwen drawled provocatively. She tilted her blue gaze toward Adam and blinked twice. "So, Adam. Ready for that ride yet?"

Adam smiled, turning the bottle slowly in his hands. "I think I'll give you another couple of days to tame that beast."

"What a shame," Gwen said, her voice throaty and come-hither. She pulled the green scarf from her hair with one long, suggestive stroke. "I've got it all warmed up and everything."

Lacy frowned. What on earth was going on here? "Gwen," she began, allowing a subtle sternness to touch her voice.

"Your stepdaughter and I met at the Cartwright this afternoon," Adam interjected pleasantly. "She had just run into my friend's sports car with her motorcycle, and she was afraid I might be a lawyer coming to sue her for every cent she has."

Gwen laughed, gathering her hair up in one fist lazily, exposing her long, lovely neck, then letting it fall across her shoulders. "Which at the moment isn't very many," she said dryly. "As they've just discovered at the Cartwright."

Gwen had bought a motorcycle? And she had hit someone? Well, that explained the ambulance chaser comment. Gwen's flirtatious manner, however, didn't need any explanation. Gwen flirted with every male she met—from poor Teddy Kilgore on up.

And Adam was a long way up. It was quite predictable that Gwen would go all Marilyn Monroe for a man like Adam, who dominated the door to the stuffy little parlor, and whose hands around the fragile neck of the bottled ship were tanned, masculine and utterly sensual.

More confusing was Lacy's own reaction. She found that she disliked the sight of Adam flirting back, which made no sense at all. She didn't want Adam Kendall. She didn't even *know* Adam Kendall anymore, really. And what she knew she didn't like. He was too arrogant, too smug, too glossy and sure of himself. Too much the stereotypical self-made man.

"So…what's up?" Gwen was smiling again. "Did I interrupt anything?" She eyed Adam speculatively. "Don't tell me you two were playing spin the bottle with one of daddy's ships?"

"Don't be ridiculous, Gwen." Lacy strode evenly to the doorway and plucked the bottle from Adam's hands. She pushed past him into the parlor and replaced it carefully on Malcolm's table. "It's late. Adam was just leaving."

"Ouch." Gwen chuckled and winked at Adam. "I guess she told *you*, huh?"

"Your room is ready for you, of course," Lacy said. Gwen's room was always ready, though it was rarely used. "Feel free to take your things up and settle in."

"Ouch," Adam echoed teasingly. For a moment his sapphire blue gaze locked with Gwen's, and Lacy intercepted a look of such sympathetic understanding that she felt a pang of isolation, a pinch of rejection. She banished the feeling immediately. She'd been rejected by her stepdaughter every day for the past ten years. This was nothing new.

"Gwen?" She raised her brows in bland inquiry. "Do you need help with your bag?"

"That's okay. I'll get the duffel later. The temperature's a little cold down here for me anyhow, if you know what I mean." Gwen tied her silk scarf rakishly around her neck and adjusted her makeup bag across her slim shoulder. "So I'll just let you two get back to saying good-night—or whatever you were doing."

She started up the staircase slowly, giving Adam a long look at her trim little backside, which was just barely covered by the turquoise cashmere. At the landing she leaned down with a grin. "But remember, Mr. Kendall. When you're ready for a ride on something a little wilder and warmer, let me know."

BY ELEVEN THE NEXT morning, Lacy had been on the telephone so long her ear was starting to hurt. But it had been worth it. She had lined up two new corporate donors for the neonatal wing; she had discussed details with Kara Karlin, who was organizing the volunteers for next week's gourmet dinner fund-raiser; and she had locked in a rate from the printer for the direct mail campaign brochure.

Best of all, she had avoided spending any one-on-one time with Gwen.

To her surprise, Gwen had risen early this morning. Lacy assumed that must be a new habit formed during Gwen's year as an au pair—the girl's previous routine had always been to stumble out of bed around noon, squinting tragically at the sun as if it were a poisonous death ray from an alien spacecraft.

Today, though, Gwen had been up at eight, showered and dressed in tight black leather pants and a flamingo-colored tube top by nine. By ten, Teddy Kilgore had arrived, and the two of them were in Gwen's room now, giggling and strumming Gwen's guitar rather badly along with the stereo.

Some absurd ember of maternal protectiveness had

flared slightly as Gwen closed and locked her door, but Lacy had smothered it quickly. Gwen was twenty-three years old—it was a little late to be laying down rules about entertaining boys in her bedroom.

So Lacy merely took a deep breath and dialed the newspaper's society columnist and tried not to listen as Gwen and Teddy laughed and strummed and played ever-wilder CDs on the stereo. She tried not to evaluate the sounds—tried not to think about how as long as Teddy was playing the guitar, Gwen couldn't be making any serious life mistakes.

It was ridiculous, she knew that. Lacy wasn't Gwen's mother. She wasn't even really her step-mother. She was merely, as Gwen had once put it, a profound pain in the ass. But, still…how could Lacy help wishing she could prevent Gwen from making some of the same mistakes she herself had made? Especially when she knew how devastating the effects of such recklessness could be.

No one was answering at the newspaper. Realizing she must have dialed the wrong number, Lacy hung up. Before she could start again, the telephone rang.

It was Jennifer Lansing. Lacy stifled a groan—she couldn't afford to antagonize Jennifer. It had been difficult enough to talk to her into helping with the hospital fund-raiser. Usually Jennifer reserved her energy for her own causes. But Lacy needed Jennifer's chilled chicken breasts to make her progressive dinner a success. Pringle Island society was divided on almost every subject, except on the subject of Jennifer's chicken. It was unanimously considered the best dish in town.

''Jennifer!'' Somehow she pumped enthusiasm into her voice. ''I was going to call you in a just few minutes. You know, I've still got you pencilled in for the dinner next week. Have you decided whether you'll be able to help us out? You know the evening just won't be the same without your chicken breasts.''

''Well, darling, that's why I'm calling.'' Jennifer's voice was syrupy, and Lacy knew immediately that she wanted something. She should have predicted this. Jennifer never did anything without bargaining for a favor in return. That was what made her such a formidable fund-raiser—she always had a pot full of golden IOUs she could call in at a moment's notice. ''I was hoping we could talk about that.''

But Lacy had played this game a hundred times, and she was ready. ''Great,'' she said pleasantly. ''Let's talk.''

''Well, you know I'm in charge of the lighthouse day Saturday.''

Lacy did know. As the director of the historical society, Jennifer was coordinating the renovation of Gambler's End Lighthouse. This weekend most of Pringle Island society would be out there in cutoff jeans and T-shirts, mixing cement, digging up weeds, picking up trash and slathering on paint. Lacy hadn't planned to attend, merely because she was up to her ears in arranging the progressive dinner.

''And, honestly, I'm just not getting the response I was hoping for. Dr. Blexrud and his wife have cancelled, and half the Boy Explorers troop is calling in sick with ptomaine—apparently they aren't quite ready to get their campfire cooking badges yet, if you know what I mean.''

"Gosh. That's a shame.'' Lacy hadn't quite figured out where Jennifer was going with this. But then she wasn't giving it her full attention anyhow. One half of her brain was registering that Gwen and Teddy had put on a sexy Eric Clapton song, and that Teddy's guitar strumming had ceased.

"So...'' Jennifer's voice was tighter now. She was narrowing her circle, coming in for the kill. "I was really hoping that maybe you could join us. I know it's dirty work, but you must have a pair of blue jeans somewhere in that designer closet, don't you, darling?''

Lacy chose to ignore the dig. Jennifer knew quite well that Lacy had never shirked hard work. They'd hammered nails and wielded shovels beside one another time and again at local volunteer events—installing the elementary school playground equipment, planting trees in the city park, cleaning up the public beachfront, and a dozen other similar occasions.

Besides, Lacy was still waiting to hear the real reason for this call. So far this negotiation wasn't up to Jennifer's usual standards.

"I'll be glad to help,'' Lacy said. "But I don't see how my one pair of hands can really compensate for the loss of an entire troop of hearty boys. Do you want me to recruit Gwen, too?''

"Umm...well, sure. That would be great.'' Jennifer paused. "And I was thinking, what about Adam Kendall? Any chance you could talk him into pitching in? If we had someone with his...his skills, well, I'm sure everything would be fine, and I would have plenty of time to cook my chicken for your dinner.''

Ahh. Lacy felt the claws sink in as Jennifer found her mark. So *that* was what this was all about. Adam Kendall. But what on earth made the other woman think that Lacy could dictate what Adam did with his weekends? If only Jennifer had seen the contempt in Adam's eyes last night as he spoke of Lacy's marriage....

''Why don't you ask him yourself, Jen? Didn't you have dinner with him last night? Surely he'd come if you told him the situation.''

''Well, let's both ask him,'' Jennifer said smoothly. ''Between us we must have enough feminine wiles to make sure he shows up.''

Feminine wiles. Is that what Adam Kendall admired now? Ten years ago he hadn't. But ten years was a long time.

A peculiar thumping had begun shaking the ceiling just above her—she could see tiny rainbows dancing on the parlor wall as the crystals in the overhead light fixture shimmied from the vibration.

Oh, no... Gwen. Gwen, be careful.

Lacy put her forehead against the heel of her hand and shut her eyes. ''Fine, Jennifer,'' she said, suddenly tired though it wasn't yet noon. ''We'll both ask him.''

GWEN FELL BACK AGAINST the mattress, sweaty, exhausted and smiling. She was going to have to take another shower, but it was worth it. She hadn't had this much fun in months.

Teddy was still going at it, though. He stood on her other twin bed, shaking his head so fast his hair whipped around wildly, jumping up and down so hard the springs were probably going to pop, playing air guitar like a madman. He actually looked more like the Tazmanian Devil than Eric Clapton, but that was okay. He was pretty darn cute, when he stopped trying to be a Don Juan and remembered to be a normal person for a while.

Finally he collapsed, too. He lay on the other bed, breathing heavily, his hair plastered to his flushed cheeks. He turned his face toward her and grinned. "You're a pretty good dancer. Next let's put on one of the rappers or something. Do you have any of that cool guy's CDs? The one with that song?"

Gwen peeled up her leather pants an inch at a time. She should have worn shorts for this kind of workout, but who would have thought Teddy Kilgore could be so much fun? She had expected to take him for a ride on the motorcycle and then spend the rest of the day fending off his slobbery kisses.

"I don't listen to rap." She raised herself on one elbow. "Hey—I'm dry as dust from all that dancing. Go get me a Coke, would you?"

He snorted. "It's your house. You get it."

She eyed him scornfully. "Chicken. What, are you afraid the Stepwitch will bite you?"

He looked incredulous. "You mean Lacy? Heck, no. Nobody's afraid of Lacy. She's sweet as hell. She's always nice to everybody."

"Sweet?" Gwen threw her forearm over her eyes. "God. Spare me."

"Well, she is. Everybody loves her. She—"

"I said spare me." Gwen flipped, turning onto her stomach. "I mean it, Teddy. Go get me a Coke, or go home."

With a great deal of grumbling about bitchy chicks, Teddy made his barefoot way out of the room. Gwen didn't move. She just lay on the bed, her face in the pillow. Her euphoric mood had sunk, dropping out of the clouds like a popped balloon. She should have known better than to mention Lacy's name. It was always the kiss of death.

Even Teddy idolized her. God, what a joke. Wasn't there a single person on this stupid island who could see that the woman wasn't even human? RoboWife, that's what she'd been. She had been programmed to make straight A's at grad school, cook Cordon Bleu dishes for dinner every night, and suck up to her husband's business partners. She had *not* been programmed to make mistakes, even little ones like buying a gross color of lipstick or letting a button fall off a blouse. She had *not* been programmed for warmth, or to kiss or hug or whisper funny stories at bedtime. She had not been programmed, in fact, to even notice any disappointing adolescent stepdaughters hanging around, blatantly hungry for attention.

Yep. Lacy had always been the perfect RoboWife. And now she was just RoboWidow. Nothing had changed.

Teddy was back, carrying an aluminum can of

Coke in each hand. Gwen took hers eagerly and knocked back a long gulp. "That's better," she said. "Thanks."

Teddy was quiet. Too quiet. Now that she looked at him, Gwen could see that he was acting kind of funny. He sat on the edge of the bed, his hair all mussed and his bare feet sticking out from his jeans like big white fish. He was frowning down at his Coke.

"What's wrong?" Gwen swung her foot over the bed and nudged his. "Don't pout. I'll find some rap music on the radio if you want."

"I'm not pouting." Teddy rubbed at the condensation on his can, still scowling. "It's just that... Something kind of funny happened.... When I passed the parlor just now, Lacy was on the telephone."

Gwen rolled her eyes. "Nothing funny about that. The woman lives on the telephone. She's a professional kiss-up, always trying to raise money for things. That's her job."

"Yeah, well, this time she was talking to a private detective."

Gwen sat up slowly, looking to see if Teddy was kidding. "A what?"

Teddy looked miserable, and suddenly Gwen remembered that he was really very young, at least two years younger than she was. It made him a lot of fun to play with, but it didn't leave him able to handle anything very dramatic.

"A private detective. Really. I mean it. I heard her

say so." He turned his big brown gaze on her. "I think she was hiring someone to look into you."

Gwen grimaced skeptically, but something weird and uncomfortable twisted inside her. "Well, that's quite a leap. Why me?"

"Because. Didn't you live in Boston? You know, when you were doing that nanny thing?"

Gwen nodded. "So what?"

"That's where Lacy was telling him to go. She said, 'I think Boston is the place to look. But be sure to be discreet. I wouldn't want her to get wind of our investigation.'" He had been doing a fairly good impression of Lacy's snotty tones, but he gave up and sighed. "Or something like that."

The twisting feeling tightened into something that felt a lot like anger. She knew Teddy wasn't making it up. It sounded just like Lacy. So. The Stepwitch was having her investigated? Why? Did she think she could make some kind of trouble for Gwen—maybe have her trust fund cut down or something? What a bitch! How could her father have been so stupid as to make Lacy the trustee of Gwen's inheritance?

But she didn't want Teddy to know how angry she was. "She's wasting her money, that's all I can say. I worked my butt off the year I was in Boston, and that's all she's going to find out. I spent the whole time changing diapers and playing patty-cake, and while it may have been boring as hell, last time I looked it wasn't illegal."

"You really don't care?" Teddy looked incredulous.

"I really don't care." She put down her Coke and stood up. She wasn't going to waste her time getting mad. It would be much more fun, as they said, to get even. She just had to think of the perfect way.

She tossed her curls defiantly and slicked her hands across her leather pants, brushing away any wrinkles. "What are you waiting for, Kilgore? Find me a rap station, and let's get this party going."

CHAPTER SIX

GAMBLER'S END LIGHTHOUSE had guarded the northeast edge of Pringle Island since 1858, withstanding a century and a half of hurricanes and ice storms, vandals and erosion and neglect. So, Adam decided as he watched a hundred or so islanders clambering across the rocky promontory, it could probably survive the Pringle Island Historical Society, too.

But the scene before him really was a zoo. Jennifer Lansing had tried to create an event that included something for everyone. The result was one part elegant turn-of-the-century picnic, one part Spring Break, one part science class field trip.

And one part—one very small part—actual work on the lighthouse itself.

He wasn't quite sure how he'd gotten into this. Two calls had been waiting for him at the Cartwright when he went back to his room from the golf course last night. The first had been a long, sugarcoated confection from Jennifer, begging flirtatiously, hinting that without his expertise—expertise in what, she didn't specify—her day would be a professional failure and a personal tragedy. The second had been from Lacy, a clipped, monotone sentence that had carried all the warmth and sincerity of a message delivered by someone with a gun pointed at her head. *There will be a work day at the lighthouse tomorrow—Jennifer hopes you'll come.*

Neither invitation had been particularly tempting. But somehow, when the morning came, he'd found himself climbing into blue jeans and polo shirt and dragging a bewildered Travis along with him out to Gambler's End.

"So which one is the lovely Lacy?" Travis showed no interest at all in the lighthouse, a two-story granite keeper's dwelling with a forty-five-foot granite tower rising from the roof. "Where is Heaven's Sexiest Angel?"

"Damn it, Travis." Adam slammed his car door. "That joke's ten years old now. Get some new material."

Travis grinned. "I never retire a joke until it stops working. And that one never fails to get a rise out of you, bro. Works just like a machine. I push here, you jump there."

Adam growled under his breath. Travis knew him too well. They had met ten years ago, in Adam's first week away from Pringle Island, when the two of them had found jobs training for hazardous repair work at a refinery in the Virgin Islands. They'd both been eighteen, both eager to get rich quick. And late one hot, exhausted night, Adam had told Travis about the girl he'd left behind. The girl he had believed was waiting for him. "She's like an angel," he had rhapsodized, beer and youth and loneliness making him ridiculous. "Only sexier."

Travis had never let him forget it.

"She's here somewhere," Adam said, scanning the busy scene without enthusiasm. "This is one of those snobby noblesse oblige days, where the rich put on expensive blue jeans and pretend to work like real folk. Just her kind of thing."

"Well, unless the Dow fell about a thousand points overnight, we're rich, too, remember?" Travis slid his fingers into the pockets of his jeans and grinned. "Rich boys. You and me. Still kind of a kick, isn't it?"

"Still kind of a joke, you mean."

"Yeah. That, too. But it sure makes it easier to pick up chicks. Sorry—I mean *angels*." Adam growled again, but Travis was already walking toward the lighthouse. "Look. There's Gwen Morgan!"

Sure enough, even Gwen was out here today. Adam looked over toward the keeper's house, where Gwen was kneeling on a small scaffold, scrubbing at the second-story windows.

She stood out in this understated, uptight crowd like a peacock at a convention of crows. Travis was moving faster now, grinning stupidly, as if caught in a magnetic field. "If you should suddenly feel the urge to get lost, Adam, I wouldn't mind a bit," he said over his shoulder.

Adam shook his head in amused resignation and obligingly slowed down. Actually, he was happy to yield the field to Travis on this one. Gwen was a knockout, all right, but her compulsive flirtations suggested a lot of unresolved baggage. She needed a counselor, a friend, far more than she needed a lover, and Travis, the professional brother, was perfect for the job.

In no hurry to reach the crowd at the lighthouse, Adam walked slowly, letting himself absorb the sights and smells of the island, which were at once both strange and hauntingly familiar. It was a hot, cloudless day, and the air out here next to the water was humid and briny. It was a unique New England beach smell. It was a smell that, against his will, against his better judgment, took him back.

Back ten long summers. Back to one July afternoon a decade ago, when he and Lacy had romped on the sandy beach of Pringle Cove, a mere two miles south of here. Under the yellow sun, they had pawed one another like tumbling puppies. They had splashed, and kissed, and wrestled in the water for the sheer joy of touching one another.

He had teased her, he remembered. He had unhooked her bikini top and held it away from her grabbing hands, but then lost it in the pounding surf. Lacy had been mortified, and he had scooped her up into his arms and carried her to the car, pressing her nakedness against his chest so that no one could see. And he had spent four days' salary buying her a new bathing suit, so that Aunt Flora wouldn't know.

Aunt Flora! Adam hadn't thought about that dried up old martinet in years. Aunt Flora the Enforcer, they had called her. Aunt Flora, who was parenting the orphaned Lacy as an act of martyred duty and hadn't approved of Adam Kendall.

He had heard that Flora had died a few years ago, but she'd lived long enough to see Lacy married to

Malcolm Morgan. She'd probably approved of Malcolm, Adam thought with a sudden upsurge of bitterness. Malcolm had been just her type. Cold, controlling, smug and repressive. And, of course, rich.

"Adam! Stop daydreaming and give me that strong arm to lean on."

Adam came back from the past with a start. Tilly Barnhardt stood beside him, and he immediately realized that under her elaborate white wig her face looked pale, her gaze slightly unfocused. He recognized the signs—she was having an insulin reaction, and she needed an infusion of sugar right away.

Quickly he held out his forearm. She gripped it with both hands, her fingers weak and trembling slightly. "Take me up to the keeper's house, will you? I need to sit down."

"You need more than that," he said. "You need something sweet. Some juice, maybe, or—"

"Lacy will have some up at the house."

"Are you sure? If we go all the way up and there's no juice—"

"Lacy *always* keeps juice nearby for me," Tilly broke in impatiently. "She's been taking care of me for ten years, Adam, while you were gallivanting around the world. So hush up and just do as I say."

Adam didn't argue further. Slowly he led Tilly toward the square granite structure, noticing as they made their way carefully over the rocky ground that she seemed much more frail than he had remembered.

He looked up and saw Lacy coming toward them, hurrying down the path with a small paper cup in her hand. Her face was as perfectly composed as ever, and in her eyes Adam could find none of the anxiety he was feeling.

"Here you go," she said gently, putting the cup into the older woman's hands and bracing it with her own. "Come on now, Tilly. Take a sip."

Almost childlike in her unquestioning trust, Tilly drank. Lacy watched calmly—so calmly, in fact, that Adam began to wonder whether he'd imagined that Tilly was in any danger. When half the orange juice was gone, Lacy eased the cup away, situated herself on the old woman's other side, and took her arm.

"Why don't we get in out of the heat," she suggested smoothly.

Ten minutes later, it was as if it had never happened. Tilly was ensconced in a chair in the front room, her blood sugar back to normal. Her color had returned, and her temper along with it. She was grumbling mightily, fussing at Lacy, asserting at the top of her voice that she was perfectly well enough to go back to painting the wooden fence along the lighthouse path.

"They need me out there," she insisted. "That jackass Silas Jared thinks he's in charge, and he's doing it all wrong. Up, down, sideways—he's got the brush going every which way. I told him, but he wouldn't listen." She sniffed and reached up to adjust her wig.

Silas Jared... Oh, yes. Adam remembered the silver-haired curmudgeon, Lacy's next door neighbor. The one with the gun. And the knife. He smiled at the thought of Tilly and Silas Jared competing for the job of head fence painter.

Lacy, however, was obviously unamused. "Your blood sugar took a dive because you had your insulin this morning, and then you didn't eat any breakfast."

Tilly glared at her, but Lacy stared back steadily, undaunted. Adam couldn't help noticing how impeccably groomed she was, even on a hot, dirty workday like this. She looked elegant, cool, utterly collected. She looked almost nothing like the sandy, tousled, sunburned and blushing teenager he had carried half-naked from the ocean ten years ago.

"Isn't that right, Tilly?" Lacy tapped her foot. "You forgot to eat breakfast, didn't you?"

"Lacy," Adam broke in, feeling sorry for Tilly, who looked guilty and cross. "Does it really matter now exactly what happened?"

Lacy didn't even look at him. "Yes," she said curtly. "It does. And Tilly knows that it does. If Tilly ate normally, and still had this reaction, it might mean she's getting too much insulin. Did you skip breakfast, Tilly?"

The staring match continued for several tense seconds. To Adam's amazement, Tilly backed down first.

"Perhaps I did forget," the older woman answered huffily, looking down and pretending to flick an imaginary speck of lint from her white slacks. "If you say so. I guess *you* know everything. I'm sure I don't remember."

Lacy sighed, and she caught her lower lip between her teeth. She looked tense. Adam would have said she looked angry if he hadn't already learned she didn't indulge in emotions anymore.

"Stay in that chair, Tilly," she ordered, her voice

low, her syllables tight. "I'll bring you something to eat. Adam, everything is under control here. There's no need for you to stay. I'm sure Jennifer would love to see you."

And then she was gone without another word. Adam watched her disappear with a strange sense of anger and disappointment. But why? She had handled the crisis capably. What more had he wanted from her? Had he wanted her to weep, to worry and wring her hands over her old friend?

He tried to be honest with himself. Was he just insulted because she had dismissed him? No. He had just wanted her to care. About Tilly. Or maybe, just a little, about him. He just wanted her to be human. They had a past, damn it, whether she wanted to admit it or not. And she definitely didn't want to admit it. He remembered her cold eyes at the auction, her stiff body when he had put his hands on her there in Malcolm's parlor. Her icy voice on the answering machine last night.

Impulsively, he turned to Tilly. "She's changed," he said roughly.

Tilly frowned. "Of course she has. She's grown up."

"Grown up?" He shook his head. "No. What she's grown is cold. Cold and hard as a rock."

Tilly waved her hand irritably, and he knew he had annoyed her. She would undoubtedly scold him now for daring to speak ill of her darling Lacy.

"Is that what you think? You think she's cold?"

"Yes," he said. "Yes. That's exactly what I think."

He was prepared for a blistering denial. But when Tilly spoke, she surprised him.

"Well, then, Adam Kendall, maybe you should ask yourself two things. One—what made her that way?" She pointed her fragile forefinger at him. "And two— what are you going to do about it?"

BY NOON THE SUN, which in the morning had been sweetly warm, was a fireball of punishing heat. All but the hardiest lighthouse volunteers had given up any pretense of working and had gathered inside the keeper's house to gossip or take siesta in the cool shade of its thick walls.

Lacy chose to keep going. No one had trekked out to the point yet to pick up trash, so she decided to do that. Lacy didn't mind that it wasn't very glamorous. She would rather be covered in mud, then broiled like a lobster in the noonday sun than join any indoor party that included Adam Kendall.

She grabbed a trash bag and trotted out to the rocky spit of land that jutted into the sound. At least she'd be alone, which she needed. She had almost broken down in front of Adam once today already—something she had vowed she'd never do. But the sight of Tilly so weak, having one of the insulin reactions, had almost undone her. The doctor had warned that it was becoming difficult to regulate Tilly's blood sugar.

Clearly, Tilly wasn't taking his advice seriously. Lacy did, though. She was tough. She prided herself on it. But she wasn't tough enough to do without Tilly.

Somehow, she was going to have to monitor Tilly's

meals. And her injections. If only they weren't in the thick of the fund-raising campaign. And if only Gwen hadn't decided to come home right now, bringing her nasty little thundercloud of hostility with her.

And Adam... Lacy sighed as she picked up a shiny, feather-tipped fishing lure and dumped it into her bag. Actually, it wouldn't have mattered *when* Adam had decided to show up. Any week, any day, any minute during the last ten years, it still would have been like throwing a bomb squarely into the center of her life.

Climbing carefully, she made her way across the black rocks. She paused often, looking for abandoned fishing line, or those treacherous plastic rings that drunken boaters tossed into the water so carelessly. She found them easily, and far too often. Her bag began to fill.

When she reached the tip of the rocky finger, she sat for a moment, catching her breath. The water was a deep, mossy green that winked in the open sunlight.

She watched it, half-mesmerized by the heat and the motion. Gradually her vision began to discern small distinctions, and she realized that the foam nearest to her was partially made up of a huge tangle of fishing line. Bending carefully, she grabbed hold of the knot and pulled.

It slid toward her, but after she had reeled in a few feet of line it balked, stubbornly refusing to come any further. The line was caught on something. Damn. She lay on her stomach, ignoring the mud against her shirt, and tried to find the obstruction.

She stretched so far her arms began to hurt, but she couldn't reach the problem. She wriggled farther, hanging over the edge, the jagged rocks sticking into her ribs unpleasantly. But still she couldn't reach it.

The minute she heard the footsteps behind her, she knew who it was. With her luck, who else could it be? *Hell's bells.* Why couldn't he just leave her alone? She sneaked a quick look down at her shirt. She was, of course, a mess.

Lifting herself to her knees, she turned to watch Adam maneuvering his way toward her on the rocks, graceful as a tightrope walker.

He reached her and smiled pleasantly. "Hi. You looked as if you might need some help."

Her first instinct, of course, was to say "no." But that would have been unforgivably rude. Not to mention blatantly untrue. Besides, he was no fool. He would know that she said "no" out of embarrassment, out of a need to avoid his company.

"Thanks," she managed to say politely. "This line seems to be hooked on something underwater, and I can't free it. "

He took the tangle of line from her hands and gave it a careful tug. "It's something pretty heavy."

With that same innate physical grace, he arranged himself stomach-down along the rocks. "Let me see if I can free it."

His reach was so much longer than hers. His hands disappeared into the water, then his forearms, as he felt for the end of the line. His entire torso was unsupported—the rock ledge ended just below his waist. The entire picture seemed to defy gravity, and Lacy's breath caught in her throat. It wasn't a long way down, just a foot or two, but *headfirst...*

Without thinking, she moved to kneel behind him. She wrapped her fingers around the firm swell of his calves and held on tightly.

He lifted his head, cocking a grin over his shoulder. "Thanks."

Lacy didn't answer. She knelt there quietly, her palms against the rough denim of his jeans, watching as he stretched his long, finely sculpted arms further down into the water. The muscles along his back bunched and broadened, accentuating the tight, tapering line down to his narrow hips.

He seemed so powerful, so strong—and yet so vulnerable, lying there in a position that seemed strangely intimate. It made her feel odd, almost light-headed. Or perhaps it was just the heat.

She rocked forward and tried to peer around him. "Find anything?"

He grunted in response. She couldn't tell if it was an affirmative or a negative grunt, so she settled back against her heels and held on.

"Here we go. It's wrapped around this...this—" He inched forward a little more. She gripped tighter as she felt every muscle in his body strain to free whatever he'd found. "Damn," he muttered. "What *is* this thing?"

The muddy bottom must have let go of its treasure with a pop, because even she felt the abrupt release, and the sudden off-balancing of his whole body as he overcame the resistance.

"Okay," he said, handing her the finally loose fishing line behind his back. "Watch out back there. I'm coming up."

She let go of his calves and wriggled to the other side of the rock, curious. He had found something— some large, strangely shaped object coated with mud. He rinsed it briefly, then used his free hand to hoist himself back onto the rock and into a sitting position.

With a bemused grin, he stared at his prize. "God." He turned it over, as if in disbelief. "This just may be the ugliest damn thing in the entire world."

She had to agree. It probably had once been a ceramic lamp. It looked like a naked woman standing on a hippopotamus. A long metal lamp harp, much corroded, stuck out of the woman's head. Flecks of mustard-colored paint clung in odd places to her body, and the hippo had obviously once been a nauseating shade of green.

"Well." Lacy cleared her throat. "You can definitely see why they threw it into the ocean."

Adam met her gaze with a broad smile. "I don't know. I was just thinking it would look mighty nice on your parlor mantel, right next to that lovely picture I bought back for you the other day."

She tried not to smile. She refused to let herself laugh. But she looked at the naked lady, and the laugh came up anyhow. It came from nowhere, and it spilled into the shimmering summer air like a visible thing. He laughed, too, and propped the lamp up beside him like a trophy.

"I found something else down there." He held out his hand, and she saw that he had been clutching a pink-veined stone against his palm. "Do you still collect them?"

The stone was small and beautiful. Vaguely heart-shaped. For a moment she couldn't speak. Long ago, he had given her so many of these lovely stones—it had become a tradition to find a new one each time they visited the beach. He hadn't had enough money to buy her expensive gifts, but he had always found these little nuggets of beauty.

"No," she said thickly. "No, I don't collect them anymore." Malcolm had been disgusted by them. Couldn't she detect that fishy smell? And what was the point? They were junk rocks, not worth a plug nickel. And so, one day, she had scattered them around her garden, where the turning, decaying seasons had eventually buried them over. She hadn't thought about them in years.

He didn't look surprised. "Well, here." He pressed it into her hand. "Start a new collection."

She didn't know what to say. The sensible part of her brain said to refuse it, to reject the stone and whatever implications he thought it carried. But a deeper part ignored that warning and instructed her numb fingers to tighten and close protectively around the stone's cool weight.

"Thank you," she said. "It's very nice."

"Lacy—" Adam's voice was low. She barely made out the word. "Lacy, maybe we—"

But whatever it was he had been going to say, she didn't want to hear it. She stood quickly, and with her empty hand she began to brush at the front of her muddy shirt. "Good heavens, I'm a terrible mess," she said brightly. "And you know, I really should be getting back in to check on Tilly. "

He stood, too. He caught her hand and stilled it. "It's all right, Lacy. Relax. You don't have to run away. It's only a rock."

She smiled again, but she still didn't look at him. "Of course it is. I know that, Adam. But Tilly—"

"Tell me about Tilly." He let go of her hand. "She scared the hell out of me this morning. She looked awful. How bad is it?"

"It doesn't have to be bad," she explained. "Not if she'd just exercise a little discipline, a little moderation. But if she doesn't... If she forgets to eat regularly, or uses too much insulin, or not enough—"

"Then it could be very bad." He looked grim, and she realized that he had already taken in the implications completely. It was eerily familiar, this easy communication, this quick comprehension. It had always been this way with them. After all, she hadn't fallen in love with him just because he had the sexiest body in New England. She had also fallen in love with his mind.

"And of course our Tilly thinks discipline is a four-letter word," he said with a half smile. "Which makes it that much tougher."

"Right." She sighed, and even she could hear the volumes of weary anxiety that were exhaled on the same breath.

Adam suddenly reached out and put his hand against her cheek. "It must be hard for you, too. But maybe I can help," he said. "Maybe together we could—"

For a split second she allowed herself to melt into the sweet comfort of his fingers. She allowed herself to consider letting him help, letting him shoulder some of this burden of loneliness and worry. But immediately the temptation terrified her. She had counted on Adam once before, and look where that had left her. She would never, ever do it again.

She backed away from his touch. "Thanks, but I really don't need any help," she said.

He raised his brows. "Don't need it? Or don't want it?"

"I don't want it," she said, enunciating the words as politely and clearly as she could. Maybe it would help to get this out in the open. Say it once, and put it behind them. "It's over between us, Adam. It's been over for ten years. I no longer need or want your help for anything."

His face was unreadable, though the sun shone on it like a spotlight. "All you want is my name on a check, is that right? A nice, big, fat check for your precious hospital wing?"

She lifted her chin. "That's right," she said. "Although I can do without that, too, if I have to. Now if you don't mind, I really need to get back."

But before she could move, a torrent of whooping and yelling came at them from the water. They both looked over to see a tiny runabout skimming through the shoals just beyond the point. Adam's friend Travis, whom Lacy had met earlier, was at the steering wheel, and he chauffeured a boatload of young beauties, all of whom were laughing and whistling at the people on shore.

Gwen was among them. In fact, she was standing on the bow, beer bottle in hand, waving and hollering something Lacy couldn't quite make out. Suddenly Gwen turned, presenting her backside to Adam and Lacy, and began to wiggle her rear end. Her hands were poised at her hips, as if prepared to pull down her bikini bottom, but Travis's hand shot out and yanked her back.

Gwen collapsed against the blond man in laughing indignation, and then the little boat angled sharply into its own wake and sped away.

Oh, Gwen... Lacy felt herself flushing.

"I'm sorry about that," she said. "Gwen is—" She reached up to tighten her hair clip and tried to think of the right word. "She's young. I'm afraid she's still got a few rough edges. Anyway, I'm sorry."

"Don't be," he said. He was still watching the water, though the boat was so far away now it looked no bigger than a toy. "I like her."

Lacy looked at him. Surely Gwen's scattergun approach to flirtation was a little indiscriminate for a man like him?

"Well, the feeling is apparently mutual," she said sardonically. "I could see that the other night, as I'm sure you could. Gwen doesn't believe in...holding back."

"No," he agreed. "She's always out there swinging, isn't she?" Finally he turned and looked at Lacy. The silver scar beneath his eye seemed more pronounced, as if the sun had highlighted it. "But she needs all that spunk, you know. She needs all that fire, because she's chosen to tough it out alone, doing battle with a world that isn't always very nice."

And because the communication between them was still unusually rapid, she saw where he was leading the conversation. She felt her back stiffen. "You seem to know a great deal about her," she said icily, "considering you met her only this week."

"I know a lot about people *like* her," he corrected. "People who decide to ride out the storm, even when it scares them, even when it hurts. People who resist the temptation to tie up in a safe harbor somewhere far from the real world."

"You are making assumptions again, Adam." She squared her shoulders. "And a lot of them are wrong."

"Are they?" The wind was blowing his hair into his eyes, and the squinting gaze he cast down on her seemed as hard and bright as blue stones. "Are you trying to tell me that when I left you didn't scurry into the first safe harbor you could find? That you haven't hidden there ever since? That you aren't scared to death to do anything spontaneous? Anything a little bit dangerous?"

"I'm not trying to tell you anything," she answered. Her fist was so tight the stone was growing hot against her palm. "I don't care what you think."

"Then just answer me, Lacy. Be honest for once in your life—if not with me, at least with yourself." He took her by the shoulders. "Do you ever, ever act without thinking? Do you ever do something just because it feels good, without asking yourself if it's smart, or safe, or *cost efficient?*"

She heard the insulting emphasis on those last words. She saw the contempt in his eyes. And it hurt.

Like the old days, like a heart breaking all over again, it hurt.

Without thinking, she lifted her hand and slapped him once, hard, across the cheek. And then she threw the little pink stone into the water. It sank immediately, back into the ocean.

"Yes," she said quietly. "Apparently I do."

CHAPTER SEVEN

GWEN WAS TIRED, and that little girl wailing over in the corner of the lightkeeper's house wasn't helping matters any.

Gwen had been out at Gambler's End practically the whole darn day. She'd arrived before noon, and it must be almost sundown now. The shadows that slipped through the window were long and cool and violet.

She hadn't meant to stay here more than a couple of hours. Just enough to keep the Stepwitch off her back. But it had turned out to be more fun than she'd expected. Travis Rourke was here, for one thing. And Adam Kendall. It was like hitting the Daily Stud Double.

So, naturally, she had hung around. And as it turned out, even the Stepwitch left before Gwen did. Lacy's mood had been so tense and icy that Gwen had felt no impulse to follow her home. Lacy in a *good* mood was scary enough. In a bad mood she could freeze your internal organs to solid ice with one look. Kind of a cross between the Snow Queen and Medusa.

But maybe, Gwen thought, it was finally time to leave. Even Lacy's company might be preferable to hanging around the keeper's house, now that Adam Kendall was gone, Travis was nowhere to be found, and that little kid was wailing up a storm.

She looked toward the source of the weeping. It was Becky Jared. At about four years old, Becky was the youngest of Silas Jared's four grandkids. She looked cranky as hell. And exhausted.

Annoyed, Gwen glanced over at the Jared adults. Couldn't they see their daughter was pooped? They were busy trying to bust open the last can of paint for the fence. Like the world was going to end if that stupid fence didn't get finished today? Didn't they know a four-year-old kid couldn't handle a day this long, in this heat?

"Becky," Gwen called, resigned to staying a little bit longer. "Want to see the coolest light in the world?"

Becky paused in her crying. She looked about ready to drop, her eyes swollen and her red curls stuck wetly to her cheeks. "No."

Gwen shrugged, as if she didn't care one bit. "Okay. I thought we might go look at the light, because sometimes from up there you can see Stormy. But if you don't want to, that's okay."

Becky hiccuped softly. She kept looking at Gwen, frowning as if torn by conflicting desires—the desire to keep crying, and the desire to see something cool. "What's Stormy?"

Gwen cast an exaggerated sideways glance at the adults, then held her hand over her mouth and whispered. "Stormy is the sea serpent, duh. Haven't you heard of her? Sometimes, when the sun goes down, she comes and plays in the sound.''

Becky looked out the window toward the western sky, which was deep lavender with big tangerine splotches. "The sun is going down right now," she said, her eyes widening.

Gwen nodded dramatically. "I know."

Becky wiped her eyes and stood, cookie crumbs scattering from her shirt onto the floor unnoticed. "I want to see," she said.

Gwen caught Daddy Jared's eye over Becky's head. He nodded with a smile, mouthed a silent "thank you," and went back to struggling with the uncooperative paint can. For Becky's sake, Gwen hid her disapproval—but honestly, why did people even have kids if they didn't want to play with them?

Becky tugged at her shirt. "I don't want you to carry me," she warned, her jaw set belligerently.

Gwen held out her hand. "Good, because why would I? You're not a baby."

That pleased the little girl. She took Gwen's hand happily and began stomping up the stairs to the light-house tower, asking a new question every ten seconds. What did Stormy look like? How old was she? Was she good or bad? Could she talk? What did she eat? Did she have big brothers and sisters?

By the time they reached the top, Stormy was five feet long and emerald green with sapphire blue spots. She wore granny glasses and a pink-flowered ladies' bathing cap. She was a hundred years old—just a kid in sea serpent years. She loved watermelon and chocolate chip cookies, and had eighteen older brothers. Becky rolled her eyes in sympathy at that sad detail.

Fifteen minutes into the saga of Stormy's life, Becky's eight-year-old brother came to get her. But Gwen was right in the middle of telling how Stormy had saved her family from the ruthless leader of the Stingrays, so Tommy Jared sat down to hear the end of the tale. Fifteen minutes later, the ten-year-old Jared twins joined them, but by then Stormy had been captured by pirates, so they all crowded around the Fresnel lens and listened.

Forty-five minutes into the story, all four Jared grandchildren were standing at the tower window, straining for a glimpse of the sea serpent's pink-flowered swim cap while Gwen told them about the time a tornado picked Stormy up in its funnel and dropped her in the Indian Ocean.

A few minutes later, Gwen noticed that another person was standing quietly at the doorway. Confused, she looked up. Surely there were only four Jared kids...

It was Travis, and he was grinning. Obviously he'd been listening for quite a while. "Hello," he said. "Tom Jared sent me to find out what terrible monster has kidnapped all his beloved children. Apparently, one by one they were sent up here, and not one of them has been seen since."

Becky shook her head emphatically. "It's not a terrible monster! It's Stormy the super sea serpent!"

"Oh, I see." Travis nodded knowingly. "Well, your father will be relieved. Maybe you'd better run on down now, because he's very, very worried."

The twins, at ten, were old enough to realize they had goofed by not coming right back, so they quickly began herding the smaller ones toward the doorway. Becky resisted the longest, and as the kids clambered down the twisting staircase, Gwen could hear the little girl begin once again to cry.

Travis joined Gwen at the window, still smiling. "So what are you? The Pied Piper or something? Those kids were hanging on every word you said."

She shrugged. She didn't want him to make a big deal out of it, just to flatter her. "Oh, everyone likes a good sea serpent story."

He laughed. "Yeah, but still—those kids have been little hellions all day. You had them lined up like chicks eating out of your hand."

Embarrassed, she nudged him with her hip. "Shut up. You're just trying to score points with me so I'll take you for a ride on my bike."

He held up his hands, disclaiming vigorously. "Not on your life, Stormy. I don't have enough insurance to risk my life with a madwoman like you."

She could have insulted him back, but she decided to drop it. Now that the kids were gone, she was suddenly feeling tired again. Which made sense— she'd worked hard all day, something she usually avoided like the plague.

He dropped it, too, and for several minutes they stood at the window in companionable silence, looking out over the peaceful sound. The sunset was in its last, most breathtaking moments, turning the water a rich purple, except where it broke in white, frothy lace around the rocks. In the sky, a couple of pale silver stars had broken through, and a ghostly three-quarter moon was rising in the east.

Gwen thought Travis looked tired, too. The sun had been brutal today. His tan had deepened to a ruddy bronze, and his hair was bleached almost white in places. Groaning softly, he leaned his elbows on the windowsill, as if his back might be hurting.

He had an awful cute rear end, seen from that angle. She sighed, realizing that she was too tired to flirt. But, strangely, that was okay. It felt nice just to stand here, two tired friends at the lighthouse window, watching for sea serpents to come swimming by.

"You know, I wasn't kidding," Travis said after a while. "You're really good with kids. I mean *amazing*. You should be a teacher or something."

Gwen shifted her weight from one foot to the other uncomfortably. She stared out at the stars, which were getting brighter as the sky darkened, like some kind of Disney special effect.

"I thought about it for a while, when I first went to college," she said. But the minute she spoke the words she regretted them. What the hell was she saying? She wasn't going to be a teacher. She remembered how her father had laughed out loud at the suggestion, then sobered, horrified to discover that she had meant it seriously.

A teacher? Good Lord, Gwen, don't be ridiculous. Do you know what teachers get paid? I didn't rear my daughter to think as small as that!

"Why didn't you do it?"

"I flunked out of college, which is one teeny little problem. And besides, my dad made it pretty clear the family honor couldn't survive having a lowly schoolmarm in the ranks.''

Travis looked irked. "It's not your dad's life, is it?"

Gwen laughed, and the sound had a slightly brittle edge. "No, but it was his name on the tuition checks, so..." She shrugged.

A small furrow formed between his eyes. "But—" He hesitated. "But hasn't your father been gone a long time now? I mean, Adam told me your dad died about five years ago, and—"

She sighed. "Yeah? So? What's your point? Don't make a federal case out of this, Travis." She wondered why she sounded so annoyed. "I just said I'd thought about it occasionally. I've also *thought* about being an astronaut, a coal miner, and a stripper. But you don't see me wearing a G-string and pasties, do you?"

He tilted his head, accepting her reprimand with his usual easy good nature. "Well, now, ma'am, as a matter of fact, I don't." He wriggled his eyebrows. "But I'd be glad to—"

Good grief, he was cute. She swatted him with a laughing exasperation. "Careful, buddy. You think I should be a teacher? Well, I'd gladly teach *you* a thing or two."

He ducked and grinned. Then he took her hand, just a comfortable, brotherly grip, and began to lead her down the winding staircase. "Let's go, Stormy. I'm whipped, and I need a shower in the worst way."

"Yes, sir, you do," she agreed, and he squeezed her hand hard, a playful punishment. If she'd had a brother, Gwen thought, smiling to herself, she would have wanted one like Travis. A little hassling, a little advice, a lot of affection with no strings attached...

Was he right about the teaching thing? *Maybe*. She didn't like much in this whacked-out world, but she did like kids. *Yeah, maybe*. If things had been different, she just might have made a pretty darn good teacher, after all.

Not that it mattered. It was way too late now. Boston College wasn't interested in a twenty-three-year-old dropout with a one-point-one grade average and a really bad attitude.

Even Stormy the super sea serpent couldn't change that.

LACY WOKE UP FEELING wonderful. That was a surprise, because she'd gone to bed feeling rotten—achy from overwork, tender from sunburn, and uncomfortable about having lost her temper with Adam, especially in such a public spot.

What had she been thinking? If anyone had seen her... Pringle Island society was small and inbred. It usually took less than twenty-four hours for a ripe piece of gossip to make its way full circle around the grapevine.

It was going to be a hectic day of doing damage control on her image. But instead of the dread she had expected to feel, she felt strangely invigorated. Almost buoyant. Apparently venting one's emotions was just as healthy as all the pop psychologists said.

She slept well, and she slept late. Before she went

into the kitchen, she turned on the downstairs stereo. It felt like a music kind of day.

But not *that* music. The classical station was playing Mozart's "Requiem," which might be beautiful but was also, she pointed out to the deejay, *darn depressing*. She turned to an oldies station, which was having a Motown party. Much better. Maybe they'd even play "I Heard It Through the Grapevine."

Though she almost never ate breakfast, today she filled a huge crystal bowl with juicy slices of every fruit in the house—kiwi, apples, strawberries, mandarin oranges, grapes, honeydew, blueberries. And then she sat on the kitchen side of the pass-through counter, feeding bits of cheese to Hamlet, and going through Saturday's mail.

The radio began playing Lionel Ritchie's "Stuck On You," and Lacy couldn't stop herself from humming along. She pitched a piece of junk mail toward the trash can, and it swished neatly out of sight.

"Nothing but net," she said. She returned to the mail, popping a red grape into her mouth and humming around it as best she could. Maybe she should slap people more often, she thought, chuckling out loud. It was clearly, in some weird and perverse way, good for her mood.

"Lacy?"

She glanced up to see Gwen standing in the breakfast room doorway, looking half-asleep and completely bewildered.

"Good morning," Lacy said politely. "Are you hungry? There's plenty of fruit."

Gwen didn't answer right away. She tightened the

belt to her terry-cloth robe, yawned, and tugged at her hair, which was looking even more electrified than usual. Her father would have been furious—leaving the bedroom in her nightclothes! But of course that was probably why she did it.

"I see that. What—" Gwen shook her head slightly, as if she thought she might be dreaming. "What are you doing?"

Lacy gestured toward the letters and bills. "Sorting the mail. Eating breakfast."

But Gwen hadn't meant that, and they both knew it. She tilted her head toward the parlor, where the radio had shifted into an old Aretha Franklin song. "I mean, what's with the music? This isn't your usual, is it?"

Lacy gave her stepdaughter a bland look. "I don't know. What is my 'usual'?"

Gwen snorted. "You know. Beethoven's Sleeping Pill Sonata."

How would you know what my usual is, Gwen? Lacy almost spoke the words out loud. *You're almost never here....*

But she didn't say it. She didn't feel like letting a tussle with Gwen spoil this lovely morning. And besides, Gwen was actually right. Lacy couldn't remember the last time she had moved the dial on the radio.

"I guess I just felt like something different today." She went back to sorting the mail. "But I'll be leaving for work soon, so if you want to change it, go ahead."

"No." Yawning, Gwen shuffled into the room and picked out a small, curved slice of mandarin orange.

"It's okay. Whatever." She made her way to the refrigerator. "I guess I'll get a glass of milk. Want one?"

Lacy looked at Gwen, surprised. Was it something in the air? This was the first time she could ever remember Gwen offering her anything. After years of unremitting resentment, why would Gwen pick this morning to suddenly turn mellow?

But maybe it *was* something in the air. And maybe, just maybe, it could be the first step toward a new...a new... Lacy was afraid to use the word "friendship." She'd given up all hope of being friends with Gwen years ago. But she had awakened this morning feeling strangely different. It was as if, all around her—and inside her, too—things were changing.

She had been honest with Adam yesterday, honest about her anger. And it had actually felt rather good. Scary, but definitely empowering. Maybe she could risk being honest with Gwen today. Maybe she could admit that deep inside she had sometimes wished for...if not "friendship" perhaps at least "truce"?

"God, I love milk." Gwen poured a huge tumbler full. "They turned the power off in my apartment four days ago, so I haven't had milk in a week."

Lacy's foolish thoughts skidded to a halt. Of course. How had she been so dense? Thank goodness she hadn't said anything stupid...about friendship or truces or secret longings. Gwen hadn't come down just to be friendly. She'd come down to demand an advance on her allowance.

And this mild version of conversational soft soap was merely because she was afraid Lacy might say no. The last time she'd needed an advance Lacy had warned her that it must not happen again—and Gwen knew Lacy had been serious. Gwen wasn't stupid. Wild and rebellious and chronically defiant, but not stupid.

"No, thanks. I already have my coffee," Lacy said, pulling herself together, feeling the peculiar euphoria begin to dissipate. She sneaked a peek at her wristwatch. She hoped Gwen would get to the point quickly. She was due to give a VIP tour at the hospital in twenty-five minutes, and she knew that a prolonged argument about the check was almost inevitable.

Gwen set her glass of milk on the counter and scooted onto one of the bar stools on the other side of the pass-through. "So," she said, overly casual. "I guess you can figure out why I've come home."

Lacy put another flyer into the "toss" pile. She didn't look up. "I deduced that it wasn't just to spend time with your family."

Gwen made a rude sound into her milk. "Family?" She took a swallow, wiped her lips with the back of her hand, and then chuckled mirthlessly. "Is that what you call us? *Family?* We're more like two miserable animals my father left behind, both locked up here in some kind of financial house arrest."

"Locked up?" Lacy smiled. "That's overstating it a bit, isn't it? You can leave any time you like."

"Ha!" Gwen sucked on her orange slice, dribbling a tiny trail of clear juice across her fingers. Malcolm had always hated Gwen's clumsiness—though once, years ago, Lacy had stood up for her, insisting that her awkwardness had its own charm, like a puppy whose feet were just a little too big to control.

"Yeah, I can leave," Gwen said, licking her fingers, as if she still were trying to annoy her father. "But leaving takes money. Which I haven't got. So I thought, since you hold the keys to the trust fund, you might want to help me out with that."

A dozen questions ran through Lacy's mind. Like...where did all this month's money go? Why didn't Gwen just get a job to help support her lifestyle? Why didn't she lower her lifestyle to match her income?

But she'd asked all those questions before, over and over in the months and years since Malcolm had died. Gwen never offered answers. Instead she just grew angry, ranted about invasions of her privacy, and generally made life such hell that Lacy finally wrote out a check to restore peace to her life.

But enough was enough. Malcolm had written the will this way because he wanted Gwen's inheritance to last. And their investment counselor had warned that if Lacy kept writing checks against the principle, it would all be gone before Gwen turned thirty.

Lacy had promised herself that she'd say no this time. No matter what.

"So? How about it, warden? Are you going to turn that key for me? Write me a check and set me free? Set us *both* free?"

Lacy put the last bill in the proper stack, squaring the edges neatly. Then she turned to Gwen with as much implacable poise as she could muster. "No," she said. "I'm not."

"What?" Gwen's eyes narrowed. "That's crazy. You can't want me hanging around here!"

"It's your house, too," Lacy responded tranquilly. "I'm delighted for you to stay as long as you want to."

"Well, I *don't* want to." Gwen shoved her milk across the counter so hard it banged into the crystal bowl of fruit, sending a clear silver ringing into the air. Milk splashed onto the pristine countertop. "As you damned well know."

"Gwen." Lacy stood, wiping the last hint of grape from her fingers with the linen napkin, then taking a kitchen rag to mop up the spilled liquid. From the parlor the Supremes were singing about baby love, but Lacy no longer enjoyed the sound. The sparkle had completely died out of her morning. "I have to get to work. We can talk about this more later, if you'd like, but I assure you it's pointless. I will not advance you any money this month."

"Damn it, Lacy, you can't refuse to—"

Lacy took a deep breath. "It's only two weeks until your next check, Gwen. Maybe you should take that time to think things through. Make a budget, maybe. Make some plans. Maybe decide where you're going with your life."

Gwen's scornful gaze raked Lacy from head to toe. "Where I'm *going?* I know where I'm going, Stepmother, dear. I'm going where the fun is. Wherever people have real lives and real relationships. Not this petrified, mummified robot thing *you and my father* called living."

Lacy lifted her chin. "Fine. But if it takes cash to

get to this Eden of yours, you'll have to wait a couple of weeks. Till your check comes through.''

Making a small, thwarted sound of anger, Gwen stood, too. They faced each other across the pass-through.

"God, you're a piece of work. You're more like a machine than a human being, aren't you?" Gwen tossed her tangled mane defiantly, but her eyes were shining with frustrated tears. "Well, I may be broke, but at least I'm *alive*. And I'll be damned if I ever let myself end up a frigid witch like you."

With one last muffled oath she stormed out, her bare feet slapping furiously against the wooden floor. As she passed the parlor, she pushed the power button to the stereo, silencing the music.

Her footsteps thumped up the stairs, a drumbeat of hostility, and finally faded. Then, nothing. Nothing but the kitchen clock, ticking away the minutes with a hollow, echoing sound.

A strangely lonely sound. Silent. Sterile.

Lacy clenched her jaw against a sudden pain. How absurd. She'd heard all of Gwen's insults—and worse—a thousand times. She'd even heard them again yesterday, from Adam Kendall.

They meant nothing. They had no power over her.

Blinking twice and squaring her shoulders, Lacy took her coffee cup to the sink, rinsed it and set it carefully in the dishwasher, as Malcolm had taught her to do.

A robot. Yes. *Frigid.* Yes. And she didn't care. *She didn't care.*

But to her horror, as she stood there, staring blindly out the kitchen window, Lacy realized that she did.

ADAM HAD ALREADY had two scotch and waters, but he was seriously considering having another.

He signaled the blond beauty who was serving the dozen or so golfers sitting around the Cartwright's lounge rehashing their day on the course. She nodded when he tapped his empty glass, then beamed at him as if he'd done something very clever.

Smart lady, Adam thought wryly. Smile therapy for wounded male egos. She probably raked in more tips in a month than most people did in a year.

"You know, bro, getting blotto isn't going to make you feel any better." Travis leaned back in his chair and puffed out his chest in a disgustingly smug way. "I beat you, and you're just going to have to live with it."

"Go ahead," Adam said. "Enjoy your victory. You'll get few enough in your life if you keep slicing your nine iron like that."

Travis snorted, tilted back and drained his fourth beer. "So *you* say. Scorecard says something else."

Adam chuckled. He and Travis had been having this argument off and on for years now—sometimes with Travis as the winner, then Adam, then Travis again.

Back in the early days, in the islands, they had played on a weedy public course whenever they could steal a free day, swatting the balls clumsily just to let off steam, and plotting how to invest their hazard pay. When their investments had begun to catch fire, they had graduated to smoother strokes at the country club every Saturday morning.

Adam could still remember the day, about three years ago, when they had realized that the money had begun to make itself, and that, if they wanted, the two of them could golf every single day of the week. It had been a heady moment—they had both laughed out loud at the sheer improbability of the miracle.

It had also been the moment when Adam knew that he would, after all, return to Pringle Island someday.

"I gotta tell you the truth, though, Adam. I kind of thought maybe your head wasn't in it today, you know?" Travis leaned forward, earnest and tipsy at the same time. "Seemed to me you might be thinking about…other stuff."

"Stuff like what?"

"Stuff like Lacy Morgan."

The waitress chose that moment to bring Adam's drink. She set it down with a lot of unnecessary fussing over the napkin and the swizzle stick. Grateful for the interruption, Adam returned her warm, attentive smile with a little extra enthusiasm.

"Well?" Travis looked impatient. "Aren't you ever going to tell me what happened? I've waited all day, but you haven't said one word about it. Damn it, are the rumors true?"

"I doubt it," Adam said. "Rumors rarely are. But I'm at something of a disadvantage here, since I have no earthly idea what you're talking about."

Travis grinned. "The hell you don't. And you can knock off that snarky prep-school sarcasm. It won't wash with me. You didn't get your money from

Daddy and Mummy. You got it by climbing into dirty tanks of oily crud with a blow torch and doing work everyone else was too scared to do.''

"Or too smart to do." Adam shook his head. "God, we were dumb, weren't we?"

"I was dumb." Travis wiggled his finger emphatically in Adam's face. "*You* were motivated. You had this burning need to make money so you could go home in glory and live happily ever after with the woman you loved."

"Like I said." Adam raised his drink. "*We* were dumb."

Travis met the toast with one heartfelt clink of beer bottle and glass, then subsided into what seemed like a melancholy reverie, no doubt reliving some of their closer calls at the refinery. And there had been quite a few. The explosion that left the scar under Adam's eye, for instance, had nearly severed the muscles in Travis's left leg.

But it was time to change the subject, before the beer had Travis so morose he became hopelessly boring.

"So," Adam said, shoving the peanuts toward his friend. "Have you had time to research the real estate situation around here yet? Or have you spent all your time on the links, trying to correct that nasty slice?"

As always, Travis shook off his blue mood easily. Adam had chosen his topic well. Travis was a real estate wiz—he'd been doubling his money every couple of years by buying and selling old houses and plots of land. Helping Adam choose an investment home on Pringle Island had been the official cause for

142 A SELF-MADE MAN

Travis's visit—though they both knew he'd go anywhere for a good game of golf.

"Yeah, I've been looking into it, but I can't rec-
ommend actually buying anything. These island people think awfully damn highly of their homes. You'd
think the dirt in their gardens was gold dust. Besides,
most of the properties have been in the family since
the ice age, you know? Even a fixer-upper out here
costs two times what it ought to."

"Only *two* times?" Adam lifted one eyebrow in a
perfect imitation of Biff, his old high school nemesis—a boy who definitely had inherited his money
from Mummy. "Surely there's enough in just one of
my Dot Com accounts to cover that, old chap."

Travis groaned. "I hate it when you do that. But
yes, of course you can *afford* to buy one. I'm just
saying it's not a good investment. The houses around
here are overinflated, just like the egos."

Adam rubbed his chin against the back of his hand.
"Still…"

"Besides, I was thinking you'd probably changed
your mind. Because of what happened at the lighthouse, that is." Travis frowned. "Hey, you never answered me about that, did you? Did it happen or
not?"

Adam sighed. "I was afraid you would remember
about that eventually. All right. Tell me what you
heard, and I'll tell you if it's true."

"Well." Travis suddenly looked a little uncomfortable. He fiddled with his empty beer bottle. "I
heard that you and Lacy had a…a…" He looked up.
"What's the polite word? What do the snobs call it?"

Adam grinned. "A contretemps?"

"Right. One of those. I heard you had a fight. When you two were out on the point." Travis leaned forward, almost knocking over the bottle. The pretty waitress cast an alarmed look their way. "I heard, bro, that she hauled off and slapped you right in the face."

"That's right." Adam sipped his scotch calmly. "She did."

Travis leaned back, letting the air out of his chest with a deep, dejected whoosh. "Man. I'm sorry, I really am. I know you had been thinking that maybe you… Maybe she… Maybe you and she…" He shrugged, as if suddenly aware that he was treading onto territory they usually roped off-limits. "Well, you know what I mean. I'm just really sorry."

"Don't be."

Travis cocked his head, obviously surprised. "Why not?"

"Because it was actually the most encouraging sign I've seen since we got here."

"Encouraging? Are you nuts? The woman wanted to draw blood. If that's encouraging, what would it take to discourage you?"

"Indifference. Apathy." Adam took his time, explaining patiently, remembering that four beers always fuzzed Travis's brain just a little. "When it comes to women, fire is always preferable to ice."

Travis nodded slowly as understanding dawned. "Oh. *Oh, yeah.* I get it." He sighed again, then rubbed at his face as if all this deep thinking were making him tired. "So. Now you've started a fire. What are you going to do about it?"

Adam smiled, stood up and tossed a generous tip on the table.

"That's easy," he said. "I'm going to buy a house."

CHAPTER EIGHT

BY EIGHT ON ANY summer Saturday morning, not one single parking space was left within three blocks of the Main Street farmer's market. Today, the day of Lacy's long-anticipated progressive dinner, things were even worse. Every serious cook in town was at the market bright and early, fighting over the best supplies.

So Lacy didn't bother looking for a space nearby. She just drove on down to the Crested Plume Antiques store at the end of Main and walked back. It was no hardship. She loved to walk, especially in the early morning, when the salt air smelled fresh, and the distant rumble of waves breaking against the shore could still be heard over the tourist traffic.

It was going to be a beautiful day—hot but breezy, with billowing cumulus clouds already stacking up overhead. She hoped the weather held, because guests at tonight's dinner—billed as The Seafood Stroll— would start at one end of the island and eat their way across town. If the night was clear, the finale would be held at the beach, where the guests would sit on blankets and drink Bellinis under the starlight, while local musicians serenaded from the dunes.

As she had expected, the scene at the market was

bedlam. Mildred Pritchett and Elspeth Jared faced off over a cart of freshly grown herbs, as tense as gunslingers. Over by the fruit stands, the three wives of the Pringle brothers, the island's premiere family, were stuffing melons and citrus into their bags seemingly at random, as if they had won a five-minute, all-you-can grab shopping spree contest.

Tilly was there, too, even though she'd already acquired the fruit necessary for her cream-puff pastry swans, and didn't need anything more from the farmer's market. She was there for the pure excitement of it all.

When Lacy walked up, Tilly was arguing heatedly with the vendor about the price of pears. Her friends were ignoring her—it was a familiar sight. But several tourists had paused to watch the battle. From the fuss Tilly made over an extra nickel, no one could have guessed she was one of the wealthiest women on the island.

"It's all right," Lacy interjected, putting her arm through Tilly's. "She'll take them, and she'll pay full price."

Tilly turned with a scowl. "I will not. He's charging a dollar and ninety—"

"She'll take them," Lacy repeated, squeezing Tilly's arm warningly. She turned to her friend as the man began huffily bagging pears. "Stop trying to beat the fellow down," she said sternly. "For you it's pure entertainment. For him it's business."

Tilly hesitated, obviously debating whether to bother taking offense. But then she laughed, throwing back her head in such enthusiastic enjoyment that her wig wobbled earthward. She reached up and anchored it back into place with one good shove.

"Oh, she's right, she's right," she said to the vendor, taking the bag of pears and giving him his money. "I love to haggle. You should see me at the bazaar in Morocco."

"I'd love to," the man said dourly.

Before Tilly could begin fussing again, Lacy steered her toward the nearby café. "Sit," she said, pointing to one of the small black iron chairs. "I'll bet the price of one of those pears that you haven't eaten breakfast this morning."

Tilly's expression was so guilty Lacy almost laughed. But it wasn't funny. It was serious. So she held back her smile and ordered scrambled eggs and whole wheat toast, ignoring Tilly's muttering about Belgian waffles and chocolate croissants.

But soon enough Tilly was happily distracted by the bustle of life around them. Anyone could tell in an instant that it was the peak of the island's tourist season. The quaint, twisting Main Street was jammed with strolling couples, sidewalk artists, skate-boarding teenagers. Within fifteen minutes, half of Tilly's friends had passed by, and she enjoyed telling them how heartless Lacy was about the pastries.

Lacy tuned her out, preferring to listen to the street musicians who had set up an impromptu stage just two doors down from the café. Three shaggy blondes were running through every Beach Boys song they knew, using only a guitar, a keyboard and a tambourine. The air rang with laughter and music, and several couples broke into spontaneous dancing.

Lacy watched them with something that felt strangely like envy. They were so blissfully uninhibited. As if it hadn't ever occurred to them that they looked silly. Malcolm would have found it undignified. But no one else did, Lacy realized as she glanced around. Everyone else seemed to find it delightful, laughing and clapping and singing along, enjoying the show.

A new couple joined the others. Lacy recognized them with a small shock. It was Gwen, dressed as flamboyantly as ever in a neon orange summer dress belted with a lemon-yellow scarf. And her partner was Adam's friend, that darling Travis Rourke, whose Hawaiian print shirt was equally exotic. They looked wonderful dancing together, Lacy thought—full of life, health and sexy charm.

Malcolm would have been livid. His daughter making a spectacle of herself in public! But Malcolm would have been wrong, Lacy realized with a cold certainty. He would have been repressively, witheringly, overbearingly *wrong*.

"What's the matter, Lacy?" Tilly put her hand over Lacy's elbow. "I'm just kidding about the Sugar Police thing, you know."

Lacy smiled. "No, you're not, but that's okay. I *am* the Sugar Police."

Tilly looked at her closely. "Still," she said. "Something's wrong. What is it, honey?"

Lacy folded her napkin several times before answering. She wasn't sure how much of the truth to give. But she needed to talk to someone, and Tilly was the only person she could come close to being honest with.

"I'm not sure," she began slowly. "I just feel a little…edgy these days."

"Edgy? About tonight? It's going to be a big hit, honey. It's going to put you over the top, and that neonatal wing is going to get built, I promise."

Lacy shook her head. "No. Not about tonight. Just generally, about everything. I feel—" She broke off, her gaze following the dancers as they moved laughingly into an updated rendition of the Twist.

How could she say this? That was the entire problem, in a nutshell. She *felt*. For the first time in years, she had started to feel again.

"I feel unsettled," she said, hoping that would be enough. "It's as if I suddenly don't have complete control over my emotions anymore. I can be happy one minute, and the next minute I'm down. It's not like me. You know I never lose my temper, Tilly. Never. But the other day, I—"

"You slapped Adam Kendall?"

Lacy sighed, abandoning all hope that she hadn't been seen. "You heard about it, then?"

"Of course I heard about it." Tilly grinned. "This is Pringle Island, sweetheart. The guy serving us these nasty scrambled eggs has heard about it."

Lacy flushed, tossing her napkin onto the table. "Oh, dear God…"

"But what's so bad about that?" Tilly took a sip of coffee serenely. "They're bored. It gives them something to talk about."

"I don't want them talking about me. And besides,

that isn't me! I don't do things like that. I don't lose my temper, I don't slap people—''

"Well, I guess you do now." Tilly looked pleased. "And be honest with yourself, honey. Didn't Adam Kendall deserve slapping?"

"No." Lacy shook her head. "Well, maybe. Yes. I don't know." She turned to the older woman helplessly. "Good grief, listen to me, Tilly. I sound like some kind of dithering airhead. This isn't me. I don't dither."

Tilly's face softened, and she put her hand against Lacy's cheek. "It's all right," she said. "You're just waking up. And you have to expect things to be a little confusing."

"Waking up?" Lacy sat as straight as she could, somehow finding Tilly's comment oddly disconcerting. It had the inescapable ring of truth.

"Yes, Sleeping Beauty. Waking up." Tilly took Lacy's hands and covered them protectively with her own cool, dry palms. "You've been a long time healing. But you were hurt, sweetheart. Horribly hurt. Losing Adam. Losing the baby—"

"Tilly, don't." Lacy felt a sudden horror that she might cry. When had she begun to shed tears so easily, like summer rain? She hadn't cried in almost ten years, until the past few days.

"Well, it was all very difficult. It was only natural that you should cocoon yourself, giving yourself time to heal. But maybe you're strong enough now to come out. Maybe you're ready to wake up, emerge from the cocoon, and enter the world again."

Lacy stared at her friend numbly. "What if I don't

want to?'' She squeezed Tilly's hands. ''What if I liked it better being asleep?''

Tilly reached over and placed a soft kiss on Lacy's cheek. ''I'm not sure it's your decision. The anaesthetic is wearing off, and life is calling. You're just going to have to get up and answer.''

Suddenly, a shadow fell over their table. Lacy didn't even look up. She knew who it was. Subconsciously, she moment she'd seen Travis Rourke, she had known Adam must be here, too.

''Good morning, Adam,'' Tilly said eagerly, immediately abandoning the earnest tone of their earlier conversation and adopting a bright, flirtatious air. ''Thank goodness! Yes, Lacy would like to dance— by all means take her away so I can order something decent to eat!''

''Tilly!'' Lacy pressed the older woman's knee under the table. She wasn't quite able to switch gears so easily. And hadn't they just been talking, indirectly at least, about Adam? About the way his reappearance was threatening to ruin Lacy's quiet, controlled existence? Or had she ever quite admitted that her painful awakening had coincided with Adam's return?

''Morning, ladies,'' Adam said equably. His mouth was tucked in at one corner, as if he were holding back a smile. ''Tilly, I'd love to oblige you, but I'm afraid street dancing is something that happens spontaneously or not at all.''

Tilly grumbled. ''Well, pretend it was your idea, then. I'm starving here.''

Adam turned to Lacy obediently. ''I know you'll

be stunned to discover that I feel a sudden urge to do the twist. Will you join me?''

What stunned her was that she felt a momentary impulse of her own—a shocking, unprecedented impulse to say "yes."

How ridiculous! This was what she had meant when she told Tilly she felt "edgy." How erratic could one woman be? Less than a week ago she had slapped this man in public. Now she was going to *dance* with him? It would look schizophrenic. It would *be* schizophrenic. The rumormongers would be weak with glee.

"I don't think so," she said, trying for an even, pleasant tone. If she ever did give in to an impulse like this, it wouldn't be with Adam Kendall. "But thank you."

"Heaven help me, apparently the Sugar Police never rests," Tilly complained loudly. "Well, thanks for trying. At least she didn't slap you."

Lacy flushed and stared at Tilly, as much to avoid Adam's eyes as anything else. How could she be so low as to bring this up in front of him? Lacy had considered apologizing to Adam at some point, but she wouldn't be forced into it by a meddling Tilly Barnhardt.

Adam raised one eyebrow. "Not yet," he said. "But after all, it's still early."

"Besides, Lacy has her mind on other things," Tilly explained agreeably. "Tonight is the last big fund-raiser of the neonatal wing campaign. The Seafood Stroll. Have you heard about it? It's five hundred dollars a head, but now that you're rich you won't mind that, will you? And besides, it's worth every penny. It's the only way to get your hands on any of my famous pastry swans.''

"I've already bought my ticket," he said with a smile. "Jennifer Lansing talked me into it. Apparently it's also the only way to get one's hands on her famous chilled chicken breasts.''

Tilly chuckled evilly. "Don't you believe it for a minute, son.''

Enough. Lacy stood. Unfortunately she stood so abruptly that she knocked over Tilly's small glass of orange juice. It made a puddle on the white tablecloth and dripped stickily onto the toe of her bright white tennis shoes. Apparently the newly awakened Lacy was just as clumsy as her stepdaughter.

"Tilly, I'd really better get going," she said, mopping as fast as she could, dispensing with grace for the moment. *Damn him,* she thought, though she couldn't quite figure out how it was Adam's fault. "I have a lot left to do before tonight.''

Adam tilted his head. The morning sun danced along his high cheekbones and lit the sapphire blue of his eyes. "Anything I could help with?''

"No," she said quickly, appalled at how those eyes seemed to reach right in and tweak her edgy nerves. "No. I'd just better get going. I've got— So many details still— There's so much—''

"Oh, for heaven's sakes, just run on, then. Adam will see me to my car.'' Tilly laughed, patting Lacy on the arm, and turned to Adam with an innocent smile. "Don't worry about Lacy. You see, she woke up rather late, and she's got a lot of catching up to do.''

PUSHING HER HAIR OUT of her face with a giant mitted hand, Lacy stared down at the cookie tray in dismay. Rows and rows of perfectly shaped question marks, which she had created herself just twenty minutes ago. Every one of them burned to a crisp.

The air in Tilly's state-of-the-art kitchen was acrid with the smell of scorched pastry dough. Lacy looked at the clock—6:45. In one hour and fifteen minutes, the first guests would be arriving. They would sit at Tilly's exquisitely set table, holding shining silver spoons and staring at the empty Limoges plates in front of them. They would be expecting one of the three young servers, all lace-capped and standing at attention, to deliver them each one of Tilly's legendary cream-puff pastry swans.

Except that there were no swans. There were only these rows of blackened swan necks. All lying charred and dead on this cookie tray.

Angie, the youngest of the three hospital candy stripers who had volunteered to serve at Tilly's house tonight, appeared at the kitchen door. She sniffed the air anxiously.

"Umm...Mrs. Morgan?" She wrinkled her nose. "Mrs. Barnhardt asked me to tell you that sometimes the oven runs a little hot."

Lacy managed a rueful smile. "Yes," she said, looking down at the pitiful swan necks. "I just noticed that."

Angie braided her fingers together, obviously in

misery. "Oh dear. Oh dear, I guess I'd better tell Mrs. Barnhardt. The doctor is with her, but—"

"No." Lacy shook her head emphatically. "No, don't tell her. I don't want her upset." She cast another glance at the clock—6:48. "There's still time. If I have enough pastry dough left, I can begin again."

She tilted the tray, sliding the ruined pastry into a plastic bag. "Here. If you'll just take these to the outside can, please? Maybe we can get the air cleared out in here before the guests arrive."

Angie accepted the trash bag and scurried away. Lacy turned back to the refrigerator, where the pasty dough was still chilling. Thank goodness Tilly had made the dough up in advance—Lacy wouldn't have dared to pass her own mediocre concoctions off as Tilly's famous specialty.

She tried to focus, but as she filled the pastry bag she noticed that her hands were trembling slightly. She didn't want to be here. She wanted to be upstairs, with Tilly. She wanted to hear what the doctor had to report. Instead, she had to stay down in the Barnhardt kitchen, working on these frivolous swans.

Oh, Tilly. Tilly, you stubborn old dragon. Why did you do something so foolish?

Earlier this afternoon the young candy striper had telephoned her in a panic. Tilly was unconscious. Lacy had guessed instantly what had happened. And when Tilly had recovered enough to talk, she herself had confirmed it. Determined to sample her own work as she baked, Tilly had injected herself with an extra dose of insulin.

The sugar and the medicine would safely cancel each other out, she had assumed. But she had assumed wrong. Instead she had collapsed, unconscious, on the kitchen floor.

That had been two hours ago. The doctor had arrived quickly, and Tilly had come around, weak, but conscious and coherent. Still, Lacy couldn't stop worrying. She had wanted to cancel the dinner, but Tilly had insisted that the fund-raising must go on. She had worked herself into quite a state fretting about it, until Lacy had finally agreed to come down and make the pastry swans.

It was so hard to concentrate. She had to try three times to get the nozzle attached to the pastry bag. Finally a replacement batch of swan necks was ready. Lacy lowered the oven temperature fifty degrees and slid the tray inside. Then she turned her attention to the swan's bodies, one hundred of which sat headless on the butcher block island in the center of the kitchen.

Wings. She had to make the wings. But she'd created only a dozen pairs of the little triangles before the knife slipped, its razor-sharp edge slicing easily through the tip of her index finger.

"Ouch!" She dropped the knife and brought her stinging finger up to assess the damage. Not a long cut, but a deep one. A bloom of bright red blood appeared quickly, and she had to whisk her hand away to avoid staining the swans.

She stood at the sink, rinsing her finger while she kept a cautious eye on the stove—7:06 and still ticking away. *God.* Could anything else go wrong?

"Mrs. Morgan?" Angie was back at the kitchen doorway, looking more diffident than ever. "Mrs. Morgan, I'm not sure what to do. A Mr. Kendall is here. He says Mrs. Barnhardt called him and asked him to come. But you had said that no one should be allow to see her—"

"I'm not here to see Mrs. Barnhardt," a deep voice corrected firmly from just behind Angie's shoulder. "I'm here to see Mrs. Morgan."

"Oh." Angie moved out of the way, watching with blatant admiration as Adam entered the kitchen. She gaped in a kind of mindless pleasure as he touched her shoulder and gave her a reassuring smile.

"Thanks," he said. "I'll help Mrs. Morgan now. We'll be fine."

He was already dressed for the dinner, Lacy saw. But he wasn't letting that stop him. As he moved into the room, he shrugged off his jacket, tossed it over the back of a kitchen chair, tugged down his tie, and began to roll up his white shirtsleeves.

He was as expensively dressed as Malcolm had ever been, she noticed. She recognized that fine double-needle tailoring, that soft-as-water linen. And yet the effect was subtly different. Malcolm had seemed to draw substance from his pricey clothes, and had stood in them stiffly, as if insisting that you notice how important he was. With Adam, the man was dominant. The clothes draped his elegant, muscular body with a sublime indifference. You knew he would be just as beautiful in jeans. Or in nothing at all.

She suddenly became aware that she was standing

there just as stupidly blank as Angie had been, with the cool water from the spigot pouring unnoticed over her finger.

No. She had to do better than this. She turned off the water and faced him squarely. "Adam, look, I'm not sure what Tilly—"

With a sudden movement, he reached past her, grabbing her forgotten mitt from the counter and sliding his hand into it smoothly. He opened the oven door quickly and whisked out the tray of swan necks. Just in the nick of time, she realized. They were the perfect golden brown. Another thirty seconds, and she would have had a second tray of blackened pastry.

"Thank you," she forced herself to say. "I had forgotten about them. I cut my finger, you see, and—"

"You sure did. Give me that." He set the tray onto the island, grabbed a couple of paper towels from the nearby roll and pulled her hand toward him. It was bleeding again, she realized. Her finger was red down to the last knuckle.

She knew how incompetent she looked. As he applied a firm pressure to her finger, she waited for him to make one of his snide comments. Ovens that overheated and knives that hacked off fingers? This was the woman all Pringle Island society had called "the perfect hostess"?

She didn't know if she could take his sarcasm on top of everything else. "Look, Adam," she said tensely, "I don't know why Tilly called you, but quite honestly I don't think I'm up to dealing with you right now. As you can see, I'm having some problems. I've been drafted at the last minute to bake something I'm not familiar with. I'm way behind schedule, and I'm worried to death about Tilly. The last thing I need is someone hanging around looking for something to sneer at.''

He didn't respond right away. He lifted the paper towels, checking her finger. "Did you put hydrogen peroxide on this?''

"Yes,'' she said, pulling her hand back. "Adam, did you hear me? I really think it would be best if you left now.''

He crumpled the paper towels and tossed them in the under-counter trash. "I'm here to help,'' he said evenly. "That's all. Tilly thought you needed a hand.''

What could she say to that? Even if he didn't sneer, he was going to distract her. But she couldn't admit that just being in the same room with him clouded her thinking.

So what could she say? To buy time, she busied herself looking for a bandage. With her back to him, she tried another tack. "And that was thoughtful of her, really. I do appreciate it, but—'' She found a package of bandages, thank goodness. "But it's *baking,* Adam. It's little swan's wings and chantilly cream and confectioner's sugar. It's not exactly your specialty, is it?''

"Because I'm a guy? That's not very enlightened, Lacy.''

"No,'' she said. "I know plenty of guys who love to bake. And I know you used to cook when you lived at home with your father. But now you— You're—''

You're more at home at the golf course, or the health spa, or the bedroom. You're more comfortable watching your portfolio expand than watching an egg timer. You're too much man for this moment. You're all gorgeous muscle and sexuality, and I don't want you here.

"You know," he said, "there were no women at the refinery. No housekeepers, no cooks, no mothers, no girlfriends. We were just a bunch of crazy boys who somehow managed to do everything ourselves. And we got pretty good at it. Actually, I'm a damn fine cook."

He looked up at the clock. "But more importantly, I'm a pair of hands," he said matter-of-factly.

Still she hesitated. "You'll miss the dinner," she said. "You'll miss Jennifer Lansing's famous chilled chicken breasts."

He chuckled and pulled his tie completely off, tossing it toward his jacket. "Not very much I won't." His grin was charmingly lopsided, just like the old days. "Come on, Lacy. Let it go. It's 7:33, and we've got a hundred swans to build."

CHAPTER NINE

VOLUNTEER VALETS WERE parking cars out at the beach, so even though Lacy arrived very late, she was able to drive right up to the champagne finale of her Seafood Stroll.

As she made her way across the boardwalk that led over the small dunes, she saw that even the weather had cooperated. A cool breeze made the yellow Tiki torches dance. The sky was clear, and a romantic blue moon-glow bathed the secluded elbow of sandy beach where the guests had gathered.

She could hear the band playing. Slow songs, of course. After scallop bisque, stuffed grape leaves, summer squash casserole, lobster salad—and of course cream-puff pastry swans dusted in powdered sugar—everyone was far too well fed to do any vigorous dancing tonight.

Though Lacy had hated to leave Tilly, she was glad she had come. The fund-raiser had been a terrific amount of work. But the work was done. Tilly was asleep with a private nurse standing guard. It was time to sit back and relax.

Lacy stepped quietly onto the beach, planning to blend in without fanfare, but her key volunteers must have been watching for her arrival. They motioned for the band to hush. Within seconds two dozen of her closest allies, men and women who believed that the neonatal unit was important to Pringle Island, had collected together for a warm outburst of applause.

Embarrassed, Lacy shook her head, hoping to stem the flow.

"Speech! Speech!"

Though she hated such things, she knew she had to manage a few words. These people had worked very hard for her project.

"Hi, everyone," she said, summoning her brightest smile in spite of her weariness. "I'm pretty sure I'm looking at the best-fed people in New England tonight." A ripple of agreement ran through the crowd. "And I'm absolutely certain not one of us will dare to step on the scales in the morning."

They laughed. A few patted their midsections and groaned happily. "But you don't have me to thank for that," she said. "Thank all these talented cooks, who created such masterpieces. And, of course, thank our generous friends, who contributed so handsomely to the cause."

The applause went up again, and the chefs involved bowed with laughing pride.

"So have a great time tonight. You've earned it. And if you stay long enough, who knows? You may even dance off a few of those calories."

She motioned for the band to begin again. The violins moved into a rendition of the Brahms Lullaby— a song they'd chosen in honor of the babies whose lives might one day be saved by the neonatal unit.

The melody was timeless. Almost unbearably poignant. Lacy felt a stinging behind her eyes, but somehow she blinked it away. It was a time for joy, and she would not spoil it with selfish sentimentality.

She moved into the crowd, thanking people individually as she went. The dancing had begun again—under such a moon, it was almost impossible not to want to take someone in your arms. Teddy Kilgore was doing a body meld with Gwen. Silas Jared was pacing off a stately waltz with his daughter-in-law. The two oldest Pringle sisters were dancing with each other. And over there, just skirting the ruffled edge where the water met the shore, Jennifer Lansing was cheek to cheek with Adam.

Lacy turned away. Perhaps a glass of champagne…

"Lacy! You're not already taken? I can't believe my luck! Dance with me!"

Travis Rourke was smiling at her, and he looked so adorable, with his sun-bronzed laugh lines radiating out from his eyes and the moonlight turning his tousled hair almost white. She couldn't say no. She didn't want to say no. After all, she was human. The moonlight affected her the same way it did everyone else.

So she moved into his arms, which were strong and warm and easy. He danced like a dream, full of a graceful vitality. She remembered how she'd seen him doing the twist with Gwen this morning, right in the middle of the street, completely uninhibited, completely sexy. The thought made her smile.

"What?" Travis grinned down at her. "Drat! Did I do something ridiculous already?"

She shook her head. "Of course not. I was just

thinking you're a lovely dancer. I saw you this morning, at the market. With Gwen.''

"Oh, yeah. Wow. She's an amazing lady. A real pistol." He paused. "Sorry, I guess you already know that. She did mention that you and she— Drat, how should I put this? I guess sometimes you just wish she weren't *quite* such a pistol, right?''

Lacy looked at him. In the bright wash of moonlight she could see his kind, perceptive features clearly, and she wondered if there was any point in pretending things were fine. Gwen, with her shoot-from-the-hip candor, had probably told him everything within ten minutes of meeting him.

"Well," she admitted, "sometimes I wish the pistol didn't seem to be loaded and pointed right at my head.''

Travis nodded, smiling wryly. "Know what's funny, though? I think she feels the same way about you.''

"About me?" Lacy expressed her incredulity politely but clearly. "I'd be very surprised if that were true.''

Travis shrugged. "I could be wrong, I guess. But I've got six older sisters, so I've seen the female psyche up close and personal all my life. I'm kind of a female-ologist, right?'' He laughed without self-consciousness. "In fact, I've got one sister who is a lot like her, I think.''

"Really." Lacy smiled, imagining the Rourke household. She'd be willing to bet those Rourke girls had doted on their sunny younger brother shamelessly.

"Yep." He danced into a twirl, apparently just for the fun of it, then settled down again. "Moira. She wasn't ever quite like the others. She didn't want to be a doctor, or a lawyer, or an Indian chief. She was always off in her own world, always dying her hair purple or piercing her eyebrow or something. Always assuming the others looked down on her. She was pretty prickly there for a few years. Darn hard to get along with."

"And now?"

"Now she's got an art gallery, a husband who's something big for Greenpeace, and three little girls who, if there is a God, will someday drive her as crazy as she drove us."

"And does she still have purple hair?"

Travis chuckled. "Sometimes. She's still Moira, after all. Which is good, because we adore her as she is. She just needed to learn to adore herself, too."

Lacy didn't answer for a moment, absorbing his message. Maybe he had a point. Gwen's mother had died when she was just a toddler—and growing up with Malcolm couldn't have been great for anyone's self-esteem. And then to get a stepmother barely five years older than herself... Even worse, a stepmother who had no idea how to handle an unhappy adolescent.

"Thanks," she said. "I understand what you're trying to—"

But just then someone tapped Lacy's arm. She looked over her shoulder. It was Gwen.

"Cutting in!" Gwen looked gorgeous in a bright green sarong, her hair spraying out from a glittery blue band like a moonlight-white waterfall. But her expression as she stared at Lacy was stony. "Sorry, Lacy. You can't monopolize the greatest looking guys all night just because you're the big boss of this fundraiser."

Lacy backed out of Travis's arms, remembering the rebellious Moira, who had somehow learned to love herself....

"You're right," she said agreeably, giving Gwen a warm smile. "Your turn." She started to walk away, but at the last minute she reached back and touched Gwen's shoulder. "Hey—I hear you helped Jennifer make the chicken tonight. That was awfully nice. Thanks."

Gwen screwed up one side of her face, rejecting the compliment as if it smelled a little rotten. "Yeah, well, it was no big deal," she said. Then she turned to Travis. "Are you going to dance with me or not?"

ADAM HAD FINALLY SHED Jennifer Lansing—no easy task. The woman had attached herself like Velcro to his arm when he walked in, and she hadn't let go. But eventually he'd been able to dance over toward Howard Whitehead, who had more money than anyone on the island and an interest in local history. As Adam had hoped, Jennifer had been unable to resist the bait, so between songs he had subtly passed her off to the millionaire.

Now, champagne in hand, he had retreated to the boardwalk, where he could hear the wind whispering through the eel grass and watch the white-capped waves rolling in toward shore in sets of three.

He could also see Lacy dancing with Travis, who was obviously knocking himself out trying to amuse her.

As far as Adam could tell, Travis was having only limited success. Lacy was smiling, but it was that too-smooth, perfect-hostess smile. Boy, she had that one down pat, like a computer-chip smile.

But it still was enough to set off a little stick of dynamite in Adam's veins. He finished off his champagne in one long tilt. She was more beautiful than ever, wasn't she? And he still had it bad.

Once, he had believed she would be his wife. Sure, they'd parted in anger. Sure, she hadn't understood why he'd had to leave. But he hadn't taken any of that seriously. She'd wait for him. They belonged together. Every plan he made, every dream he dreamed, had been built around that fact.

The night he had discovered she *hadn't* waited, that she was married to someone else, he'd drunk himself into a fury. And from there he'd kept drinking, until his rage had eventually subsided into stupor of self-pitying grief.

He must have been insufferable. Travis had finally taken the bottle away. "An angel? Man, you're scaring me now," he'd said. "Next time we have a day off, you're gonna get yourself a date, bro. You're so horny you're starting to hallucinate."

But he hadn't been hallucinating. She had been like an angel. Blushing, passionate Lacy Mayfair had been able to bring him to his knees with one shy glance from those wide gray-blue eyes. And apparently poised, icy Lacy Morgan could do it, too.

Yeah, he had it bad all right. He had come home to Pringle Island looking for closure—and perhaps a small, satisfying pinch of revenge. He had been so confident, certain that the faithless bitch who had broken his heart had no power over him anymore.

But who was he kidding? No power? Dreams of white lace, golden rings and "forever after" might be dead. But dreams of hot nights, sweet, velvet skin and hard, sweating sex were definitely alive and kicking.

Kicking him right in the gut.

He'd just about decided to cut in on Travis when he heard footsteps behind him on the boardwalk. He turned to see a middle-aged man in a suit coming up slowly toward the beach.

"Hello," the man said politely. "Maybe you could help me. I'm trying to find Mrs. Malcolm Morgan."

Adam looked him over. Clean cut, mid-forties. Fairly nice suit, though of course nothing like the designer duds worn by the guests at this snobby little soiree. A decent fellow. Working guy. But something was eating at him right now. The man looked tense, as if he was nursing bad news.

Suddenly Adam had a pretty good idea who he might be. "Is your name Frennick, by any chance?"

The man smiled, clearly surprised. "That's right. Has she told you about me? I'm sorry. I thought she wanted this kept confidential— And I don't think we've met—"

"We haven't. And she hasn't. I heard about you just tonight, from Tilly Barnhardt. She's an old friend of mine. I'm Adam Kendall."

Frennick shook Adam's hand. "Oh, okay, then. Still, I think I should report to Mrs. Morgan...."

Adam nodded. "She's over there—" He was surprised to see that Lacy was no longer dancing with Travis. Instead, Gwen was hanging all over him. "Well, she was."

At that moment, Gwen looked up. She squinted toward the boardwalk. With a startling suddenness, her expression turned thunderously black. She said something to Travis, shaking her head emphatically as he started to follow her. Then, lifting the hem of her sarong into one fist for faster movement, she started stalking toward Adam and the newcomer.

"Mr. Frennick!" She climbed the three stairs to the boardwalk. Her eyes were blazing. "You may not remember me, but I definitely remember you. I know what you are, what you do. You're a snoop, that's what you are. My father used you all the time. And now that Stepwitch is using you, too, isn't she? Well, you can just stop following me around, buddy, because—"

"Gwen." Adam interrupted as soon as he realized that the older man was too stunned to set things straight. "Mr. Frennick isn't following you around. He's here to see Lacy."

"Well, sure he is!" She didn't take her eyes off the other man, as if she could scowl him into retreat. "He's got to report to her, doesn't he? So did you dig up plenty of dirt, Mr. Frennick? Did you find out about the time I bounced a check at the grocery store?"

Frennick looked miserable. "Miss Morgan," he began awkwardly. "I can assure you that I—"

But Lacy, ever the alert hostess, had obviously noticed the fuss and had smoothly made her way across the beach, over to her stepdaughter. Her smile was still lovely, but it seemed strained, artificially fixed in place.

"Gwen, keep your voice down," she said firmly, holding out her hand at the same time to greet the newcomer. "Hello, Mr. Frennick. I apologize for my stepdaughter. Gwen, I can't imagine where you got the idea that Mr. Frennick has anything to do with you."

"Don't you dare apologize for me!" Gwen was practically in tears. "You're not responsible for what I do. You aren't my father. You aren't even my mother. You have no right at all to have this guy snoop around my life."

"I'm not doing any such thing," Mr. Frennick insisted, recovering his poise now that Lacy was here as backup. "I am a licensed private investigator. I did legitimate business work for your father, Miss Morgan. And now I'm doing legitimate work for your stepmother. It has nothing at all to do with you."

Gwen frowned, and Adam saw the first hint of uncertainty flash through her expression. "Of course you'd have to say that."

"He says that because it's true." Lacy faced Gwen patiently. "This has nothing at all to do with you, Gwen. You have my word on that."

"Your word?" Gwen muttered something unintelligible under her breath. "Fine. What *does* it have to do with?"

Adam wondered how Lacy would handle that question, which was thrust at her like a dare. But he shouldn't have worried. Naturally, the composed, articulate Mrs. Malcolm Morgan was equal to any challenge.

She put her hand gently on her stepdaughter's elbow. "It's personal, Gwen. I'm sorry, but just as it would be wrong for me to pry into your life, it would also be wrong for you to pry into mine, wouldn't it?"

For a moment Adam thought Gwen was going to refuse to back down. Not because she thought Lacy was lying. He could tell that, in spite of the rude mutterings, Lacy's word did carry a lot of weight with her stepdaughter. Still, Gwen clearly hated losing face.

Luckily, Teddy Kilgore chose that moment to come looking for a dance. "Gwen," he called up from the base of the boardwalk. "Gwen, come on down! They're playing our song!"

Gwen wasn't stupid. She saw her safe exit, and she took it, though she cast one last daggered look at Lacy before haughtily descending the stairs to meet the boy waiting there.

But the resentment bounced off Lacy like the impotent nonsense it was. She turned to Adam. "Thank you," she said formally. "Now if you'll excuse me, Mr. Frennick and I—"

Adam shook his head. "I think I'll stay. I want to hear what Mr. Frennick has to say."

She frowned, and he could see the surprised annoyance racing through her mind. Was she going to have to fend him off as well?

"It's all right," Adam said, cutting through the impending protests. "I know about Tilly's baby."

"What?" She was good, but he noticed that she couldn't quite hide her shock. "You do? How?"

"Tilly told me tonight, when I went up to check on her. It seemed to be weighing heavily on her mind, perhaps because of the insulin episode. She told me she got pregnant sixty-two years ago and gave the child up for adoption. She said she had hired a private detective to locate her daughter, and that you were urging her to start the investigation. She wanted my advice."

"Oh." Lacy looked at Frennick. "Well, I—"

"She didn't seem to think any investigation had actually begun yet." He raised one brow. "Apparently she was mistaken. I can't imagine Mr. Frennick would track you down here, in the middle of the night, unless he has news of some kind. I want to hear it."

Obviously Lacy knew when she had lost an argument. She lifted her chin slightly, but she didn't in any other way exhibit discomfort.

"All right, Mr. Frennick," she said. "Apparently Mrs. Barnhardt has confided in Mr. Kendall. So tell us both. Have you found Tilly's daughter?"

"Yes, I'm afraid I have." The sad-eyed man took a deep breath. "Her adopted name was Caroline Scott. Up until two years ago, she was a nurse practitioner in the Boston area."

Lacy's eyes grew very dark. "What happened two years ago?"

"Two years ago," he said slowly, "she died."

HER EVENING SHOES in her hand, Lacy had covered at least a quarter of a mile along the wet sand before Adam caught up with her. Lost in her own unhappy thoughts, she had been blind to everything around her, deaf to all sounds, including apparently the one of a man running up behind her.

So she was surprised when he grabbed hold of her elbow, exerting just enough pressure to slow her down, then ease her to a complete stop.

"Hey," he said softly. "Talk to me."

She didn't turn around. She didn't have control of her face right now. "I don't want to talk," she said. "I want to be alone."

"Sixty-two years is a long time, Lacy," he said. "Tilly knew this was one of the possible outcomes. You must have known that, too."

"Of course I did." But she hadn't ever really believed it. Fate would not be so cruel, she'd thought. After sixty years of regret, sixty years of longing, surely Tilly would get another chance. And now to learn that her daughter was gone forever—that there would be no reunion, no second chances...

Oh, she had been so naive. Lacy stared out at the ocean, which seemed massive tonight, swollen waves moving inexorably toward the shore, equally indifferent to the human pleasure going on back at the party, and to the suffering here in her heart. She had heard that some people were comforted by the immensity of it, the sense of something more eternal than trivial human concerns. But tonight it simply made her feel small and helpless.

"Tilly is tough," Adam said bracingly. "She can take it."

"I know." Her breath hitched. "I know."

And she did. She knew all about being tough. About enduring what you had to endure. But she had wanted something better than that for Tilly. She had wanted a rainbow, storybook ending. She had wanted laughter and joy, forgiveness and relief. She'd wanted Tilly to have a chance to shower her child with the millions of hugs and kisses she'd been holding inside her for sixty-two years. Since the day her child had been born—and then whisked away.

Lacy knew how all that love, locked inside you with nowhere to go, could swell and ache until you thought you'd go mad.

"I'm not going to tell her." Lacy said, talking fast, as if she weren't sure her voice would hold out. "That's why I began the investigation secretly. So that if the news was bad in any way—if her daughter couldn't be found, or didn't want to be found…or if the worst happened…if she were…"

Her words seemed to strangle on themselves. Falling silent, she wrapped her arms over her chest, holding onto her own elbows as if she could keep herself from falling apart.

"Lacy." Adam put his hands on her shoulders and turned her toward him, though she tried to resist. The moonlight fell full on her face, and, looking at her, he groaned low under his breath. "Lacy, don't. Don't cry."

"I'm not crying." She shook her head angrily, ignoring the tracks of wetness that felt oddly cool as the evening breeze touched them. "I don't cry."

He reached up with his fingers and brushed the wetness away slowly. He ran his thumbs under her eyes, drying them. But as soon as he had wiped away one wet streak, another appeared.

"I don't," she repeated tonelessly. "I don't know what this is. I never cry. *Never.*"

"I know," he agreed softly, still stroking the ever-renewing dampness with a velvet rhythm. "It's all right, Lacy. It's all right."

Was it? Would it ever be all right again? She didn't believe it, but she discovered that she loved the sound of his voice saying so. She found herself leaning, by minute fractions of invisible inches, into the warmth of his palm. His drifting fingers offered a kind of comfort she craved without knowing its name.

Gently, as if following a diagram of tenderness, he touched his lips to her forehead, her temple, her closed eyelids, the trembling corner of her mouth.

And then, as though the map had led him to an inevitable destination, he kissed her. She felt his heat pulsing, poised above her, and then his soft strength pressing in, seeking some truth, some answer that only her lips could provide.

She tasted salt tears and ocean mist. And Adam. She tasted Adam.

Adam... Whispering his name, she reached up and touched his hair. It was soft—she could feel cool moonbeams sliding between the silken strands. She touched the pulse beating hard in his jaw. And then she found his shoulders. She clutched them as a sudden weakness swept away the strength to stand alone.

"Lacy." He breathed the word against her wet mouth, and the heat tingled there until she pressed against his lips again.

A rushing need arced between them, and desperately the kiss deepened. She felt the stars move, caught somewhere in the deep, forgotten places of her heart.

Oh, God, she remembered this. And this was just the beginning. There was more. More melting, more surrender, more hot, shivering pleasure...

But after that, the pain.

And not just the simple pains—the trivial embarrassment, the disappointment, the gossip. No, after a complete surrender of the heart, you were at the mercy of an entire torture chamber of sophisticated suffering.

Rejection, which made you a lost child again. Loneliness that turned your blood to ice. Emptiness that gutted your soul.

No. She pulled back slightly. Never again. It wasn't that she wouldn't risk it. It was that she couldn't. She simply didn't have the strength anymore.

Somehow, ignoring every primitive instinct in her body, Lacy forced herself out of his arms.

"What is it?" Adam's voice sounded hoarse. "What's wrong?"

"I need to get back," she said, taking another step away from him. She felt the cool water lick her hem, and her toes sank into the firm, wet sand. But she picked up her poise like a shield and held it in front of her.

She smiled politely. Distantly, though her lips felt warm and swollen. "I know you were just trying to comfort me, and I thank you, really I do. But I'm fine now. And the others will be wondering where I've gone."

On cue, the breeze shifted, and it brought with it a few silver notes from the band, as light and mystical as if unseen fingers played on chimes of glass. And then someone shrieked playfully, and other voices laughed.

Adam gave no sign at all of hearing any of it.

"That wasn't *comfort,* Lacy. That was sex. Or it soon would have been. You know as well as I do what was happening here."

Lacy allowed herself a graceful laugh, so small and refined that she herself only half-heard it over the sound of the incoming tide.

"Oh, I don't think it would have gone *that* far," she said. She gestured toward the distant flickering orange tiki lights. "This is hardly the time or the place for such…indulgences. It was foolish, though. I'm sorry. I shouldn't have kissed you. I can't imagine what I was thinking."

"You weren't thinking at all." Adam narrowed his eyes, but she knew he was angry. Even after all these years, she still knew every nuance of his voice. "You were *feeling.* Remember feeling, Lacy? You really should try it more often."

CHAPTER TEN

LACY TRIED TO FOCUS on the neonatal brochure that lay open on her desk. If she didn't get it right today, she'd never get it mailed out in time. And, since they were still about fifty thousand dollars short of their goal, it was important.

In the short term, it was even more important than the news Mr. Frennick had brought. And it was definitely more important than Adam Kendall, or any of the confusing emotions surrounding that foolish kiss. She tried to put all of it out of her mind.

"I'm not sure we have enough white space here yet," she said, looking over at Kara Karlin, who had been working with the copywriter.

"Really?" Kara grimaced. "Oh, dear. I'm sorry."

Lacy flipped the tri-fold paper, checking the other side. The pictures were great—happy mothers and their robust infants. Very upbeat, rather touching. But the type… "It's not a big problem. Could we just rewrite some of this text, using bullet points instead of full paragraphs? That ought to make it a little more readable."

Kara frowned down at her own copy. "I'm sure we could." She took a deep breath. "And I was wondering—do you want to include a coupon for people to cut out and send in if they'd like to donate?''

Lacy shook her head. ''That's not always a big success. Too many coupons get tossed in the trash.'' She knew why Kara had suggested it, though, and she smiled over at her sympathetically. ''Sorry, Kara. There's just no substitute for the face-to-face ask.''

''I know.'' Kara sighed. ''I just hate that. I'm so bad at it.''

''You're getting better all the time. Which reminds me. Has Mr. Seville made a decision yet?''

Kara shifted uncomfortably. She folded and unfolded her brochure. ''No, and I'm a little worried about that. He was at the Stroll Saturday night, and when we were out at the beach, I heard his wife complaining about Gwen.'' She looked up, her gaze apologetic for having to mention it. ''You know how stuffy Mr. and Mrs. S are. And Gwen was—well, she was dancing, and... I just thought it might be a good idea for you to call Mrs. S. You know, see if you can smooth her feathers.''

Lacy almost laughed. ''You mean I'm just stuffy enough to make her feel better about us?''

Kara looked stricken. ''Of course not! I just meant that you were dignified. Calm and professional and—''

''And stuffy.'' Lacy smiled. ''Don't worry, Kara. I know what you meant. I'll call her. In the meantime, see what you can do about the brochure, would you? I'd like it to go out by Friday.''

As Kara exited, she nearly collided with Tilly, who had come barrelling through the doorway without looking to the right or the left. Kara began to apologize as Tilly anchored her wig with one be-ringed hand, huffing indignantly.

"Well, just watch where you're going, for Pete's sake," the older woman said irritably.

Lacy looked up. "What are you doing down here? Didn't you promise me you'd stay in bed today?"

Tilly waved health concerns away with her usual disdain. "I can't be in bed right now! I'm fine! And besides, we have a disaster."

Kara paused, her own highly emotional temperament always ready to wallow happily in the gory details of a new crisis. But Tilly didn't want an audience. She glowered at Kara fiercely, and the woman hustled on, murmuring another apology.

Lacy folded the brochure calmly and slipped it into the next day's tickler file. "That's nice," she said, swiveling back around to face her friend. "I hadn't had a disaster in the past ten minutes, and I was getting bored."

Tilly flopped onto the sofa dramatically. "You think I'm exaggerating. But you'll be sorry you made fun of me when you hear how bad the problem is."

"Okay. I'm ready. Tell me about the disaster, and then I'm taking you home."

"You know how we've been counting on Howard Whitehead for twenty-five thousand?"

Lacy nodded. Howard Whitehead was an obscenely rich gentleman of about fifty-five, who had a rather lascivious eye for much younger ladies. In fact, Tilly had once nastily speculated that he'd agreed to help build the neonatal wing because he expected to be using it on a regular basis.

But Lacy knew that he genuinely loved his native Pringle Island, which was why he had promised to be one of the wing's biggest individual sponsors.

Still. If Howard were backing out... Lacy began to feel nervous for the first time.

"Don't tell me," she said, closing her eyes and leaning back in her chair. "Don't tell me we've lost him."

Tilly waved her hand airily. "*We* haven't lost him, child. *You've* lost him."

Lacy's eyes snapped open. "I have? How? I haven't even spoken to him in a week."

"Exactly." Tilly kicked off her shoes and put her feet up on the chair in front of her. She tsked dramatically—and Lacy began to suspect that she was enjoying this. "Apparently the old lech is miffed because you ignored him at the Seafood Stroll. He says you didn't even say hello, and that halfway through the dance you just disappeared."

Lacy groaned. "Oh, good grief."

"Well? Did you?"

"Did I what? Forget to say hello to Howard?"

Tilly scowled. "No, you stubborn minx. Did you leave the party?"

"Yes." Lacy pretended to be searching her mind. "Yes, I may have. I was tired. I needed a few minutes alone."

Tilly eyed her carefully. "Alone with Adam Kendall?"

So that was where this was leading. "Tilly." Lacy

thumped the desk softly in exasperation. "If you already knew I was with Adam, why didn't you say so?"

"I wanted to see if you'd tell me."

"Well, I won't." Growling under her breath, Lacy rotated her Rolodex to the *W*s, then picked up the telephone and began punching numbers. "So stop this infernal digging."

"Who are you calling?"

Lacy turned sideways, facing the big floral poster on her other wall. She wanted Tilly's prying eyes out of her line of vision. The number was ringing. One. Two... "I'm calling Howard Whitehead. I'm going to invite him out to dinner to talk about the donation."

"Okay," Tilly said agreeably. "But not Friday night. You're booked for Friday night."

Lacy set her jaw, then shifted slowly to glare at Tilly, the phone still cradled between her cheek and her shoulder. "I am?"

Tilly began arranging her pleated skirt carefully, as if everything important in life depended on it. She didn't look at Lacy. "Yes. I invited Adam to dinner Friday. At my house. Friday at seven. I told him you'd be there."

"Why, you—" But Howard had finally answered the telephone. Lacy kept her most scorching glare fixed on Tilly while she chatted smoothly, explaining how sorry she'd been to miss Howard at the Stroll, and how eager she was to sit down and tell him all about the progress on the neonatal wing. Would he like to have dinner some night soon?

"Not Friday," Tilly reminded her.

"You would? Well, that's lovely." She didn't take her gaze from Tilly's for a single second.

"Not Friday," Tilly mouthed again in an urgent whisper.

"Why, yes. Yes, of course," Lacy told Howard Whitehead sweetly. "Friday would be just fine."

OUTSIDE THE WINDOW OF Adam's hotel suite, Pringle Island was enduring one of its famous summer monsoons. At only four o'clock in the afternoon, the sky was as dark as midnight, and the glass panes ran thickly with mud-colored rain.

Inside the suite, Adam was putting a golf ball into an overturned trash can. Travis sat at the desk, alternately watching their stock quotes flow across his laptop computer and sifting through a stack of real estate listings.

They should have been on the fifteenth hole by now. Adam missed a five-footer, which he tended to do when he was edgy. He hated being cooped up inside.

"What the hell is going on out there?" He set up for a two-footer, and he missed that, too. *"Damn it."* He slapped the ball the last two inches, making the trashcan ring. "On the late news last night, the weatherman predicted zero percent chance of rain today."

Travis chuckled, tapping his keyboard without looking up. "Oh, yeah. Like they ever get it right."

"They ought to." Adam leaned on his putter and stared out the window. "What a bloody mess."

"How about this one?" Travis shuffled papers.

"Restored 1853 four-bedroom cottage, two acres, overlooks the Sound." He squinted at the listing. "'Hist Grk Rev.' What the heck is 'Hist Grk Rev'?"

Adam didn't turn around. "It's real estate talk for 'costs too much.' Nope—I'd rather be on the beach than the Sound. Besides, what would I do with four bedrooms?"

"Same thing you do with one, bro." Travis waved the paper at him, leering. "Just four times as often."

Adam took an imaginary swing at an ugly ceramic planter next to the window. "You seriously over-estimate me, my friend. You always have."

"The hell I do." Travis turned back to the computer. "Whoops. Lost about ten grand while we weren't looking. Told you we should sell that pharmaceutical stock."

He waited fifteen seconds for a reaction, which never came. Then he leaned back in his chair, put his bare feet up on the desk and sighed. "All right. Come on, out with it. What's the matter? I've brought you about maybe twenty terrific pieces of property here, and you've found something wrong with every one of them. What's eating you? Is it the Friday thing?"

Adam prowled to the window, idly swinging his putter. Not much to look at down there. What little he could see looked wet and distorted, as if it were viewed through a melting funhouse mirror.

But Travis was waiting for an answer. If only he had one. He was itchy, all right. He was in a royally bad mood. But what exactly *was* wrong with him?

The Friday thing. Could it really be no more than that? Was he sitting up here pacing this hotel room like a caged animal, acting unforgivably snarly and impossible to please—all just because Tilly had called to say that Lacy couldn't make it to the dinner?

Surely not. Surely he wasn't that far gone.

"No," he said, swatting at the drapes, using his putter like a hedge clipper. Once, fifteen years ago, he'd used plenty of hedge clippers in this town. He'd probably mowed the lawns of half those houses Travis was now trying to talk him into buying. "Of course it's not 'the Friday thing,' as you so quaintly put it. I don't give a damn where Mrs. Morgan eats dinner Friday night."

Travis tilted his head, smiling dryly. "No? Well, what, then? Are you upset about the situation in the Middle East, maybe?"

Adam scowled over at him, but it was difficult to maintain his façade with someone who knew him so well. Too well. Travis looked just the way he always had—scruffy blond hair brushing the collar of his unpressed Hawaiian shirt, blue eyes twinkling, knowing way too much. *God.* Adam would be paying for those drunken confessions for the rest of his life, wouldn't he?

He gave one last pretend swing at the planter. At least, it was supposed to be a pretend swing. Unfortunately, he miscalculated, and the hideous thing smashed into about fifty miserable pieces.

"Great," he said through gritted teeth. "Just great."

"Oh, well." Travis shrugged. "I didn't like it, either."

Disgusted, Adam dropped his putter in the bag,

came around the mess and lit restlessly on the arm of the sofa.

"Okay," he said, as if Travis had interrogated him to the limits of his endurance. "So maybe it *is* getting under my skin a little."

"Really?" Travis smiled. "You think so?"

"It's just that she's so damned predictable. Howard Whitehead is sixty if he's a day, and he's a lecherous old coot. But he's got the biggest checkbook in town, so…" Adam let his voice dwindle off, realizing that he had begun to sound a little too bitter.

Travis glanced back at the computer screen. "Whoops. Made twenty grand. Told you we should hang on to that pharmaceutical company." He tilted his head, grinning.

Adam growled irritably. "Who cares about the damned drug company? You're the one who opened this topic, buddy. How about sticking to it for thirty seconds?"

Travis's grin deepened, until about a quarter of his freckles sank into his dimples. "I *am* sticking to it. What I'm saying is, are you *sure* that Whitehead has the biggest checkbook on the island? Our portfolios are pretty similar, and they're nothing to be ashamed of. Unless I'm mistaken, your wallet makes a fairly respectable bulge, if you follow my drift."

Adam hesitated. "I'm not sure I do. Are you saying I should try to *buy* a date with Lacy?"

Travis heaved a long-suffering sigh that came from the depths of his soul. "I'm saying you're getting on my last nerve here. I'm saying you need to sort things out with this lady once and for all, before you drive yourself stark raving insane, and take the rest of us with you.'' He gestured toward the broken planter. ''It might be cheaper, anyhow. In the long run.''

An hour later, still wearing his rain-sodden coat, his hair plastered to his head, Adam made his way to Lacy's office and dropped a check for fifty-thousand dollars on her desk.

She stood as he entered, but she stayed safely behind her desk. She was beautiful and remote, all dressed in gray, her hair tied back in a severe twist that showed off small diamond stud earrings. She glanced down at the check, and then, without betraying the least surprise, looked up at him, a silent question in her eyes.

''Double,'' he said flatly. ''I'm doubling Whitehead's bid.''

She didn't touch the check. She just looked at him, and her eyes were very dark, very large. Her face was icy pale.

''Something tells me,'' she suggested politely, ''that, in return for this generous donation, you're going to want more than our usual thank-you note.''

''That's right,'' he said. ''I am.''

''It comes on a lovely linen stock,'' she said. ''Suitable for framing.''

''Got plenty of those,'' he said. He wiped the wet hair from his eyes and met her gaze steadily.

''A permanent VIP pass? Free lunches in the hospital cafeteria for life?''

He shook his head. ''More.''

Still she didn't pick up the check. She stood as still and bloodless as a statue. Her fingertips rested lightly on the surface of the desk, but her arms were held with an unnatural stiffness, and he knew her serenity was accomplished by a force of will alone.

She smiled, as if he were a difficult but valued patron. Which, he supposed wryly, pretty much summed it up.

"I'm afraid you'll have to tell me, then," she said reasonably. Her voice shook only a little. "What exactly do you want in return for this check?"

"Dinner," he said. "With you on Friday night."

CHAPTER ELEVEN

AT SEVEN O'CLOCK Friday evening, it was still daylight. The sun poured lovingly over the exquisitely planted window boxes along Main Street, and picked out the odd sparkle here and there in the cobblestone road.

Tilly had, at the last minute, declared herself too tired to host a dinner, and had insisted that Lacy and Adam eat out. She'd already made a reservation for them at the Lost Horizon Tavern, which sat at the end of Main, overlooking the yacht basin. Lacy had glared at her silently, but she hadn't said a word.

They were a little early, so they walked slowly, taking their time. They didn't talk much, though occasionally one of them would acknowledge a passing acquaintance. By now, word that Lacy Morgan had actually slapped that handsome new man in town had reached every ear. Avid curiosity lay behind every friendly face that stopped to say hello.

It was all horribly awkward. But neither of them would admit it, so they kept strolling silently, each waiting for the other to break first.

Strange, she thought. Once, window shopping along this charming street had been a favorite pastime. They had walked hand in hand, stopping at each storefront, picking out glamorous items to "buy" for each other. "How about that necklace?" Standing behind her, Adam had wrapped one arm tightly around her waist and, with his free hand, pointed at a huge purple tanzanite on a sparkling gold chain. He had traced a slow, sexy circle around her neck with his index finger. "You can wear it instead of a nightgown."

But now, though they passed diamond brooches and velvet gowns, titanium golf clubs and sapphire cuff links, miniature yachts and crystal goblets, neither of them said a word. She wondered if he had discovered, as she had, that it was all really just so much junk.

Finally they reached the restaurant, which was tucked out of sight behind a winding entryway heavily planted with moonflowers, hollyhocks and bright pink peonies.

She had eaten here a hundred times. She knew that the clam chowder was divine, and the bluefish pate was only so-so. She knew that Marvin, the maitre d', was getting arthritis in his left knee. She knew that the ladies' room needed repapering.

But suddenly she almost couldn't bring herself to go in. With an intensity that startled her, she remembered how mysteriously elegant this restaurant had seemed to her ten years ago, hidden away in its shadowy exclusivity. It had stood for everything Adam wanted to be able to give her, but couldn't.

He had always promised he'd take her here someday. She glanced over at his handsome, remote profile. Did he remember that?

"Mr. Kendall! What a pleasure to see you!"

Obviously Adam had been here, too, sometime since his return. Marvin welcomed him warmly, fawning over him with the tone he usually reserved for members of the Pringle family, or visiting dignitaries.

"And Mrs. Morgan! Welcome."

He took them to a table on the terrace, overlooking the harbor, where dozens of boats bobbed sleepily in the sun. Lacy gave Adam a sidelong glance. This was royal treatment, indeed.

After they had ordered drinks, Adam leaned back and smiled. "So," he said pleasantly. "Does conversation cost extra?"

She smiled back. Oh, how civilized they were! "Of course not. What would you like to talk about?"

"How about telling me why you said yes?" He tilted his head speculatively. "Quite honestly, I was expecting you to tear the check into pieces and throw it into my face."

"Really?" She sipped her white wine before continuing. "Why? What would that have accomplished? You had already insulted me. If I had refused to take the check, it merely would have meant that you had insulted me for free."

He looked at her quizzically. "Why does it have to be interpreted as an insult? Why not a compliment? After all, I wouldn't pay fifty thousand dollars for the pleasure of just anyone's company."

"But I don't *sell* my company, Adam. And you know that. Pretending you believe that I do qualifies as moderately insulting, wouldn't you say?"

He chuckled, shaking his head admiringly. "You're sharp, Lacy. But then you don't ever let anything as useless as emotions blunt your thinking, do you?"

"No, I don't." She put her wine down. "As you seem so fond of pointing out. But frankly, I think we've covered this ground quite thoroughly, don't you? Maybe we should choose another topic."

"Okay." He extended his hand, palm up, toward her side of the table. "Your turn."

"How about the neonatal unit? We're very excited about that. Since your donation has put us a good bit over our goal, the hospital board is debating how to use the extra money. They seem to be evenly split between upgrading the faucet fixtures and buying more televisions for the waiting rooms."

"I'd vote for the faucets myself," he said in mock seriousness. "You can't go wrong with good plumbing." He paused. "I take it the medical aspects were already fully financed?"

"Of course. They came first. Your money was purely gravy. Delightful to have, but not strictly necessary."

"How lowering," he said. But he was smiling, and she knew his ego hadn't really been pricked at all. In fact, he was clearly enjoying himself. Well, good, she thought. He might as well get his money's worth.

Even so, it was difficult to think where she could safely take the conversation next. His easy good nature was making it difficult to stay annoyed. She was, in fact, in danger of enjoying herself.

She was glad to see Marvin approaching, wine bottle in hand.

"Sorry to disturb you, Mrs. Morgan," Marvin said somberly as he poured a new glass for her. "But Miss Morgan and her friend are just finishing their meals, and she said that you'd be handling the bill." His mouth was tight and pained. "I thought I'd better check with you."

Controlling her surprise, Lacy looked toward the main room of the restaurant. Sure enough, Gwen and Teddy Kilgore were at one of the center tables. Gwen, who was dressed in blue leggings under a pink chiffon sheath covered in crystal dewdrops, waved merrily. Teddy looked down at his plate, obviously miserable.

"That'll be fine," Lacy said, waving back with moderation. She smiled at Marvin. "Just put it on our account, please."

When they were alone again, Adam seemed to be studying her carefully. "So this motherhood thing must be quite an experience," he said.

She knew she blanched. The blood quite simply left her face. She had no control over it whatsoever. "What?"

"Motherhood." He glanced toward where Gwen and Teddy sat. "Or stepmotherhood—whatever you call it. It must have been a pretty wild ride, especially with a stepdaughter who's so...frisky."

Relaxing, Lacy looked over at Gwen, too, seeing her this time through Adam's eyes. She saw so much beauty, so much energy, so much pure willful stubbornness. And yet, paradoxically, she saw such childlike vulnerability. Adam had been right about Gwen, she realized. The young woman led with her chin, leaving herself completely unprotected. But she lived. She lived big.

"Actually, I've been thinking about that a lot," she said. "And to tell you the truth, I don't think I've been much of a mother to Gwen at all."

He remained impassive. "No?"

"No. She didn't want a mother. She was thirteen, and she was entering puberty with a vengeance. The very idea of having a stepmother only five years older than she was mortified her. So she froze me out. Completely."

The food arrived, and Lacy dropped the subject while the waiter was within earshot. She was a little embarrassed to have said so much, anyhow. What was it about Adam that made her act so out of character?

She hoped that he would just move on to something else—before she really said too much.

But he didn't. He cut off a piece of his filet mignon—the Lost Horizon specialty—and urged her to go on.

"So she resented the heck out of you. That's probably pretty natural for a thirteen-year-old. But it never got any better?" He seemed truly interested. His expression was merely curious—not judgmental.

"No. If anything it got worse. Malcolm hated all the turbulence in the house, so he sent her away to boarding school." Lacy pushed her fork around in her vegetable couscous, but she didn't feel much like eating. "Gwen never forgave me for that. She felt that I had completely pushed her out of the family."

She took another sip of wine and looked out at the water. The sinking sun had turned it the color of strawberry ice cream. The masts of the boats were so many bold black crayon marks against the pink sky.

"I didn't understand it at the time, but I can see now that I failed her badly. I should have stood up to Malcolm. I should have insisted that we all stay together and work things out."

He raised one eyebrow. "You should have stood up to Malcolm Morgan? You were eighteen, Lacy. I've seen grown men quake before Malcolm when he was in a temper." He chewed a slice of filet thoughtfully. "Of course, he was always pretty crazy about you, wasn't he? Maybe you could have—"

They were getting into dangerous areas here. Malcolm had always been conspicuously paternal toward Lacy, even when she was only a lowly salesclerk at one of his many stores. Adam had resented it with all the normal territorial outrage of a teenage boy. "The old lech has got a thing for you, damn it," Adam had complained, pulling her up against him possessively. "But he'd better stay away from my girl."

"Perhaps I could have," she said. "But I just didn't have the courage. I was—" The conversational waters were getting even more risky now, she knew. She must pick her next words carefully. "I was rather self-absorbed, I'm afraid. I didn't recognize how much she must have been hurting."

But, to be fair to herself, how could she have seen it? She was blind with her own pain, numb with her own unbearable losses. She had been like a mindless creature, existing only from one moment to the next. It had taken every ounce of her energy just to survive.

And by the time she emerged from that nightmare of misery, it was too late. She and Gwen were strangers. Or worse. Gwen's resentment had matured into something that felt a lot like hatred. They had become civilized enemies. And Malcolm's will had eliminated a lot of the "civilized" part.

A sudden vibration against her thigh shocked her out of the wretched memories. She slipped her cell phone out of her pocket, checked the number and, seeing that it was the hospital switchboard, flipped it open to answer.

She didn't say much—she mostly listened. After a few moments, she flipped the telephone shut and looked over at Adam.

"I'm afraid I'm going to have to get over to the hospital," she said with a sigh. "They've had a minor emergency."

His brows pulled together in immediate concern. He gestured for the check. "Is everything all right?"

"Yes, fine. It's actually a big to-do over nothing. A small fire broke out in one of the new rooms—a staff member probably had been using it for a cigarette break." She arranged her knife and fork on her plate and pushed back her chair. "It was extinguished quickly, but somehow the press got wind of it, and they're looking for an official comment. Unfortunately, that's my job."

He put a couple of big bills on the table. "I'll drive you over."

"No, that's okay." She pointed to his half-eaten

steak, the untouched summer squash casserole. "You should finish your dinner. I can get a cab."

He shook his head. "I'm afraid I have to insist," he said politely. "Even allowing for inflation, surely fifty-thousand dollars buys more than two bites of steak and a salad."

She didn't have time to argue. If she didn't hurry, Kara Karlin might end up talking to the television reporter, and everyone in town would go to bed thinking the hospital had burned to the ground. And besides—she didn't really want their date to be over so soon....

"All right," she said. "Thanks. I'd appreciate a ride."

Within minutes his rented Mercedes was speeding past the now-darkened shops of Main Street—and almost immediately they saw a very odd sight. An obviously tipsy Gwen was doing a tightrope walk down the center yellow line in the middle of the street, and Teddy was tugging at her sleeve, apparently begging her to get back up on the sidewalk to safety.

Lacy sighed. Somehow, she knew, Gwen's rebellious behavior was at least partly her fault. If only she'd had the courage to put aside her own unhappiness and focus on Gwen for a while. It might have done them both a world of good.

Adam seemed to read her mind. "Don't beat yourself up too much, Lacy," he said as he sped past the two foolish young people and steered the car toward the hospital. "I'll say it again—you were only eighteen. You were almost as much a kid as she was."

That was a generous thing to say. If she weren't

careful, she would end up liking this man. Being with him like this felt dangerous—but strangely nice.

"I don't beat myself up," she said. "But neither do I let myself off the hook entirely. Either extreme—either wallowing in guilt or dodging it—is a little too weak for my taste."

He just drove, then, for several very long seconds. The silence was so loaded she had to will herself not to speak recklessly, just to break it. She focused instead on the silver ribbon of road that stretched out before them and tried to clear her mind.

Finally, as he brought the car to a stop at a red light, he spoke.

"Can you really do that, Lacy? Can you put yourself above the reach of all emotional weakness? Are you sure you're really as cold-blooded as you think?" He looked over at her, his extraordinary blue gaze so probing she had to force herself not to squirm. "Or have you just managed to persuade yourself that you are?"

She stared back at him, somehow realizing that the question was a good one. And for some reason, she wanted to answer it honestly.

"If you persuade yourself long enough," she said slowly, "there ceases to be any difference between the two."

APPARENTLY NOTHING VERY interesting happened on Pringle Island on a summer Friday night. A small cigarette fire in a trash can in an unoccupied wing of Pringle Island General Hospital had brought out every journalist in town.

Adam stood by and watched Lacy's first two interviews, admiring her adroit handling of the TV reporters and enjoying the sight of her beautiful face with the bright camera lights on it. But when the print media descended, determined to get to the bottom of what they were sure was a shameful scandal, Adam wandered off in search of the hospital vending machine.

It was half-empty, and he began to wish he had pocketed the rest of his filet, gravy and all. Cheezy Crunches, which seemed to be made of salted cardboard wrapped around orange lint, were a damn lousy substitute for perfectly grilled red meat.

He choked down two of them, then began lamenting the forfeit of that nice bottle of Chardonnay. Finally he ambled into Lacy's office and waited patiently—all right, almost patiently—on her sofa, reading a couple of full-color brochures that made the neonatal wing sound like the greatest thing to hit Pringle Island since refrigeration.

An hour later, she showed up at the door, looking drop-dead gorgeous in her silver dinner dress, with its low-cut neckline that was lined with tiny rhinestones. At least he assumed they were rhinestones. Malcolm hadn't been *that* rich, had he?

"I'm so sorry," she said, coming in and kicking off her silver sandals wearily. "I had no idea there would be so many of them."

"I've been fine," he said. But, come to think of it, he did seem to spend a lot of time perusing her magazines while he waited for a chance to be with her. What exactly did that mean, he wondered? Then he decided he didn't want to know. A man who had spent fifty thousand dollars for one dinner he didn't even get to eat—well, that was a man who needed to have his head examined.

"I've been looking at these brochures. They make the new wing sound so exciting I feel the urge to donate all over again."

She chuckled, plopping down on the sofa beside him. "That's the general idea." She leaned her head against the cushioned back and shut her eyes. "There's a pen on my desk. Feel free to use it."

"No way." He tried to make himself stop staring at her. But he'd been looking at dream pictures for so long. He couldn't help wanting to compare them to the reality. The smooth, pale column of her throat. The soft, downy curve of her cheek. The polished, intelligent brow. The full, sensual mouth, now tinted a very expensive peach. "I haven't gotten my money's worth for the first check yet."

She opened her eyes slowly and caught him staring at her. He wondered what his expression must have been, because a sudden wariness tightened the muscles around her mouth.

She eased herself to an upright position. "Maybe you'd better tell me exactly what you think you bought with that check, Adam."

He smiled. "I hear some of the old rooms are being converted as part of the new neonatal unit," he said. "How about a tour?"

She looked at him closely, as if she mistrusted his motives, but he arranged his face as angelically as possible. He blinked innocently, and finally she laughed. She was clearly thawing, he thought. The idea pleased him far more than it should have.

"Oh, all right," she said. "But I'm not putting my shoes back on. My feet are killing me."

"What?" He reared back in horror. "The exquisitely groomed Mrs. Morgan walking barefoot through her kingdom? Letting the peons see her bare feet? Surely this is a first. Should we call back the press?"

"What nonsense," she said, climbing up off the sofa with a little groan. "The new wing is completely empty. No one will see me."

And so they wandered through half-darkened halls, her rhinestone neckline winking as they passed under the dim blue lights placed high above the doors. The place was eerily empty, just as she had predicted, just room after room of silent, gleaming sterility.

Finally she made one last turn, and they found themselves in a surprisingly chaotic area filled with ladders and drop cloths, tools and boards and brushes.

"A work in progress," she said with a smile. She pitched her voice low, though they were clearly alone. "But there is one finished room, which we use to impress our best donors."

He smiled. "That would be me, I suppose."

Though she was turning away, he could see by the curve of her cheek that she was smiling, too. "Yes, Mr. Kendall. That would be you."

She opened one of the doors that lined the corridor. She flicked a switch and turned on a small, soft-glow lamp beside a bed that didn't look at all like a piece of stereotypical hospital-issue equipment.

"This is one of our birthing rooms. If a mother is at risk in any significant way, she will deliver here, in close proximity to the neonatal equipment."

"Nice," he said. He went over and sat on the edge of the bed. It was wonderfully inviting, the sheets fine linen, the mattress firm but comfortable. On the far side of the bed sat a small rocking cradle. He touched it, and it swayed gently under his fingers. "All the comforts of home."

"We hope so," she said, looking around the room with an obvious sense of pride. "For many of these mothers, this will be a terrible time, a time of great fear. Some of them will be delivering prematurely. Others will be facing different complications. There are so many ways things can go wrong...."

She took a deep breath. "We can't work miracles. But we are hoping to help in any way we can."

He followed her gaze, taking in the details, and he realized that her pride was well justified. The room was warm and cozy, completely nonthreatening. A comfortable chaise longue sat in the far corner, a place for concerned relatives to nap, or spend the night if necessary. But behind the little human touches, he could see that state-of-the-art hospital equipment had been tucked into every possible cranny.

This was not just a feel-good room, not just a room for impressing rich benefactors. It was a working room. A room for saving lives.

"You've done a wonderful job, Lacy," he said sincerely. "It's going to be a very special place. I wouldn't be surprised to find a miracle or two in here someday.''

But he wasn't sure she heard him. She was moving about the room restlessly, touching first one thing and then another, straightening the little bedside clock, adjusting the shade on the glowing lamp.

''Thank you,'' she said. Her voice was muffled, and he couldn't quite read her tone. ''I hope you're right.''

She was near him now, tugging at the lacy ruffle around the cradle as if she couldn't bear for it to be one millimeter askew. She touched the soft, tiny sheet with such tenderness that he felt impertinent just watching her, as if it were a violation of her most private thoughts.

Suddenly he realized that her eyes were shining in the lamplight. Her lips were held together tightly, as if closed over an unspeakable pain. At that moment, he felt as if the ten years between them no longer existed. Whatever caused it, her pain was his own. And he couldn't endure seeing her like this.

Impulsively he reached out and took her hand.

''Lacy,'' he said with a sudden, insane flood of emotion. ''I missed you. All these years... You know that, don't you? I missed you so much I thought I would die.''

Slowly she turned to face him. Two tears rolled down her cheeks, but her expression was still one of unfocused bemusement, as if she were lost in a world of her own.

''And I missed you.'' She touched his face with an

indescribable sadness. "I missed you so much I *did* die."

His insides twisted into a knot so cruel he almost groaned out loud.

"No, you didn't," he said fiercely, pulling her hand closer. "Damn it, Lacy, you *didn't*. I know how to bring you back. Let me."

Under the force of his grip, she lost her balance and dropped onto the bed beside him. She didn't protest as he took her slender, motionless body in his arms, folding her up against his chest.

"Please let me, Lacy. Let me show you the way back."

He wasn't sure what exactly he intended to do. Did he think that sex was the answer—that a few hours of slow, patient lovemaking here on the bed of this strangely silent hospital birthing room would melt the ice in which she had encased herself for so many years?

Perhaps he was just crazy enough to do it. Ten years without her had starved him, made him reckless with desire.

But before he could even sort out his thoughts, he felt her shoulders begin to shudder.

"Adam," she said hoarsely. She tried to pull away.

But he wouldn't let her. He held her close as another spasm moved through her, this one more violent, seeming to rend her with its merciless force.

"It's all right, Lacy," he whispered. "Go ahead. Let go."

She held back another second, maybe two. And then, with great, gulping sobs, as if she were a child again, without the power of restraint, without any arts of self-protection, she began to cry.

He clutched her tightly, letting her flood his shirt. He stroked her damp hair. He whispered soft, meaningless noises.

It wasn't what he'd expected. But maybe, just maybe, it would do.

CHAPTER TWELVE

As SHE NEARED the Cartwright Hotel's Olympic-size swimming pool, Gwen unbuttoned her yellow lace cover-up and tossed it over her shoulder rakishly. She looked like a million bucks in this swimsuit, and she wanted Travis to get the full effect.

But the annoying man wasn't even watching. Gwen was only about ten minutes late, but Travis was already in the pool, motoring some little kid around on a raft. She let out her chest-expanding lungful of air and scowled over at him. She was accustomed to a little more attention than this.

Actually, though, he looked kind of cute. His hair was wet and slicked back, showing off his great bone structure. And his bare, tanned shoulders were downright yummy.

She'd been focusing her attentions mainly on Travis—frankly she just didn't have the energy now to get into anything as mysterious and sticky as the Adam-Lacy thing. Besides, though Adam was a walking, talking hunk of sex appeal, he was kind of hard to get to know. Travis was much cozier.

Maybe in a little while she'd have to forgive him for not noticing her dynamite bikini.

"And the shark grabs hold of your raft. He's push-

ing you out to sea!'' Travis was making ridiculous
growling noises—since when did sharks *growl?*—and
scissoring his feet with great, dramatic splashes, thrilling the little girl, who was probably about six and
still wore water wings.

Gwen's irritation evaporated. She dropped the
cover-up, her orange towel and her fat romance novel
on one of the deck chairs and walked over to the pool.
She squatted, leaning over the coping.

''Excuse me? Mr. Shark? Remember me? I'm the
girl you had a date with?''

He glanced her way, smiling delightedly.

''Ah! The shark sees a new victim! Miraculously,
you are saved!'' Travis grinned at the little girl, giving her raft an exciting, wake-producing shove, which
made her squeal even louder. He turned, then, and
began lumbering through the water toward Gwen, still
in shark mode. When he reached the side, he put his
hands up and grabbed her around the waist.

''Come, my pretty. Come live with me in the water
and be my Shark Queen.''

She held back. ''I don't want to be a shark. Too
much work. They never sleep.''

He looked hurt. ''But we have to be sharks. That's
what DeeDee wants us to be. And we're officially her
champions today, because her brothers are giving her
a hard time about her water wings.''

She glanced over at the little girl, who was pad-
dling furiously, obviously trying to get away from
three preteenaged boys who were splashing her and
calling out singsongy insults.

''That's DeeDee?''

Travis nodded. "And those are DeeDee's brothers. I call them Dum-Dum, Doo-Dah and Diddley-Squat. They're obnoxious as hell. They can't help it, of course. They're eleven, twelve and thirteen."

Gwen sighed. "And how is it we come to know DeeDee?"

Travis grinned beguilingly. "I met her ten minutes ago. While I was waiting for you."

"Oh, so now this is my fault?" But she looked over at DeeDee one more time. The little girl appeared absolutely miserable, her hair sticking to her flushed cheeks as she ducked the incessant splashes. Gwen squinted toward the three hooting, whistling young ruffians.

And she was hooked. Just as Travis had obviously known she would be. She took a deep breath. "Okay. Stand back, Mr. Shark. I can take care of this."

She stalked over toward the boys. "Hey. You."

They paused, stunned to see this blond lady in a million-dollar bikini talking to them. Gwen allowed herself a good internal chuckle, thinking that her bathing suit was turning out to be useful after all. The thirteen-year-old was actually blushing. He probably had a poster on his door of some actress in a bathing suit just like this.

He glanced around dubiously. "Me?"

"Yeah, you." She smiled. "I'm looking for someone to show my friend over there how to do a jack-knife off the high dive. And when I saw you, I said, now there's a young man who could do it." She let the smile broaden flirtatiously. "You can, can't you? I mean, you're not afraid or anything, are you?"

The kid was scared, all right. He was scared green. But his little brothers were giggling, poking him in the ribs, egging him on. And, nasty little bully that he was, he didn't even have the guts to admit he was a chicken.

"Sure," he said, elbowing his brothers back angrily. "Shut up, you two. I can do it."

But he couldn't. He got all the way to the edge of the board, took one long, shuddering look down the forty-two feet of empty air, and froze. He stood there forever, while his brothers called up taunts, trying to work up the guts. But finally he backed down the ladder, red-faced with shame.

Less than two minutes later, all three boys left the pool without another word, leaving their little sister to play peacefully under the benign eye of her parents, who had been comfortably buried in their novels and apparently unaware of the entire drama. Gwen strutted back to Travis, a smug smile on her face.

He was chuckling as he pulled himself out of the pool and began to dry himself off with a towel. "That was vicious," he observed appreciatively. "Absolutely diabolical."

She buffed her nails against her chest, then blew on them playfully. "Just a little something I picked up at boarding school," she said modestly. "The theory is this. If you're getting picked on by a bunch of bullies, you find the biggest, ugliest bully of them all and you carve him up for luncheon meat. Suddenly everyone else just can't wait to leave you alone."

He whistled. "Where'd you go to boarding school? Alcatraz?"

"Pretty close." Gwen arranged herself on the deck chair, making sure all her curves were displayed to maximum advantage. "Daddy didn't much care where he sent me. He just didn't want to have an audience while he tried to thaw out his freeze-dried bride."

Travis dropped onto the adjoining lounger. He cocked his head quizzically. "Lacy?"

Gwen put her sunglasses on—sometimes talking about all this made her eyes sting, and she wouldn't want him to get the wrong idea.

She nodded. "Yep. Lacy, the Lovely Lady of the Manor. She didn't want any little brats hanging around, either—especially not a brat who knew she wasn't really a lady at all. She was just one of the salesclerks from Daddy's five-and-dime, playing dress up."

Travis didn't smile this time. His eyes darkened.

"That's kind of a crummy thing to say," he observed quietly. "And you know, I wouldn't have pegged you for a snob."

To her surprise, his gentle criticism hurt. Really hurt. She couldn't say why, actually. Ordinarily she considered her day a success if she had offended everyone in sight.

But Travis was different. He didn't seem to look at her as just a sexy chick, or as a rebellious hellion, or even as a royal screwup who would have been A Disappointment To Her Father. He didn't pigeonhole her at all. He just accepted who she was and seemed to like her anyhow.

She found that she wanted him to go on liking her.

"You're right," she said finally. "I don't know why I said that. I don't really give a damn that she used to be poor. I don't even believe she married Daddy for his money. She spends almost nothing of what she inherited. It's just that—"

She stopped for a minute. She was about to say things she never said, even to herself. And she had no idea why.

"It's just that it would've really helped to have a friend in the house, you know?" She drew in a breath, and stared off into the middle distance. "I would have liked for her to like me. But she didn't. And she doesn't. And she never will."

She finally faced Travis, whose expression was understanding without being sappy and sympathetic. "And that's that, I guess." She shrugged. "No big deal. *C'est la vie,* right? I just wanted you to know it wasn't really about the money."

"Okay. Clarification noted." Travis smiled. "So. Want to be a teacher?"

The abrupt change of subject left her off-balance. She frowned. "What?"

"I said, want to be a teacher? The country club rec director is looking for someone to give swimming lessons to the little kids. I told him I thought you'd be great at it. He wants to interview you at three."

She took off her sunglasses so that he could more clearly identify the intensity of the scowl she was giving him. "You've got a lot of nerve. You think you can arrange my career? First of all, buddy, you don't even really know me."

He laughed and lay back on his lounger. Mad as

she was, she couldn't help noticing he had a fabulous body. "Oh, yes, I do," he insisted. "You're Moira, with a pinch of Kelly, and a dash of Ellyn thrown in."

"What the hell is that supposed to mean?"

"It means you should stop grumbling and go to the interview." He shut his eyes, still smiling. "It means, my belligerent blond bombshell, that you are a natural born teacher."

LACY SIFTED through the pile of catalogues on Tilly's bed, looking for the one on double-handled, chrome-plated faucets.

It was one o'clock Saturday afternoon, and Tilly had insisted on looking at the various options for up-graded faucets. The board of directors—of which Tilly was a member—would vote on Monday, and she wanted to be prepared. If Lacy hadn't brought them here to the Barnhardt house, Tilly would have dragged herself over to the hospital, though she wasn't anywhere near strong enough for the trip.

So of course Lacy had come, struggling up the stairs under an armload of plumbing catalogues.

Tilly Barnhardt was an infuriatingly stubborn woman, Lacy thought to herself now, as she handed the catalogue across the bed. But then, perhaps that was what kept her going. That indomitable will had overcome a great many challenges in the eighty-six years of Tilly's life. It just might get her through this new trouble, too.

"What are you smiling about?" Tilly fixed Lacy with a stern glare over her reading glasses. "And what's wrong with you today, anyhow? You look different. You look…younger. Happier." She smiled coyly. "Well—maybe I've answered my own question! Could this have anything to do with dinner at the Lost Horizon, by any chance?"

Lacy made a dismissive sound and looked back down at the paperwork. "Nonsense. I don't look one bit different today. You're making this up. You're just determined to believe that your matchmaking last night worked some kind of miracle."

"Well, did it?"

Lacy tried to school her features into perfect normalcy. "No," she said curtly. "No miracles."

Tilly snorted. "Then why do you look like that?"

"Like *what?*" This was ridiculous. Tilly was just on a fishing expedition. She couldn't have any way of knowing that anything important had happened last night. She couldn't in a million years have guessed that Lacy had spent an hour weeping her heart out in Adam Kendall's arms.

And what had that meant, anyhow? She hadn't been able to cry over the baby in years now. But suddenly, in that room, with Adam by her side, the tragedy of the whole thing had overwhelmed her, and she had simply opened like a faucet.

He had been so kind. He hadn't even forced her to explain. He had simply absorbed the tears without question, comforting her without attaching any strings.

And somehow, when it was over, she had felt younger. Lighter. As if, in the old cliché, someone had taken a weight from her shoulders.

Tilly studied her face for several long seconds.

"Clean," she said finally. "It's a funny word, but it's the right one. You look clean, the way the sky looks after a good storm."

That was much too close to the truth. Lacy felt herself flushing. "Matilda Hortense Barnhardt, if you don't stop—"

"Knock, knock." Adam appeared in the doorway, holding a bunch of yellow-faced daisies. "Am I interrupting?"

Tilly crowed with pleasure and held out her hands for the daisies, which were her favorite flower. "Not at all! I'm so glad you're here. Tell the truth, Adam. Doesn't Lacy look clean today?"

Adam smiled curiously over at Lacy, who buried her face in her hands, abandoning hope. "Why, yes," he said, playing along, although he clearly had no idea what was going on. "She practically sparkles. Freshly waxed and lemony fresh, too, if I'm not mistaken."

"Oh, you're no help." Tilly handed the daisies to Lacy. "Go put these in some water, dear, would you please?"

Oh, no you don't, you old devil, Lacy thought, giving Tilly a hard stare. She wasn't going to be shuffled out of the room so that Tilly could pump Adam for information about last night.

"I'll call the nurse," she said sweetly. "She can do it. I need to get these catalogues put away."

So the nurse came, the daisies departed, and Lacy busied herself at the edge of the room, letting Adam and Tilly visit comfortably—but never quite giving Tilly enough freedom to say anything embarrassing.

Through it all, Lacy was acutely conscious of Adam's presence. He was dressed more casually than she had seen him before—and the sight of his familiar body in soft, well-worn jeans brought back a flood of memories.

For the first time, though, she didn't slam the door, shutting the memories out. She let a few, a very few, seep in through a small, tentative crack in her fortress. Remember the day he had bought ten packages of gum at Morgan's Five-and-Dime, paying for them one at a time, so that he could talk to her while she was working?

And the day she had picked him up at the concrete plant. The other guys had whistled at her, and some of them had come up to flirt. One young boy, observing Adam's scowl, had asked innocently, "What's the matter? Is she your girl?" Adam had growled back tersely, "That's right. Pass it around."

And remember the day they had made love in the car, and—

No. Not that one. She closed the door of her mind and pressed her whole weight against it. Not yet.

Suddenly she realized that Adam was talking to her. She looked up hastily, well aware that this time her face really did look different.

"What? I'm sorry. I was in another world."

He was standing by the bed, smiling pleasantly. "I was just leaving. I hoped you'd walk me out to the car."

She looked at Tilly, who clamped her mouth down

over a disgustingly gleeful smile. The net effect was classic cat-with-canary. Lacy wouldn't have been surprised to see yellow feathers sticking out between her lips.

"Of course," she said, ignoring Tilly. Ignoring, too, the absurd flutter in her chest, as if she'd suddenly hatched butterflies in her heart. She moved Tilly's buzzer closer on her bedside table. "You can ring for the nurse if you need anything," she said. "But of course I'll be right back."

"Of course," Tilly said smugly, though how she could talk around all those feathers was a mystery to Lacy.

Adam didn't speak until they were out of the house, walking toward his car. Lacy didn't know how to break the silence, so she simply followed him mutely, waiting. But she found herself oddly contented just to be near him.

Oh, God. What was happening to her? She wasn't letting him get under her skin again, was she?

Finally, when they had reached the edge of the drive, he turned around. "I've heard from Mr. Frennick," he said. "There's news."

"Mr. Frennick?" She shook her head, not understanding the significance. "*My* Mr. Frennick?"

"*Our* Mr. Frennick now," he said. "After he brought the news about Tilly's daughter, I hired him to do a little more investigating. And he's found something. If you're not busy tomorrow, I'd like to take you to Boston."

Her mind was moving slowly, she realized. She couldn't quite figure out what he was getting at.

"What could he have found? What's in Boston? Tilly's daughter is dead. He wasn't mistaken about that, was he?"

Adam shook his head. "No, he wasn't mistaken. Tilly's daughter is dead." He took her hand and held it between his own. "But her granddaughter is very much alive."

ACCORDING TO MR. FRENNICK, Tilly's granddaughter was thirty-one years old, newly divorced from a criminal lawyer who had been caught with his habeas all over the corpus of one of the prettiest paralegals in Boston.

But the divorce hadn't left Claire Scott Tyndale exactly destitute or downtrodden. She was a reporter for one of the Boston television stations, and she lived in an upscale redbrick town house not far from Faneuil Hall. She drove a silver BMW, was the outgoing president of the local League of Women Voters, and had recently adopted a springer spaniel named Winston.

She was also, according to Mr. Frennick, approximately seven-and-a-half-months pregnant.

But as thorough as the investigator's findings were, they didn't quite prepare Lacy for the shock of seeing the beautiful woman who opened the town house door. Nothing could have.

"Yes? Can I help you?" Claire Tyndale looked at them with large, brown, impatient eyes. Eyes that were so much like Tilly Barnhardt's that Lacy found herself momentarily speechless.

Claire frowned, glancing appraisingly over Lacy

and Adam. "You don't look as if you're selling any-thing," she said. "Which is good, because I'm not buying."

"We're not," Adam assured her. He smiled, and instantly some of the impatience left the woman's face. No one, Lacy realized, could be completely un-moved by Adam's smile. "I'm Adam Kendall, and this is Lacy Morgan. We're friends of Tilly Barn-hardt. She's connected to your mother's family. Does that name ring a bell to you?"

Claire shook her head thoughtfully. "No. I'm pretty sure I've never heard of her. How did you say she was connected to me?"

"Through your mother," Lacy answered. "But it's actually quite complicated. And it's rather personal. Could we come in to talk about it? Or, if you'd be more comfortable somewhere else, we could go get a cup of coffee."

Claire hesitated, her mobile face clearly running through every nuance of their faces, their accents, their clothes—even their car, which was parked be-hind them on the street. Trying, no doubt, to decide whether they were some sophisticated brand of con artist.

Lacy accepted the woman's perusal uncomplain-ingly. She would have done the same thing, in Claire's position. Adam had been in favor of calling first, explaining the basic facts over the phone before they arrived. But Lacy had wanted to see Claire with her own eyes. She'd wanted to do her own sizing up before they risked revealing Tilly's secret. If Claire had been a different kind of person...

But how could she have been any of those things? She was Tilly's granddaughter. Tilly's no-nonsense intelligence shone from her brown eyes, and Tilly's unpretentious friendliness played about her generous, mobile mouth.

"My goodness," she said finally, opening the door wider to let them in. "This is all very secretive." She nudged a curious puppy out of the way with one bare foot. "You'll have to forgive the house. I kind of let things go on the weekend."

And it was a mess—the kind of mess you might expect from a hard-working journalist who wasn't expecting company. Newspapers were stacked high in one corner of the room she led them into, a nearly empty cup of coffee sat next to the crumbs of whole wheat toast, and along the back wall a large-screen television showed a pregnant woman down on all fours, saying perkily, "Lift, and hold. Lift and hold. Again! You can do it, ladies!"

Claire groaned and, grabbing the remote, zapped the woman into a sudden black oblivion. "Prenatal exercises. Humiliating stuff. But they say it helps with the pain, so I do the damn things every day." She grinned at Lacy and rested her hand protectively on her stomach. "Spencer and I hate pain."

Lacy smiled back, still getting used to looking at Tilly's eyes in this young, glamorous face. Even in maternity sweatshirt and leggings, with her brown hair pulled back in a ponytail, Claire was stunning. Suddenly Lacy could see how very beautiful Tilly must have been when she was young.

Claire swept magazines from the sofa, and urged

them to sit. She settled in the leather armchair off to one side, and the little black-and-white spaniel immediately jumped up and tried to find a flat place on her tummy. "Down, sweetie," she said, laughing. "This lap is already taken."

A clear glass vase full of daisies sat on the table next to her, and Claire pulled a browning flower from the arrangement absently. "Well, are you ever going to tell me what this is all about?"

Daisies. A lump forming in her throat, Lacy looked over at Adam, silently asking him to make the explanations. He was just that little bit more removed from the situation emotionally. He could tell it better, without sentimental side trips or irrelevant details. Like daisies.

He told it perfectly. Logically, carefully, honestly. Lacy felt herself holding her breath until he was finished.

Claire must have been holding her breath, too, because when Adam came to the end of his story she let out an audible whoosh of air. "Wow," she said under her breath.

Then there was only silence. Claire twirled the dying daisy slowly between her fingers, staring out the town house window, apparently needing a minute to absorb it all.

Somehow Lacy forced herself to wait. As much as she loved Tilly, she was merely her friend. Claire was blood of her blood.

Claire had to be the one to speak first.

"You know. It's too bad she didn't do this sooner." Claire finally looked at them again, but the lighthearted warmth had gone out of her face. Her resemblance to Tilly was much less noticeable now. Tilly never looked this stern, no matter how hard she tried.

Lacy leaned forward. "She wanted to. So many times she thought about it—"

"*Thought about it?* My mother spent an entire year looking for her birth mother." Claire's voice had taken on an edge. "Did you know that? She even posted notices on the Web. Joined all kinds of search groups. No one ever answered."

"Tilly is eighty-six," Lacy said defensively. "She doesn't even own a computer, and—"

Claire stood, dropping the daisy into a small wicker trash can near her desk. "I wonder if your friend Tilly had any idea how much pain there is for an adopted child. Does she have any idea how difficult it is to go through life believing you weren't wanted?"

"Of course she does—"

"I don't think so," Claire said. "Otherwise, how could she have done it?" She touched her stomach. "Given up her own baby—"

"It was a different time," Lacy said. "It was sixty years ago. You have to understand—"

"I don't *have* to understand anything," Claire corrected flatly. "But I do. I understand that some people simply don't take their responsibilities to other people very seriously." She still held her stomach, almost unconsciously molding her palm to the perfect mound there. "I just threw out a husband who was one of those careless, self-centered people. Frankly, I'm not inclined to bring anyone else like that into my life right now.''

Lacy wanted to protest. Careless and self-centered? That was not Tilly. She wanted to make this woman see the truth—wanted her to know Tilly as she did. And to love her as she did. But what were the magic words that could break down this wall of resentment?

''We understand how you feel, Ms. Tyndale,'' Adam said, rising politely. ''And we certainly don't want to push you into anything you're not comfortable with. We just wanted you to know that your grandmother is out there, and that she has been looking for you.'' He held out one of his business cards. ''What you do with the information is entirely up to you.''

Lacy looked at him, knowing that he was right, that a calm withdrawal now was their only option. Claire's allegiance was with her mother, who had suffered from her sense of abandonment. She wouldn't be moved by tales of Tilly's heartache, which in Claire's eyes were probably her just deserts.

Still, Lacy found that she couldn't help wanting to plead with the young woman, to remind her of Tilly's age, to warn of her worsening illness, to tell her of her spunk, her love and her loyalty.

She wanted to make her understand how thrilled Tilly would be to know that a new baby was on the way. How unfair it was to deny the old woman the knowledge that her line would go on....

Lacy was surprised at the heat of her emotions. This wasn't like her. When had the need to maintain a detached restraint become so burdensome? It had once come so easily.

"Lacy?" Adam was near the door, waiting. "We should go. We'll miss the ferry."

But she couldn't leave without trying one more time. Even knowing she shouldn't, Lacy walked straight up to Claire Tyndale and touched the woman's cold, unyielding hands.

"I can't tell you what the right answer is for you," she said. "I know that forgiving people who have hurt you can be very difficult, almost impossible. But Tilly is elderly, and she isn't well. She won't be around forever. If you hold this grudge too long, you may not have another chance. And then I'm afraid you might discover that forgiving *yourself* is the most difficult thing of all."

THE FERRY RIDE BACK TO Pringle Island was sunny and calm. By this late on a Sunday afternoon, most of the tourists were heading in the other direction, leaving the quaint, quiet island to begin another work-week in the big city. So Adam and Lacy had the boat almost to themselves.

They stood together at the railing, watching the steel-gray waters of the Atlantic part before the heavy prow of the ferry. At the moment, Pringle Island was just a dark line on the horizon, but Lacy knew they would make land before long, and her time alone with Adam would be over.

After talking to Claire, they had gone to lunch at a sidewalk café. The meal had passed quickly. Lacy had almost forgotten what an entertaining conversationalist Adam could be. They had talked about cars and politics and theater and Pakistan. And, of course, Claire.

Amazingly, there had been no awkward moments, no tension of any kind. It was as if they had no ugly past between them. Lacy had been very sorry when Adam looked at his watch, and said that it was time to catch the ferry.

"It was a lovely day, wasn't it?" She wrapped her hands around the railing and leaned her head back to let the salt-laden wind sing through her hair. "I enjoyed myself." She tilted her head to look at him. "And I've decided that I feel optimistic about Claire, in spite of everything."

"You do?" He smiled. "You seemed worried when we left."

"Yes, but I've been thinking. They belong together, don't you think? I know she's angry right now, but their shared genetic heritage is so strong. Look at her! The brown eyes, that strong, stubborn jaw. And what about the dog? You know Tilly loves animals. And the daisies. The daisies were—" She paused. She didn't want to sound absurdly superstitious, but... "They were a good sign, I thought."

He raised his brows. "So you think DNA will win the day?"

"I think *love* will win the day." Turning away, she studied the churning water beneath them. "Sometimes it does, you know."

She looked up at him, then. The salty breeze was feathering his hair forward onto his face, and he looked so much like the old Adam—*her* Adam—that she could hardly keep from reaching out and touching him.

"Yes," he agreed carefully. "Sometimes it does."

His eyes were dark, and steady as they watched her. He eased a strand of hair away from her cheek, and then, slowly enough to give her plenty of warning, plenty of time to stop him, he leaned forward and kissed her.

It wasn't a long kiss, or a demanding one. But it was enough to send little electric shimmers of light through her body. As he pulled away, she touched her lips, feeling the last of the shimmers die away slowly.

"What was that for?"

He smiled. "Actually," he said, "I don't really know. Did you mind?"

She shook her head. "No," she said. "It makes no sense at all, but no. I didn't mind."

After that, they stood without speaking for a few minutes, watching as the long, skinny fingernail of land came closer, looming larger on the horizon. The boat began to slow.

"I want to apologize for Friday night," she said abruptly. She'd been trying to say this all day long, but she hadn't been able to find an opening. It had been as if they'd made an unspoken pact to keep the day peaceful, and she hadn't known how to break it.

"Don't be silly," he said. "No apology is necessary."

"But all that weeping. I honestly don't know what got into me. I think maybe I was just terribly tired."

"I'm sure you were. You'd been worried about

Tilly. And of course you've been working very hard to meet the goal for the neonatal wing.''

She cringed inwardly at the mention of the fund-raising. ''That's another thing. I should have thanked you long ago for your incredibly generous donation. I feel rather uncomfortable about it, actually. I know that the...unresolved issues between us were driving that donation, and I wish I hadn't accepted it. But I've already reported it to the foundation, and now I don't see how—''

''Relax, Lacy,'' he said. ''It's okay. I am glad I wrote that check.''

''But I shouldn't let our personal situation get mixed up with business, and—''

''You know, if I feel I got my money's worth, I don't see why you should continue to agonize over it like this. Didn't you tell me that you're much too tough to indulge in unnecessary angst?''

''Yes, but...'' She shook her head helplessly. ''I would have said I was too tough to break down the way I did Friday night, too. Or even that...that episode out at the beach. Or the kiss just now.'' She twisted her wedding ring on her finger, trying to get it to a comfortable spot. ''In a way, it's a little frightening. It's as if I hardly recognize myself anymore.''

He caught her gaze and held it.

''But I do, Lacy,'' he said slowly. ''For the first time in a long time, I recognize you.''

She gripped the rail harder as the ferry lurched into its moorings. The water beneath them boiled and rocked, upset by the sudden jarring of boat and dock.

She had to close her eyes against the dizziness of interrupted rhythms.

"Yes," she acknowledged, for what was the point in denying it? "But that may be what scares me most of all."

CHAPTER THIRTEEN

NOW THAT THE BORING struggle of raising money was over, it seemed as if the entire island was excited about the neonatal unit.

Or maybe they were just excited about the upcoming gala family day, which the hospital's board of directors had decided to host in celebration of the successful fund-raising campaign. It would be held at the local amusement park, which dated back to 1924 and had been recently renovated by the historical society.

It would be the first time the amusement park had been open in fifty years. People who had dodged Lacy's fund-raising efforts for months were suddenly calling, volunteering to host booths, bring food, or tack posters around town.

Three radio shows, two TV stations and the local newspaper were all planning to run stories on the event. The baby boutique on Main had offered to be a sponsor, and so had the biggest pediatric group in town, the local toy store and even Tina Seville's preschool, which was so elite that one of their diplomas cost more than most BAs these days.

So when the telephone rang again, Lacy assumed it was another reporter, or another sponsor looking to get in on the action. She smiled wryly. If only it had been this easy to get everyone's attention back when they had needed money!

She picked up the telephone with two fingers. She was making deviled eggs for the celebration, and her hands were messy with mayonnaise.

But it wasn't a reporter. It was Adam.

"Hi," he said, and just that one syllable made the tips of her ears tingle. She hadn't talked to him since the day they'd gone to Boston—five whole days ago. Funny how, after doing just fine for ten years without hearing his voice, suddenly five days seemed like an eternity.

But that one little kiss had been strangely addictive. She kept reliving the sweet shimmers it had sent through her. And she knew she wanted more.

"Hi, yourself." She heard the girlish note in her voice, and she hated it. She wasn't a girl. She was a twenty-eight-year-old widow. If she weren't careful, pretty soon she'd be wearing baby-doll minidresses and pigtails, and flirting with teenaged boys, the way Mary Lou Geiger did at the burger joint.

"I was just calling to see if you could use any help getting ready for Saturday." He was smiling—she could hear it in his voice. She could picture the smile exactly. One side of his mouth cocked slightly higher than the other, notching his cheek and making tiny laugh lines radiate almost invisibly around his eyes.

"Thanks," she said, "but I think I'm fine. No crises yet, thank heavens."

"No pastry swans? I make a mean pastry swan."

"So I hear." She licked the mayonnaise from her

index finger and rotated the telephone to a more comfortable spot. "But the food for this event is a lot simpler. And most of it's being donated."

"Okay. But I'm also calling to see if you'll do me a favor."

"I'd be glad to." She spooned the egg mixture into the cookie shooter—a secret Tilly had taught her years ago—and attached the small star nozzle. It made the prettiest deviled eggs, each shaped like a little yellow sunburst. "I certainly owe you one. What do you need?"

"A date."

She laughed, but something nervous danced briefly against her heart. She squeezed the cookie shooter so hard the egg mixture poured all over the plate.

She began spooning it up hastily. "You don't need anyone's help to get a date, silly. Jennifer Lansing has herself gift-wrapped daily and delivered to your door. And I've heard that the Cartwright has become *the* most popular lunching spot for the Junior League. And there's this sudden new interest in golf—"

"Lacy." His voice was still smiling. "I don't need you to *arrange* my date. I need you to *be* my date."

"Oh." She held onto the cookie shooter, trying not to grin. It was stupid to be so pleased. Much smarter would be to say no. *No, no, no.* "For what?"

"For Saturday."

"Oh, I'll be there all day," she said, stalling. "You won't be able to miss me."

"Not good enough. I must have a date. There's nothing more pitiful than going to an amusement park alone. Who will tell me I'm brilliant when I shoot down all the ducks? Who will console me when I can't toss the ring around the bottle? Who will be my valiant protector on the Ferris wheel?''

She laughed. ''You know it would be the other way around. I'm terrified of heights.''

''Yes,'' he said. ''I do know. And that's why I want you to be my date. As I recall, protecting you on the Ferris wheel was one of the easiest jobs I ever had.''

Memories spun around in her mind, little breathtaking pictures of colored lights, swirling treetops, cold wind and warm arms. *Say no,* her cautious training ordered her. *Just open your mouth and say no.*

''All right,'' she said. ''But I make no promises about the Ferris wheel.''

She had barely hung up the telephone when she heard the front door slam. Not just an accidental, whoops-the-door-slipped noise. This was a deliberate, furious explosion of wood that made the whole house shake.

Gwen was home. Passing through the foyer, she cast one dark, furious look toward the kitchen, and then, with a low, inarticulate cry, she turned away. She thundered up the stairs and disappeared into her room, slamming that door, too, with equal force.

Calmly, Lacy made another deviled egg star. And then another. She'd had years of Gwen's tempers, and she had long ago learned to ignore them. Eventually it would pass. Gwen would never tell her what had happened, and Lacy would never ask.

But after a few minutes her rhythm with the cookie

shooter faltered. She stared out the window, oddly uncomfortable.

Somehow, today, the well-rehearsed roles of hostility and indifference didn't seem right. With a sudden insight, she recognized for the first time that she *wasn't* indifferent. She had just pretended to be—out of cowardice, out of confusion, out of fear that she had no idea how to be a mother to this troubled teen. It was easier to be a stranger.

But, however they might play at it, she and Gwen weren't strangers rooming in the same boarding house. They were family, of sorts. And what kind of family would ignore the grief and fury Lacy had just now seen on Gwen's face?

The answer was obvious.

Malcolm's kind.

But Lacy wasn't Malcolm's kind. And neither, poor child, was Gwen.

Lacy set down the egg mixture and wiped her hands. Gwen needed her. Well, she needed someone, anyhow—and Lacy was the only one in the house. That degree of storming around was a message. Maybe all her life Gwen had been slamming doors because she needed rather desperately to say something that was very difficult to articulate.

If Lacy went up there right now, a fight was almost inevitable. Gwen would probably rebuff Lacy's questions, rudely reject her concern. But at least she would know that Lacy had heard—heard both the slamming door and the message that lay behind it.

And she would know that Lacy, who was, after all, her only remaining family, *cared.*

Lacy went up the stairs softly and knocked on the closed door. "May I come in?" There was no answer. The door wasn't locked, so she turned the handle carefully. "Gwen? Are you all right?"

Her back rigid against the headboard, Gwen sat cross-legged on the bed, her pillow bunched up in her lap. Her face was streaming with tears.

For a minute, Lacy hardly recognized her. It wasn't merely the distortion of the weeping. It was everything.

Gwen wore pink. Not electric pink, not streetwalker pink, not drunken rose pink. Just pink. The dress was strangely sedate, with small white buttons from neck to hem, and puffed sleeves that reached below her elbows. A good girl's dress, the kind of dress you wore to meet your fiancé's grandmother.

And her hair was demure, too, confined by a white ribbon into some semblance of a braid. Lacy glanced down. Flat white pumps. And panty hose. *Good God.* Where on earth had Gwen been, Lacy wondered, costumed like a Pringle Island debutante?

"What's the matter?" She didn't advance into the room. Better to take it one step at a time. She could tell that Gwen was shocked to see her there at all.

"What the hell do you care?" Gwen pushed her fists into her pillow and fought back more tears. "Just get out of my room."

Lacy held her ground. She hadn't expected it to be easy.

"Is there anything I could do to help?"

Gwen laughed, but the sound was strange, as if it had been grafted onto a sob. "Oh, I think you've done

plenty, Stepmother dear. Just plenty.'' She glared at
Lacy wetly. ''Tell me, when you were trashing me to
Tina Seville, did you already know I was going in for
an interview? Did you do it just to make sure I
wouldn't get hired—or did you do it just for kicks?''

Lacy didn't answer at first. Too many landmines
lurked in those sentences. She had to pick her way
across the message first, trying to find them all. Apparently Gwen had tried to get a job at Tina Seville's
preschool. That was surprising all on its own. Except
for her summer stint as a part-time swim instructor at
the Cartwright, on the rare occasions that Gwen
looked for work, she always looked *off* the island.

But there was more. Apparently, Tina had reported
something Lacy had said, something negative about
Gwen...

Lacy's face flushed. She remembered calling Tina
last week, trying to smooth the older woman's feathers about Gwen's behavior at the Seafood Stroll.
What exactly had Lacy said? That Gwen was
young—Lacy used that one often, aware that her own
severe demeanor made most people forget there was
only a five year difference between Lacy and Gwen.

And she might have agreed that Malcolm would
not have approved. She remembered Tina calling
Gwen a strumpet, and Lacy had only mildly de-
murred, her thoughts on the check Tina had promised
to write.

Lacy was suddenly intensely ashamed. She should
have boxed Tina Seville's ears, not poured honey into
them. And all for a check. Thirty pieces of silver...

''At least you have the grace to look embarrassed,''

Gwen said bitterly. "Not that it will do any good now. Tina Seville said she wouldn't hire me if I were the last applicant on Pringle Island. She could never consider hiring any girl whose own stepmother believes she is a strumpet."

Lacy considered defending herself. She hadn't said that—Tina had. But what difference did it make, really? Morally, she was guilty. She had allowed Tina to say it in her presence. She hadn't leaped to Gwen's defense, although she knew full well that Gwen had done nothing wicked.

Gwen had kissed Teddy Kilgore a few times in public, injected a few blatantly sensual moves into their dancing. Once, obviously just to annoy Tina, Gwen had winked over her shoulder at Dalton Seville and tossed a sexually exaggerated, full-lipped pucker his way.

A few moments of sophomoric mischief. But without a doubt entirely innocent. Only someone as chronically uptight as Tina would give a damn about any of it.

"I'm sorry," she said. "I had no idea you were thinking of applying at her preschool. And honestly, I'm quite surprised. Of all the places you might work, that would be the most—"

"Inferior?" Gwen made a furious sound and stabbed at her pillow. "Beneath me? Just a teacher's assistant? With my background, my breeding, my *potential?* God, you're such a snob, Lacy. You're just like my father."

Lacy frowned. "Don't put words into my mouth. I wasn't going to say any of that. I was just going to say that it seemed like a bad fit. Tina's preschool is filled with the children of the same stuffy, snobbish social climbers you have always said you hated.''

"I don't care about their parents," Gwen said defiantly. "It's the kids who matter. You wouldn't understand about that, because you hate kids. You don't know a damn thing about them. You never have."

"I'm sorry," Lacy said again, nearly defeated by this impenetrable wall of resentment. And by the fact that Gwen was right. Lacy *didn't* understand kids. She had always told herself it was because she'd been denied the chance to learn. But now she realized that had just been a rationalization. Her chance had been right here in the house.

Gwen had been her chance, and she had let it slip through her fingers.

"I wish I could pay you back for this," Gwen said now, blackly. "I wish I could spoil some dream of yours, just so you'd know how it feels. But I can't, can I? Because you don't have dreams. All you care about is money, and status, and being the most perfect little priss on this pissant island."

"Gwen—"

"Get out," Gwen said, her voice once again tight with tears. "Get out of my room, and don't ever come in here again."

She meant it, that was clear. She hated Lacy. She had no desire to be "heard" any further. Lacy moved back a step, as if the force of that hatred had a physical energy.

She paused one last time before completely closing the door.

"I truly am very sorry," she said again. "I honestly had no idea you wanted to work for Tina."

"But I did." With a low, painful moan, Gwen buried her face in the pillow. "That's how big a fool I am. *I did.*"

ALL AFTERNOON SATURDAY, Lacy kept watching for Gwen, hoping she might show up. From the moment the amusement park opened at noon, Pringle Island society and tourists came streaming through the turnstiles, hand in hand with their children, their boyfriends, or their brothers, eager for some good old-fashioned fun. From her position as ticket taker at the merry-go-round, Lacy saw almost everyone she knew.

Everyone but Gwen.

Finally Lacy gave up. Apparently Gwen's fury had not subsided. She'd just have to think of some other way to make amends. Maybe by tomorrow Gwen would have cooled down enough to listen to reason.

Adam arrived at six, the time at which Lacy's shift was scheduled to end—and their date was scheduled to begin. She'd been surreptitiously checking her watch for the past hour—the slowest hour in history. And then he was fifty-seven seconds late. She hadn't realized she could hold her breath that long.

She was up on the platform, helping Becky Jared into the saddle of a big horse covered in blue roses, when she saw him. She smiled at him across the little girl's wispy, carrot-colored curls. When he smiled back, she felt a strange swooping sensation in her midsection, as if they had started the carousel turning prematurely.

Danger. Her instincts sent up the alarm. *Hold on, hold in, hold back.* But she couldn't. She simply couldn't. Tilly had been right—like it or not, her safe emotional hibernation had finally ended. She could no more keep Adam Kendall's smile from setting her heart spinning than she could stop the moon from rising over Pringle Sound tonight.

She patted Becky's head, handed her the reins and picked her way around the colorful horses toward where Adam was waiting. He was holding two hot dogs and one gigantic Coke with two straws.

"Hi," he said. "Hope you're hungry."

She looked at the hot dog. It was covered in mustard, just the way she used to like them. "Good heavens," she said, her mouth watering at the wicked, wonderful smell. "I haven't had a hot dog in ten years."

"It shows." The comment clearly wasn't a compliment.

"What do you mean by that?"

He did a quick scan of her body, then gave her a strangely intimate smile. "It means you weigh fifteen pounds less than you did in high school. It's not natural." He held the hot dog toward her. "Eat."

She took it, registering another small ripple of pleasure. Actually, she weighed twelve pounds less, but it was close enough. Close enough to prove he remembered her body very well.

She bit into the warm, juicy hot dog and closed her mouth around a delighted groan. "Umm," she mumbled. She chewed, swallowed, and knew she'd have to eat the whole thing. "This will be dinner, then. It blows my calorie budget till about...August." She grinned. "At least I'll be a cheap date."

He chuckled. "Good. I could use a break. You'd never guess what my dinner date cost me *last* weekend."

"Let me try." She bit into the meat. Now that she'd surrendered to the guilt, the hot dog tasted like heaven. "Maybe about...fifty thousand dollars?"

"Exactly. Amazing, isn't it? I calculated it. It came to about three hundred dollars a minute."

Lacy took a sip of the Coke, then tilted the drink in his direction. "Wow," she observed comfortably. "A bargain."

Two heartbeats. Three. "Yes," he said, his eyes darkening just a little. "Actually, it was."

The carousel had stopped. Becky Jared was crying, and, looking over, Lacy noticed that Silas Jared was staring at Adam, obviously forgetting that his granddaughter needed help with her dismount.

"Hi, Silas," Lacy said pleasantly. "You remember Adam Kendall, don't you?"

He scowled. "You bet I do. And I hope that Adam Kendall remembers my gun. And my knife." He shook a finger toward Adam. "You'd better treat our Lacy right, Mr. Kendall. I don't allow anyone to upset her."

Before Adam could answer, the old man turned away and began attending to his granddaughter, who had moved from squealing joy to shrieking panic in a mere thirty seconds.

Adam sighed. "Have you been designated the official town treasure, or what? Everybody here acts as if I'm about to draw a mustache on the Mona Lisa. I don't think I've ever in my life received so many dire warnings about behaving myself."

"Sure you have," she said, licking the last of the mustard from her finger. "Have you forgotten about high school? You had a standing three o'clock appointment in Dean Bittner's office."

He laughed. "Good old Bittner. Where is he these days?"

"Right now I think he's manning the haunted house. We asked ourselves who we could get to act mean and scare the kids to death, and somehow his name came up."

Adam wiggled his eyebrows, a mischievous grin tilting the corners of his eyes. "Too perfect. Come on. Let's go."

He took her hand, and he started to move across the amusement park. But then, so suddenly she bumped into him from behind, he stopped. He held her hand up slightly, twisting it back and forth, as if he couldn't believe his eyes.

"Your ring," he said. "Where is it?"

She curled her fingers. "I took it off." He looked at her, a question in his eyes. "I didn't want to lose it," she explained. "Out here. All this dirt. So many people. Knocking into things—"

She was overexplaining, so she stopped herself.

"Good," he said succinctly. He ran his finger slowly over the untanned line of skin. And then, as if he had satisfied himself of something, he turned around again and, still holding her hand, took off toward the haunted house.

He walked so fast she almost had to break into a trot to keep up with him. It felt so familiar—her hand in his, following where he led. She felt her blood speed up, tingling faster through her veins, responding to the running. And to him.

"Coming through." He shouldered his way through the crowd, pulling Lacy behind him. Curious eyes followed them. At first Lacy murmured apologies, wondering what her friends must be thinking about this unprecedented loss of dignity.

And then she caught sight of Jennifer Lansing, who stood over at the hot dog stand, watching their progress with an unmistakable distaste. Her eyes were narrowed, her mouth pursed tight, looking harsh and pinched.

Lacy hesitated, stunned by the pure petty ugliness of Jennifer's face. Was that what *she* used to look like? Suddenly Lacy found the possibility horrifying. She stopped apologizing for running, for nicking the more sedate visitors who blocked the way. It was an amusement park. It was a beautiful, cloudless summer Saturday. Surely it was all right to run.

When they reached the haunted house, Lacy saw that Tina Seville was just coming out. The woman paused, giving Lacy a double take as if she couldn't believe her eyes.

Poor Tina. She was just about to discover what bad luck it had been to run into Lacy at this particular moment, in this particular mood.

"Tina," Lacy called out, louder than she'd ever raised her voice in public before. Even Adam turned around, wondering what was up.

Tina lifted her brows delicately. "Lacy," she said, blinking her subtle disapproval. "Are you all right?"

"I'm fine," Lacy said, her breath coming a little harder from the race across the park. "I'm glad you're here. I need to talk to you."

Tina smoothed her teal silk pantsuit, which must have become slightly wrinkled in the haunted house. "Right now?" Her voice expressed the most polite incredulity.

"Right now," Lacy confirmed unflinchingly. "It's important. It's about Gwen. I wanted to tell you that I don't appreciate the way you insulted her at the interview."

Tina frowned. "I did?"

"Yes. You did. Even worse, you put words in my mouth. You told her that I had said some cruel things—things I wouldn't have dreamed of saying."

Tina looked appalled. One didn't discuss such things in a public forum. One didn't discuss such things at all, if one could possibly avoid it. Lacy was vaguely aware of Adam standing at her shoulder, still clutching her hand. She had the sense that he was extremely amused.

"My dear," Tina began stiflingly. "I remember distinctly that I merely said she had behaved like a—"

"Exactly," Lacy broke in. "*You. You* said those things, Tina. Not me. My only mistake was in letting them pass. But that's about to change. I wanted you to know that you won't be able to get away with insulting my stepdaughter in my presence any more. I happen to think she's a very bright, very brave young woman. In fact, I think you would have been very lucky to have her at your school, and if you are too narrow-minded to see that, it's your loss, not hers.''

Tina looked like a comic book picture of outraged indignation. ''Lacy.'' She was practically speechless. ''Lacy, what on earth has gotten into you? Have you lost your mind?''

Lacy smiled, strangely exhilarated by the encounter. It felt like the first time in ten years that she'd heard her own voice, her own words, issuing from her own lips.

''Lost my mind?'' She felt the warmth of Adam's hand as he gave hers a supportive squeeze. ''No, Tina,'' she said. ''On the contrary, I think I've finally found it.''

She heard Adam chuckle as Tina moved away stiffly, her chin lifted so high it stretched her neck, carrying her wounded dignity on her padded shoulders.

''Well done,'' he said softly.

But was that true? She wondered if remorse would start to set in, now that the adrenaline of the encounter was ebbing. Cautiously, she listened for her internal censor, expecting to hear it scolding her. But she heard nothing. Nothing except a strange, vibrant humming, like the sound of something electric and powerful coming to life.

''Thanks,'' she said. ''It felt— It felt good.''

''Of course it did.'' Adam smiled. ''But now I'm thinking maybe we should skip the haunted house.

Once you've faced down a monster like that, I'm not sure there's anything left that can scare you.''

THREE HOURS LATER, when the park was finally closing, Lacy knew that Adam had been very, very wrong.

She wasn't beyond being frightened. In fact, she felt more vulnerable than ever. Jennifer and Tina and the whole notion of relentless propriety might have lost power over her, but a million new terrors had risen to take their place.

For instance, now that it was dark the blue moon shone in Adam's hair, and she was afraid of the way her fingers kept straying there, combing the moonlight through the soft strands.

She was afraid of the way she was nestling under his arm, just exactly the way Hamlet fitted himself against her knees at night—open, unguarded, limp with trust and comfort.

She was afraid of the shimmering current of electricity that zipped through her veins when he leaned over and kissed her neck. Or her shoulder. Or the inside of her wrist. All of which he had done, over and over, until she was shivering with a fear that was intensely sensual.

Most of all, she was afraid of the way everyone was leaving.

She was afraid of being alone with him here in this fairyland of strung lights and twirling horses, treading paths of colored tickets that had fallen to the ground like confetti.

Already she felt its magic closing in on her. It made her feel wild inside, sensual and reckless and edgy.

"Come on. It's the last ride." He steered her toward the Ferris wheel, which stood so tall it seemed to pierce the blue-black velvet of the sky. "I won't let you fall."

And so she climbed in and let the wheel slowly lift her up to the stars. The wind was cold up here, and he wrapped both arms around her, causing her heart to thump crazily in her chest.

She looked down, all that long, dizzying way down. And she saw things...

She saw herself making love to Adam—here on the dangerously swaying, windswept wheel; down there, astride the hard, plunging carousel horses; and over there, in the funhouse, where the mirrors would reflect their nakedness into a limitless infinity.

And then, as suddenly as they had appeared, the visions departed. The wheel rolled back to earth. But as she climbed shakily out of the small metal bucket, she finally knew what frightened her the most.

She was falling in love with Adam Kendall all over again.

CHAPTER FOURTEEN

"YOU KNOW, YOU DON'T really have to stay," she said as they walked away from the Ferris wheel, listening to the men shut off the switches and circuits behind them. Theirs had indeed been the last ride of the night. "There are quite a few maintenance men still here. And a security guard. I'll be fine."

"Don't be silly." His arm tightened around her shoulders. "I want to stay."

She didn't protest further. They wandered together, doing all the practical things. Checking bathrooms for stowaways who didn't want to go home—and they even found some. Two teenaged boys scattered, laughing, at their approach, and made for the gates.

A fog began to roll in from the Atlantic, but still Lacy and Adam made their rounds. They checked the food stands, making sure the fried batter machine had been turned off and the popcorn stashed away. They patrolled the picnic tables, gathering abandoned sweaters, lost watches and sunglasses and keys and locking them in a lost-and-found box.

But through it all they kept coming back to each other. A touch as their hands reached across a table. A kiss as they met beneath a tree. A quick waltz as they passed the merry-go-round, which still played its lilting organ music, though the horses were frozen in their spots.

Each touch lasted longer than the one before. Each kiss probed deeper. His hands grew urgent. Her body began forming a small, intense whirlpool of need. She didn't see how they could go on much longer without…without…

As they passed the funhouse, she almost turned in at the door, obsessed with her earlier vision of the two of them in there. She was mesmerized by the thought of being surrounded by endlessly repeating sexuality. She wanted to lose track of what was real and what was not.

But he kept on going. The fog was thick now, swirling as they moved through it. They were only a hundred yards from the gate.

"Adam," she said.

He turned, his face partly obscured by the thick silver mist. "What?"

"I want you," she said quietly. "I want to make love to you. Now." She took a deep breath. "Here."

He touched her face. "I know, sweetheart." His voice was husky. "I know."

He took her hand again, and he led her down a small side path overhung with elms. Tiny white lights twinkled on the branches, like fairies hiding. Their footsteps were muffled, and the night was very still, cloaked in silence by the gathering fog.

She was slightly disoriented. She wasn't sure where they were headed. But then, out of the mist, a glowing red heart appeared—and she found her bearings.

They were at the entrance to the Tunnel of Love.

The heart was crudely made of neon, she knew, and it wasn't even particularly pretty. But at this moment, draped in fog, and beckoning from the darkness, it seemed completely magical.

He paused just under the heart. It cast a wine-colored glow over his face. His strong, handsome, so familiar face... She touched it, just to assure herself that he was real.

"Lacy." His voice was a strange combination of tension and tenderness. "Are you sure about this? If we were caught... The gossips would have a field day."

"I'm sure."

"We could be seen," he said. "An argument with Tina Seville can be survived. But this..." He shook his head, and she saw the ghost of a smile through the shifting fog. "I'm not sure you could maintain your status as the official town treasure after this."

"I don't care." And it was true. She wasn't a painting, or a statue, or a monument. Not tonight. Not with him. And she didn't belong to the city. She belonged to Adam Kendall. She always had.

"I don't care," she repeated. "I want you to make love to me."

"Then come." He turned. "Follow me."

He led her into the tunnel, and for several curving yards they followed a misty footpath lined with tiny glowing pink lights. It led them to the boats, which waited at the dock, lined up dark and empty and mysterious, as if waiting for ghostly guests who inhabited the park after the crowds went home.

Lacy hadn't ever seen this ride before. The park

had been abandoned her whole lifetime, until today. But now she saw that the boats were obviously designed for romance, their heart-shaped backs forming a secluded bubble of privacy. The seats were wide, generous benches thickly padded in red velvet.

Looking at the seats, Lacy had another of her flashing, breathtaking visions. This one was so vivid that her knees suddenly went weak. She wrapped her fingers around Adam's hand.

She felt him turn, and she knew there was a question in his eyes.

"I'm sure," she said again, not taking her gaze from the lightly rocking boat. "I'm so sure I can hardly breathe."

For answer, he raised her hand slowly and kissed her fingers. His warm lips grazed the newly bare spot where once Malcolm's wedding ring had been.

Then he helped her aboard. The boat tilted under their weight then righted itself. The restless water lapped at the side of the boat with small wet sounds.

He guided her to the seat and knelt before her. He began to undress her—partly, anyway. He took his time, showing the same expert and imaginative understanding of the need for quick flight that he had learned back in their teenage years, when every encounter had been stolen, every coming together accomplished only with great risk.

She wore a long summer dress that buttoned from scooped neck to swirling skirt. He unbuttoned from the top, slowly making his way to her rib cage. Then he worked from the bottom, releasing her up to her hips. He peeled the dress away from her shoulders, pushing it down onto her elbows, and unclasped the lacy white bra that fastened between her breasts. Then, opening her skirt, he slid her bikini pants over her legs, dragging them across her bare feet with a tormenting, sensual tickle.

Just three inches of midriff remained covered. The rest was his.

He ran the palm of his hand slowly over the swell of her breast. "So soft," he said thickly. "I knew it was true. I remembered it too well. You're as soft as an angel."

Every breath she took was a struggle. Desire was thickening her blood, tightening her lungs. But he went so slowly, as if he needed to relearn her with his hands. He stroked her softly in slow, complicated patterns from shoulder to breast, sometimes rising up to her neck, sometimes dipping down behind her dress to her arching back. Then up again, as if to home, to settle possessively around her swollen, aching breast.

Finally, he bent his head, brushing his lips across her skin. Warmth flooded her veins, and she shivered and closed her eyes. It had been so long—and the years had been so cold. She was weak with relief to learn that her body still knew how to react, still knew what to do.

"Relax," he whispered, as if the ghosts in the other boats might hear them. "Lean back."

She obeyed him. She let her bare shoulders rest against the quilted velvet of the boat's padded walls. Her hands fell weakly at her sides as he moved in closer and touched her thighs. He lifted her legs, arranging them gently along his shoulders. And then he bent his head again.

Had it been dark in this tunnel? Suddenly, though her eyes were closed, she saw bright light, and a whirlpool of colors. His mouth was warm, his lips velvet soft, but his tongue was hard and knowing. She felt herself straining, grasping the safety bar overhead as if she might indeed be swept overboard by these pounding waves of desire.

At the last moment, he pulled back. She tossed her head against the velvet, protesting silently, and tensed her legs, trying to hold him. She had been so close— so close to some perfect, rainbowed release that she hadn't known in ten long, terrible years. He couldn't deny her now....

He stroked her hair back from her forehead, murmuring comfort. She reached for him, and realized that he had freed himself from his blue jeans. He even had a condom ready. Apparently he had grown wiser over the years.

But had she? If he hadn't brought protection, would she have been able to stop now? Or would she do what she had done ten years ago—seek joy in his body, comfort in this sensual abandonment, pushing away all fears about tomorrow?

"Adam, hurry," she said desperately. "I need this. I need you."

He was ready. He pulled her close, and then, in one easy shift, smoothly reversed their positions. The boat rocked, and then somehow he was against the seat, half sitting, half leaning—and she was astride him, her knees cushioned by quilted velvet, her unbuttoned dress flowing out behind her.

He slipped his hands under her dress, lifted her, and positioned her above him. But though his muscles trembled, humming with the effort required for restraint, he didn't thrust. He let her decide when it would happen, let her absorb him at her own pace.

She forced herself to move slowly, deliberately, making every inch a torture of pulsing heat and swollen pleasure. She took a deep breath and tuned her senses to a deep, dark, interior frequency, where she could almost feel their veins throbbing against one another.

She moved her hips once. He groaned. And then she didn't dare move any more. She was too close to the edge.

It was a small, wonderful miracle, and she wanted it to last forever. She had been so afraid. So afraid that this would not happen, or that she would have to fight for it, making him work, too, muscles straining, to bring her back to life. And yet, here it was, as near at hand as a ripe apple poised to drop with the first kiss of wind. As pure and unstoppable as a gushing mountain stream.

"It can't be this easy," she said softly.

He reached up and cupped his hands around her breasts. "When it's right, it's always easy, sweetheart."

She let her head fall back, in love with the touch of his fingers as they found her nipples. "But it's been…so many years…."

"A lifetime couldn't come between us." He

dropped his hands and placed them around her waist. "Hold on to me, Lacy. Let me show you how easy it can be."

Where did he get the strength? She wasn't sure whether he moved her hips with his wonderful hands, or whether he created the rhythm with his own body. She knew only that a wild tension moved through her, and none of the effort was hers. It was like flying, like being thrust ever higher into a black night sky.

So high. So high it couldn't last. And yet it did. With that amazing, graceful strength, he drove her to the edge of the sky, until she wanted to scream with the fearful exhilaration, until she was longing for the fall.

She gripped his shoulders, crying out, muscles begging for release. Her breasts brushed his chest, and for the first time, his rhythm grew strained. He called her name, and she helped him, rocking her hips to add her strength to his.

For a long, crystalline moment, movement was all they knew. Their bodies rocked, the boat rocked, the whole world rocked around them.

And then there was nothing but the long, helpless fall, dropping through a tunnel glowing with small pink fairy lights and hearts as red as neon.

When it was over, she collapsed against him, their drenched bodies meeting slick and warm and spent. It was several minutes before she could breathe without effort, and she felt his heart thumping fast beneath her ear.

"Thank you," she whispered when she could talk. She ran her hand up inside his shirt, relishing the smooth, damp curves of his chest. "Thank you for giving that back to me."

He touched her hair softly. "I didn't give you anything, Lacy. It was always yours. Even at eighteen, you had so much power, so much instinctive sensuality.... I've never known another woman like you." He growled with animal appreciation. "You drove me crazy then. You drive me even crazier now."

She noticed the casual reference to all the other women he had known. But she didn't let it sink in. She refused to brood about how he had spent these past ten years, years when she was locked in a frigid, loveless servitude to Malcolm.

Instead she wriggled subtly against him. Once wasn't going to be enough, she realized. With Adam, once hadn't ever been enough.

Memories surged back to her suddenly, the echo of his delighted laughter that first night, as he had realized what she wanted. She had turned away, embarrassed, but he had flipped her over with a low, sensual laugh, ready to bring her the miracle again, some new and wonderful way.

"Never be ashamed of wanting more," he had said. "I love to love you, Lacy. Any way you want it, as many times as you want it. Do you understand that? Nothing is too much to ask."

Emboldened by the memory, she shifted one more time, hoping he still felt the same way. She wanted more. Much more. She had so many years to make up for. It was like trying to fill a sun-parched lake.

He chuckled, tightening his hand on her back.

"I'm not eighteen anymore, you know," he said,

but his body proved him a liar. He was as ready as she was, and the heat was building fast.

But then they heard voices. Someone was whistling, and he sounded to be just outside the Tunnel of Love.

Lacy lowered her head in an agony of frustration. "Oh, no," she murmured against his arm. "Make him go away."

He laughed quietly. "God, I hope it's not Silas Jared and his knife."

But the whistling man wasn't going away. Instead, the whistling was drawing closer—a maintenance man, she thought dismally. Probably headed here to tie down the boats and shut off the power to the neon heart.

She forced herself to lift away from Adam, though the disappointment of the physical disconnection was almost painful. She pulled up the dress he had so thoughtfully left accessible, and began closing the buttons with fingers that felt rubbery and ineffectual.

Suddenly the entire tunnel was flooded with light. She glanced nervously at Adam, who was just buckling his belt. He scooped up her underclothes and handed them to her in a tight ball of satin.

"Your call," he said with a smile. "Want to brazen it out—or try to save face?"

She worried her lower lip. "Is there any way to save face at this point?"

"Maybe. You go first. If he's a gentleman, he'll walk you out to your car. Then I'll follow later. With any luck, he'll never know I was here.'

She hesitated. She didn't want to leave him, not

even to salvage her reputation. She didn't want to leave this little cocoon of safety.

But the voice was only a few yards away now.

"Go ahead." Adam kissed her. Hard, fast, full of promise. "Tomorrow?"

She nodded, smiling bravely. "Tomorrow."

And then she peeked over the heart-shaped shell of the boat, much to the surprise of the maintenance worker, who stared, gaping, as she climbed up onto the dock.

"Hello," she said pleasantly, calling on her long habit of unruffled composure to manage the rather surreal moment. She brushed tiny flecks of red velvet from her arms. "Could I impose on you to walk me to my car?"

ADAM PULLED INTO THE Cartwright parking lot slowly, his mind only half on his driving. The other half was still back at the park, reliving those incredible moments with Lacy. And then reliving them again. And again. Frankly, he wasn't sure he'd *ever* get that part of his mind back.

But somehow he forced himself to focus. The fog was fairly thick, even this far inland, and he had to park carefully. He was halfway into a space before he saw a motorcycle angled weirdly between two slots, overlapping the lines.

Must be Gwen, he thought, more amused than annoyed as he backed out again. Hers wasn't the only motorcycle on Pringle Island, especially on a summer weekend, but he was pretty sure it was the only brand new bike with that many dents already crumpling the chrome. She was a really, really bad driver.

What was she doing here? It was after midnight—and she didn't have a room of her own at the Cartwright anymore. Actually, that was probably a dumb question. She'd been putting some pretty slick moves on Travis all week. This was probably just the last move. Check and checkmate.

Too bad. Adam wasn't ready to turn in yet. His system was still way too geared up. He had been hoping that Travis might be in the mood to shoot some pool in the bar, or maybe even drag out some of those real estate listings Adam had rejected before. Adam had a feeling he might be less picky now—now that he had a stronger incentive to stay.

But if Gwen were up there with Travis, Adam was going to have to manage on his own. Maybe that was better anyhow. He hadn't ever been the kiss-and-tell type, but he felt kind of itchy and feverish tonight, and he wasn't sure he could talk about anything but Lacy. Once he started talking, he'd probably be like some insufferable drunk, holding forth about boats and angels and hot dogs and miracles, to any poor fool who'd listen.

So maybe it was a good idea to spend some time alone first, sorting things out. He picked up his mail from the front desk, strolled into the bar, bought a scotch and water and carried it out to the pool area.

The pool closed down at midnight, so he had the wide, damp deck to himself. He claimed one of the dozens of empty chairs and settled in. The huge, brightly lit blue rectangle was oddly mesmerizing, with the tendrils of silver fog floating just above it. He stared at it and found himself thinking how much he'd like to make love to Lacy in that glowing blue water.

The images were so pleasant that he was damned annoyed to hear the *click clack* of high heels approaching. There was nowhere to hide, and he was not going to make small talk to some flirtatious female right now. He'd have to pack up his drink, his fantasies and his itchy libido, and go somewhere else.

"There you are. Finally!"

The woman was closer now, and in spite of the fog he recognized that trademark waterfall of blond curls—not to mention the grape-colored minidress with a wide yellow belt. It was Gwen.

"The guy at the desk told me you were out here. I've only been waiting for you for about *two* hours. Where have you been? Didn't that stupid park thing end at ten?"

His internal Geiger counter, refined over years of dealing with all kinds of women, recognized the signs of an imminent eruption. Her whole body was tense, her voice was vibrating, and her jaw was set like a slab of concrete. He knew females, and this particular female was in the throes of a major snit.

He didn't take it very seriously, though. From what he'd seen of Gwen, she always operated at a pretty high pitch. Reluctantly, he abandoned his plan to sneak off. He sat back against his chair, resigned to trying to calm her down if he could.

"Sorry," he said. "I didn't know you needed to see me. I stayed late to help Lacy close up."

That was obviously the wrong thing to say. Gwen's eyes narrowed, and she shifted some kind of package from one hand to the other roughly, making a brief, guttural noise. "Help her close up? That's what you call it these days? That's rich."

What was she carrying? She was clutching the damn thing as if it held a bomb. Adam scanned it as inconspicuously as he could. It looked like a manila envelope, legal-sized, bulging with papers of some sort.

And why was she positively humming with hostility? He had thought, early on, that she might try to make a play for him. It had been a bit tricky, deflecting her without deflating her, but he thought he'd been successful. She had simply rotated her radar, aiming it toward Travis, without any hard feelings.

So what was this all about? He wondered if she'd been drinking.

She glared at him, apparently disgusted with what she saw. "God, what a disappointment you turned out to be," she said. "You came here like this big bad-ass ex-boyfriend, acting as if you had her number and were ready to call it. But I knew you wouldn't hold out for long. You've been here, what, a month? And she's already turned you into another one of her drooling lapdogs."

"I have to take issue with that," he said lightly. "I'm quite sure I never drool."

"Yeah, right. You do, buster, you do. They all do." She plopped down on the chair next to his and slid her overstuffed envelope onto the table between.

"But I bet you'll dry up once you've had a look at this."

His instincts prickled. He looked at the envelope, but he didn't reach for it. "What is it?"

"It's my father's will." She crossed her legs, flashing a long expanse of trim thigh defiantly. "I think you'll find it very interesting."

He watched her steadily. "Why?"

"Because it tells you a lot about Lacy. About who she really is. Things you ought to know."

"I already know she inherited a lot of money when your father died, Gwen." He paused. "So did you. That doesn't make you evil, does it?"

She arched one brow so high it tickled the corkscrew curls that dangled over her forehead. "Yeah, but do you know *how* she got the money?"

He didn't want to think about all this. He suddenly hated this angry little girl who was trying to stir up old muck. He would never *like* knowing that Lacy had been Malcolm Morgan's wife, but he had come to terms with it. He was ready to put it behind him.

"Of course you don't," she said. "But that's because you haven't looked at the will." She nudged the envelope closer to him with one long orange fingernail. "As I said, I think you'll find it very interesting."

"I find it none of my business," he said coldly. "The only interesting thing here is why you would want me to see it."

She laughed, a bitter sound that echoed off the expanse of pool water. "Oh, but it *is* your business, Adam. It is most definitely your business. Let me help you. The lawyer language makes it sound very complicated and academic, but I can cut to the chase.'' She folded her hands in her lap and cleared her throat, as if getting ready to participate in an oration contest.

''Here's how it went. Lacy was pregnant when she married my father. He wanted her to get rid of it. At first she said no, but then he rewrote his will, saying that if she bore a child during the first calendar year of their marriage, she wouldn't inherit a dime.''

Gwen tilted her head, apparently studying the effect of her words on Adam. ''Not a dime. See what I'm getting at? Daddy alters his will, and then…presto-chango…suddenly there isn't any baby anymore.''

He looked at her for a long moment. Her eyes glittered in the patio lights, and he suddenly wondered if maybe it wasn't just fury that drove her. Maybe it was pain. Maybe she hated Lacy because she had once wanted to love her.

It was a phenomenon he recognized all too well. Thwarted love turning into bitterness. He'd been there. Done that.

''Gwen,'' he said. ''Don't do this. Surely, deep inside, you don't want to hurt Lacy with such malicious gossip. Don't you think it's possible that somehow you've misconstrued—''

''*Misconstrued?*'' She stood abruptly, making the light, webbed chair rock on its plastic-pipe legs. ''I didn't misconstrue anything. I was there, remember? Nobody came right out and told me—I was just this annoying little kid—but I heard their arguments. You wouldn't believe it, knowing her now, but Lacy cried a lot back then.''

He made a sound, though he hadn't meant to.

"Yeah, it was pretty grim," Gwen agreed. "He really knew how to put the screws on. At first it was just a suggestion. Maybe it would be for the best to get rid of the pregnancy. Then it got tougher. That was how he worked. He tried to sweet-talk you into doing things his way, but if you wouldn't play along, he got mean in a hurry. That's when the lawyer came."

Adam had quit making sounds at all. He thought maybe he had stopped breathing.

"You don't have to believe me," Gwen said. "Read the will. And if you think I faked anything, check at the probate courts. It's on file there, all spelled out in black and white."

She started to walk away, obviously aware that she had caught her fish, and content to leave him writhing on the hook.

She paused after a few feet and turned. "Come on, Adam, you do the math. If she had a baby, she didn't inherit." She shrugged. "Well, I see a mighty rich widow, but I don't see any baby. Do you?"

CHAPTER FIFTEEN

LACY STOOD IN HER BACK garden, cutting daisies and delphiniums for the foyer arrangement. Hamlet lay on the grass beside her, playing his Great Hunter game, skulking through the sweet alyssum in search of imaginary prey.

She ought to be at the hospital. For years she had worked on Sunday afternoons, getting more done on that one quiet day than she did in the five bustling workweek days put together.

But she didn't feel like being cooped up in an office. The sun was brilliant overhead, and the air smelled of the ocean. If she was very quiet, she imagined she could hear the breakers as they hit the shore of Pringle Sound two miles away.

Yes, only the outdoors could hold her today. She felt restless, giddy, wonderfully alive. She had more in common with the butterflies that winged through the buttercups than she did with the men and women who prowled the hospital corridors, checking charts.

And besides…she was hoping that Adam would call. She glanced over toward the back porch railing, where she had propped the portable telephone. Surely it would ring soon. In the meantime, she kept cutting yellow daisies and laying them carefully in her basket.

Just when she was thinking of going in to put the flowers in water, she heard her front gate creak. She looked up and saw Adam coming toward her, dappled in sunlight. At the sight of him, she clutched the last delphinium so tightly it was a miracle its slim stem didn't break.

"Adam!" She felt herself flushing, as if the very sound of his name had developed sexual undertones for her. She smiled, suddenly bashful, an emotion she hadn't ever expected to feel again. "I was hoping you'd come."

He halted several feet away from her. Something was wrong with that, she thought, momentarily confused. She had expected to be embraced. Her whole body had been pulsing toward him. But he stood apart, and he held himself very straight.

"I came to say goodbye," he said. His voice was formal, too.

She frowned slightly, wondering if she had misunderstood. "You're leaving? Where are you going?"

"I have to get back to New York," he said stiffly. "I've already stayed longer than I should have, longer than I had planned."

A small stripe of shadow passed across the garden. "To New York? You mean…permanently?"

"Yes." He met her eyes, but his were as blank as if he were sleepwalking. She could read nothing, nothing that would help her to understand. "Or at least for a while. I've lived there two years, which is longer than I've lived anywhere since I left Pringle Island. It might be time to move on again. I'll have to see.''

She must have been clenching her hands. The delphinium drooped, its stem finally surrendering to the pressure. "But, Adam, last night, I—" She tried again. "We—"

"I'm sorry about last night, Lacy," he broke in, his voice rough. And for the first time his eyes showed something. They looked, suddenly, both bruised and bottomless, as if he hadn't slept much. "I shouldn't have let that happen."

Little sparks of fear were flashing inside her. He sounded so serious. So unhappy. Why had he turned sad and tight like this? Why hadn't their lovemaking left him giddy and filled with sunshine, the way it had left her?

"Why not?" She closed the distance between them, and put her hand on his arm. "Adam? What happened between us was wonderful, wasn't it?"

He looked away. "It was a mistake."

She felt herself stiffening. She didn't want to react that way, but it was such a long-standing habit. She felt her face settling in smooth, tight lines.

"That's not really an answer, is it?" She bent to drop her flower in the basket, then rose to meet his gaze. "*Why* was it a mistake?"

He squinted once, as though the sun were hurting his eyes. "I guess it's a mistake because I'm leaving," he said slowly. "Because, wonderful or not, it can't in the end amount to more than a one-night stand."

A one-night stand? What a horrible expression. But it hadn't felt like that last night. Last night, she had felt cared for. She had felt cherished, something she hadn't experienced in years—but a feeling she remembered with perfect clarity nonetheless.

She had felt loved.

Could she have been so wrong? Was she really such a fool as that?

She spoke with a forced calm. "Are you trying to say that you came to town with the express intent of seducing me, and stayed only long enough to accomplish your goal?"

"Okay," he answered wearily. "Let's say that. Let's say I'm a bastard. And then let's say goodbye."

A month ago, she would have done exactly that. She would have nodded coolly, picked up her wicker basket of daisies and retreated into the house, where she would have smothered all thoughts of him in relentless work. She would have raised another million dollars for another worthy cause. Abandoned women, perhaps, this time.

But not now. She wasn't just an obedient mannequin anymore, willing to pose first one way and then another to please her audience. Willing to cover up any emotions she might possess, just to make things more comfortable. By God, she deserved an explanation, and she wasn't going to make it easy for him to duck out of here without giving her the truth.

She took a deep breath. "I don't believe it. Last night didn't feel like an end. It felt like a beginning. Something has happened since then to change your mind. I have a right to know what it was."

Still he didn't speak. Her pain blended with her anger to make her bold. She grabbed his arm, not imploringly this time. Forcefully. "Damn it, Adam. *Tell me.*"

He stared down at her with haunted eyes. "I've read Malcolm's will," he said quietly. "I know. I know about the baby."

She froze for one long, cold moment. Heart, pulse, sight, hearing—all suspended. And then she felt her blood rush back, hot and painful, through her veins. Her hand fell from his arm.

"I didn't want to tell you," he said harshly. "I didn't want to have this conversation. What's the point? It's over—over so long ago, and I never even knew." His voice had a terrible torn quality. "Please, don't make me say things I'll regret. I know you must have had reasons...not just the money. I know I'll never really understand what you went through. I don't judge you, Lacy. I was gone, and you were alone, and..."

He closed his eyes, covering the clear blue, turning his eyes into mere collections of bruised shadows and dark lashes. "I don't judge you. But I don't think I can live with it, either."

She wondered whether she could speak. Her throat felt so swollen there was no room for words. But she forced the sound through. "How did you happen to find Malcolm's will? Were you having me investigated?"

He shook his head. "Gwen brought it to me. She thought I should know."

Gwen. Lacy sank one more level into the abyss,

remembering Gwen's last words. *I wish I could spoil some dream of yours, just so you'd know how it feels.*

"She hates me," Lacy said. "Can't you see that? She would do anything, say anything, invent anything, just to hurt me."

"But she didn't invent that will." Adam ran his hand through his hair. "She didn't invent the pregnancy. Did she, Lacy?"

Lacy met his gaze somehow. She should have told him last night. If only she could turn back the clock, and tell him these things while she was in his arms. Then she never would have had to know he was capable of judging her so harshly.

"No," she said. "She didn't invent the pregnancy. That was real. For a little while."

Such a very little while. The anguish of those last hours came back to her now, and with them came a bitter sense of the injustice of his interrogation. How dare he take this tone with her? She didn't need his understanding, didn't want his comfort. And she darn sure didn't require his forgiveness.

He had no right to judge her. His opinion on all this might have mattered ten years ago. But not today. Not when it came ten years too late.

She drew herself up and faced him squarely.

"You say you never knew. But you *could* have known, Adam. If you had called. If you had written. You should have considered that possibility, don't you think? Before you left? You weren't that naive. You knew how babies were made."

He made a low sound between tight lips. "I know

I share the blame in this, Lacy. I know. I told you I don't judge you.''

She almost laughed. But it would have sounded terrible, black and warped, so she stopped herself.

''Oh, yes, you do,'' she said. ''It's obvious that you've convicted me, and sentenced me, without even once asking me what happened. So do you know what? I think you're right. I think you *should* leave. After all, that's your specialty, isn't it?''

He made an abrupt gesture toward her, but she backed away. ''That's not fair,'' he said tensely. ''When I left here ten years ago, I was coming back. You knew I was going to come back to you.''

''No, I didn't.'' Her voice wasn't right—it was much too sharp, knife-edged and brittle—so she pitched it lower and began again. ''I had begged you to say, but you didn't care about anything but getting your hands on money.''

''For us,'' he said harshly. ''Damn it, Lacy. For *us*.''

''I didn't want money, Adam. I wanted you. But you couldn't believe that, could you? You resented my holding you back.''

''No. That's not how it was. We both said things we didn't mean. But you knew how I felt. You knew I'd be back.''

''But when?'' She felt her breath coming heavily. ''When, Adam? One year? Five? Ten? You didn't even tell me exactly where you were going—''

''I didn't know. Not until later. And by then you were already—''

''Be honest with yourself for once, Adam. You

didn't want me writing, calling, begging you to come back. You were determined that you wouldn't return to Pringle Island until you could come sweeping back in glory, dazzling everyone with your newfound wealth.''

She narrowed her eyes. ''You dare accuse me of committing terrible sins for money, Adam? Well, what about you?''

He was frowning, as if her unbridled anger surprised him. It surprised her, too. She'd been sitting on her emotions for ten years now. How convenient for everyone else! But she was through repressing her feelings. And what she truly felt right now was fury.

''You have no right to judge me, Adam. You lost your rights ten years ago, when you got on that ferry and floated away from this island, leaving me to deal with the consequences.''

''Lacy—''

But she wasn't going to listen. She picked up her basket roughly, spilling daisies on the carpet of grass. ''For five years I let Malcolm pass judgment on me. I let him tell me whether I was good or bad, valuable or worthless. But I'm never going to let anyone do that again. Not even you. *Especially* not you.''

''Lacy, you don't—''

''Go,'' she said fiercely, hoping the anger would hold, keeping the pain at bay until she could get inside. ''Just take your self-righteous ignorance and go back where you came from.''

GWEN LET HERSELF INTO the house quietly at about noon. She was dog-tired. She'd spent the night on the couch at Teddy Kilgore's house—which meant she got no rest at all. Her conscience was strangely uncomfortable, making sleep difficult for hours. And then Mrs. Kilgore, an early riser, had begun banging around in the kitchen at the crack of dawn.

So though Gwen had absolutely no interest in meeting up with the Stepwitch, she had dragged herself home anyhow. Maybe she'd feel better if she could just crash in her own room for a while. Maybe she could shake this queasy feeling that she'd done something really awful.

But no such luck. She opened the door, and the first thing she saw was Lacy. She frowned. What was going on? Lacy was about halfway up the staircase, leaning on the banister, bending over sideways, as if she were having a heart attack or something.

She walked over to the side of the stairs and looked up. Lacy's face was half-hidden by her loose brown hair, but what Gwen could see looked downright scary. Ashen, strained…desolate.

Gwen's conscience started wriggling miserably. Adam must have been here. And it must have been a pretty terrible scene. But so what? That was what she had wanted, wasn't it? She ought to feel victorious. Instead, the sight of Lacy's beautiful, broken face was strangely unsettling.

She had never seen Lacy look anything but utterly poised, completely in control. She hadn't, somehow, quite believed that Lacy was capable of real suffering. But this was the real thing, all right. It was so real it was sickening to see.

"Lacy?" She touched the banister, several treads

down from where her stepmother stood. "Are you all right?"

Lacy lifted her head a fraction of an inch. "Yes," she said in a muffled voice. "I'm just going upstairs."

Gwen wrapped her fingers tightly around the smooth wood. Her throat felt unexpectedly dry. "Has Adam been here?"

Lacy nodded. But slowly, as if the movement hurt. *Oh, God.* Gwen suddenly felt like a criminal. This wasn't how it had felt when she imagined this moment in her dreams of revenge.

"Lacy, I—"

But what was she going to say? That she was sorry? She never said she was sorry—not for anything. Besides, it would sound pretty stupid. Sorry wasn't going to change anything. The damage was done.

And it wasn't just damage. It was total devastation.

"It's all right, Gwen," Lacy said. She looked up, and she tried to offer a smile, but it was so forced that it made Gwen wince.

"I know you took the will to Adam. I think I even know why you did it." She was breathing heavily, and her words had a half-numb sound. "I know that you hate me. How could you not? I failed you. I came in here, I took the security and the respectability that your father could offer me, but I didn't take the responsibility. I should have come here prepared to be a mother to you, and I didn't."

"Hey, I made it pretty clear I didn't want a mother."

"I know. But you didn't mean that. Everyone

wants to be loved. But I was too wrapped up in my own problems to see clearly. And then, when I miscarried…'' Her voice stumbled. ''When I lost the baby…''

Whatever momentum had been driving her seemed to evaporate with the sound of that one little word. She swallowed a lonely, strangled sound and bowed her head again.

Without realizing it, Gwen had edged around the banister, and stood now on the lowest step, looking up.

''You lost the baby?'' She moved two more steps, up the treads, until she and Lacy were only three more steps apart. ''You *miscarried* the baby?'' She stared at Lacy, trying to remember the day she had gone to the hospital, but she couldn't. It was all a blur, lost in a fog of time.

''Oh, my God. I always thought— Lacy…why didn't you ever *tell* me that was what happened?''

Lacy shook her head. ''I never told anyone. Your father didn't want anyone to know, especially you. I had no idea you had overheard anything…anything about…''

Slowly, she sank to a sitting position, as if her strength had completely ebbed away. ''But none of it matters anymore. It's over. It's been over for a long time. I just didn't want to face it.''

''Oh, Lacy,'' Gwen blurted urgently. ''I'm sorry.''

She covered the distance between them without thinking. Kneeling on the tread just below Lacy, she touched her shoulder hesitantly, as if she weren't sure the gesture would be welcome. She couldn't remember when she had last touched her stepmother.

Amazingly, Lacy didn't pull away. Gwen put her arm around Lacy's shoulders, registering a low ache of surprise to discover that she was so slight and fragile. Lacy had always seemed so powerful, so much larger than life.

But Gwen had been wrong about so many things. She felt tears starting behind her eyes. She had been such a fool.

"It wasn't all your fault," she said softly. "I've been a horrible bitch. I made things so much more difficult for you. Oh, Lacy. I'm so terribly sorry."

"I know," Lacy said, almost inaudibly. She buried her face in her arms. She wasn't crying, but Gwen knew that meant only that her misery was beyond tears. "It's all right, Gwen. I know."

Tentatively, Gwen wrapped her other arm around her, too. Lacy didn't protest. Instead, she turned slightly, tilting her head into Gwen's arm. That one vulnerable gesture somehow spoke a benediction of forgiveness.

Gwen shut her eyes, absorbing Lacy's warmth, the way any child draws comfort from acceptance and love. It spread through her like honey, sweetening things that had long been too bitter to bear. Oh, she had wanted this for so long. To be held. To be forgiven. To be family.

And then someone was crying, but it still wasn't Lacy. It was Gwen, who, in spite of everything, had finally taken the first step on her long way home.

CHAPTER SIXTEEN

"FRANKLY," GWEN SAID as she squatted down to hand the tape to Lacy, who was already kneeling on the far side of the package they were wrapping, "I don't see why you're going to all this trouble just to *give* this painting away."

Lacy smiled and wrapped the tape carefully over the brown padded paper. "Well, frankly *I'm* glad we *can* give it away. I'm surprised anyone agreed to accept it."

"Yeah, who took it, anyhow? The New England Museum for the Blind?"

Lacy chuckled. Gwen's unique and spicy brand of companionship had made the past two days much easier. Once she and Gwen had finally begun talking— really talking—they had discovered that they actually had a great deal in common. Their mutual dislike of *Saturday Morning: Half Past Paradise,* for instance. Gwen admitted that she used to avoid the parlor altogether just so she wouldn't have to look at the thing.

Lacy cut the edge of the tape and rocked back onto her heels, surveying the little parlor. The portrait of Malcolm and Lacy had already been banished to the attic, and the room looked strangely clean without the two overbearing paintings dominating the walls.

"Having second thoughts?" Gwen was perched on the edge of Malcolm's desk, watching Lacy while she munched on sunflower seeds. "You know you don't have to leave on my account. We might just have a great time, being single chicks here together. Of course, we'd have to work out a date-night schedule, so we didn't cramp each other's style—"

"No, no second thoughts." Lacy placed the roll of tape on the end table and stood slowly. "I'm sure I'm making the right decision. It's way overdue."

She was pleased at how confident she sounded. She only hoped that eventually she could actually *be* that certain.

She had decided two days ago, right after the episode with Adam, that she was going to move to Boston. She had hidden away on this little fantasy island long enough.

Nothing tied her to Pringle Island anymore, not now that Malcolm was dead. Not now that Adam was—

She shied away from that thought. It wouldn't help to think about Adam right now. She had to keep her thoughts aimed forward.

She would miss Tilly, of course. And even, strangely, Gwen. But Boston was only a ferry ride away, and they could keep a constant flow of visits both ways quite easily.

She would leave the house, and all the money, to Gwen.

She had found a new job easily. Her fund-raising efforts for the hospital had been so successful that, about a year ago, a friend in Boston had tried to hire her to do community relations for the public television station there. She had, foolishly, turned him down—just as she'd turned down every other job offer through the years.

She had never admitted it to herself, but she knew now why she had always said no. She had wanted to be here, right where he had left her, in case Adam ever decided to come home. She had been as pitiful as the captain's wives who had once paced the widow's walks on top of these old Pringle Island houses, watching for their husbands to return from sea.

But no longer. She wasn't going to cower here for another decade, nursing her broken heart, feeding it bits and pieces of memories. The stables, where she and Adam had first made love. The ferry landing, where she had wept and clung, and begged him not to leave. The chapel where she had married Malcolm, her heart full of tears. The hospital where she had lost the baby, her soul cauterized and disbelieving.

And, of course, the Tunnel of Love, where she had dreamed her most beautiful dream one last time.

That was what Pringle Island was to her—a mausoleum of memory. If she stayed, she would always live with ghosts.

So she wouldn't stay. She had called her friend in Boston, and the job was still open. She had taken it on the spot.

Was she scared? Yes. Was she excited? Not yet. But the excitement would come, in a little while, when the wound Adam had inflicted wasn't so fresh. When it didn't hurt quite so much.

"Lacy, I've been thinking." Gwen was swinging her feet from the desk, admiring her chartreuse sandals, which she had paired with a sexy green sundress. She was almost herself again, Lacy thought—although she noticed a hint of maturity in Gwen's expression that seemed new. It suited her.

"You're going to knock over one of those bottled ships if you're not careful," Lacy said.

Gwen scowled. Mature or not, she still hated to be bossed around, apparently. So Lacy held up her hands placatingly. "Okay, okay. They're your ships. Break them all if you like. So, tell me. What have you been thinking?"

Gwen looked hesitant. "Just...are you sure you don't want me to talk to him? I mean, I really caused this whole thing, and I could explain that I—"

"No." Lacy propped the picture carefully against the doorway, ready to be picked up later in the day. "I meant what I said, Gwen. I don't want you to talk to Adam about this. What happened between us isn't your fault. It's a flaw, a fatal flaw, in our relationship. It's over. Period. I'm ready to move on."

"Yeah?" Gwen tossed her curls behind her shoulder. "Well, you don't sleep. I hear you tossing in there all night."

Lacy sighed. "I will," she said. "It's just going to take some time. Besides, I'd rather do without a little sleep than go beg a man to forgive me for something I never did. Wouldn't you? And he's probably back in New York by now anyhow."

"He's not." Gwen smiled hopefully. "Travis told me he doesn't leave until Friday. So..."

"No." Lacy gave Gwen her most repressive glare. *"N. O."*

Gwen subsided briefly, obviously trying to think of a good argument. But just then the telephone rang shrilly. Gwen jumped for it, knocking over one of the ships, just as Lacy had predicted.

Lacy lunged to try to catch the bottle, but she wasn't fast enough. The ship crashed to the floor, and pieces of glass flew everywhere.

"Oh, my God," Gwen said, horrified, staring at the mess. She looked toward the doorway, as if she half-expected her father to come bursting in, vibrating with fury. He would have eviscerated her over this. "Oh, my God."

But Malcolm was gone. No one would berate her for her clumsiness.

Murmuring reassuring noises, Lacy bent down to check the broken bits. Amazingly, though the glass had completely shattered, the ship was fine. Lacy picked it up gently, realizing that this was the first time she'd been able to appreciate just how delicate and beautiful its artistry really was.

For the first time, it was free.

There was a message in that, she thought, touching the tiny, intricate masts and the perfect, wind-swollen sails. The bottle hadn't been protecting the ship. It had merely been confining it.

But, all amateur philosophizing aside, the telephone was still ringing. Lacy reached across Gwen, who was bending down, hurrying to scoop up the broken shards of glass as if she still feared she'd be caught.

"Hello?"

"Is this Ms. Morgan?"

Lacy recognized the refined, well-modulated voice immediately. It was Claire Scott Tyndale. Lacy could even hear the spaniel, Winston, yipping in the background.

"Yes." She set the ship down carefully on the mantel, where it pointed its prow bravely forward. "Hello, Claire. I'm very glad you called."

A pause crackled over the telephone lines. "I almost didn't," Claire said finally, her manner as straightforward as ever. As much like Tilly as ever. "I wasn't sure. I'm still not sure. But I've thought over what you said. And if you still think it's a good idea, I'd like very much to meet Mrs. Barnhardt."

Did she think it was a good idea? It was the best. Her mind raced ahead, thinking of Tilly's joy.

"Ms. Morgan? Do you think Mrs. Barnhardt would still like to meet me?"

"Tilly," Lacy corrected encouragingly, a real bubble of happiness rising in her for the first time in two days. "No one calls her Mrs. Barnhardt, Claire. Especially not her own granddaughter."

LACY WASN'T AT THE hospital. Kara Karlin told Adam that he had just missed her. She had taken some letters to the printer, and then she had planned to pick up some dinner and take it to Tilly's house.

But Tilly said she had come already, and then left again. Tilly obviously knew that things had gone badly wrong between him and Lacy. Her manner was frosty and politely furious. It had taken all his humble coaxing to make her tell him that Lacy had been headed to the printer.

It took another five minutes of assuring Tilly that he meant Lacy no harm, but finally she thawed. The printer, she said, was on Main Street. Lacy often picked up a summer salad at the deli next door, unless if was after nine, in which case it would be closed, and then she might try the Chinese take-out place, which was—

Adam looked at his watch. Eight-thirty. He thanked Tilly, kissing her cheek quickly and then hurrying out to his rental car, which he'd left running in the drive. If he took the back roads, maybe he could catch her.

Main Street at dusk had a gilded old-world charm, with the lights just appearing in shop windows. The quaint streetlamps were still pale flames against the deep blue sky, and the sinking sun painted the cobblestone street in shining gold leaf.

This late on a weekday evening, many of the stores were already closed. Only a few people still ambled along the sidewalks, mostly stragglers, or joggers or window-shoppers on their way to a late dinner at the Lost Horizon.

Was she one of them? He pressed the brake, slowing to check every passerby. Old ladies on the iron benches, eating ice cream. Two teenagers, kissing feverishly in a shadowed alcove. A father rolling two babies in a stroller. Three middle-aged woman, suntanned and laughing loudly, obviously walking home in a pleasant post-margarita high.

But where was Lacy? Could Tilly have been wrong? What if Lacy was on the other side of the island—or back at home, refusing to answer the telephone? Frustration made him thump the wheel. Surely Tilly wouldn't have deliberately misled him, as punishment. Surely she could tell that he meant only to—

And then suddenly, there she was.

She stood alone, in front of Island Travel, looking at posters of downhill skiers and big red cruises. She wore a loose-fitting summer dress of the purest blue. Her hair was unbound, falling to the tips of her shoulder blades. Even from the back, she was the most beautiful woman he had ever seen.

For a moment he could only idle there in the middle of the street, frozen in place by the sight of her. His mind raced, wondering how he would manage to say the things he needed so desperately to say. Wondering if she'd even be willing to listen.

Someone honked, annoyed to find him blocking the way. Lacy turned at the sound, and she saw him. He quickly slid the car into the nearest empty parking space, afraid that she might run from him.

But she didn't. Though it took him an endless two minutes to park and walk back, she was still standing in front of the travel agency, her plastic container of summer salad clutched in both hands. He had thought of a dozen persuasive beginnings. But when he looked into her wide blue-gray eyes, with their deep shadows of unhappiness circling them, he couldn't remember a single one.

"Hi," he said. He looked awkwardly at the travel posters. "Thinking of going somewhere?"

She gave him an empty gaze. "Yes," she said. "Actually, I am. I'm leaving in just a few days."

He felt a cold spasm in his gut, thinking of how it would have felt if Tilly had told him that. *She's gone,* Tilly could have said. *She left yesterday, and no one knows where she is.* He imagined the frustrated panic, the sense that he'd tear the entire globe to little pieces if that's what it took to find her.

Was that how she'd felt when he left ten years ago?

"Where are you going?"

She just looked at him. *It's none of your business,* the silence said, though she didn't speak the words.

"Lacy." He couldn't let this happen. What were the magic words that would stop it? "Lacy, I came to find you because I wanted to tell you that I'm sorry."

"For what?"

"For all the stupid, cruel things I said." He shook his head, as if he could shake the past away. "I'm so sorry, Lacy. Can you ever forgive me?"

"There's nothing to forgive," she said coolly.

"Yes, there is." He was horrified to realize that, except for the dark shadows around her eyes, she looked exactly like the ice maiden he had met at Tilly Barnhardt's fund-raiser a month ago.

Oh, God. Had she retreated into that frozen shell once more? She would have built the fortress thicker this time, and she would be prepared for any attack he might have planned.

"Yes, there is," he repeated. "I was—I was a bastard. Everything you said was true. I was judgmental and sanctimonious. I should have trusted you."

"Nonsense." She shifted her box to a more comfortable position. "We slept together, Adam, that's all. It doesn't place you under any obligation to *trust* me."

"No." He held her eyes with his. "But being in love with you does."

She made a low, cynical noise, and he saw her move as if to turn away. Desperately, he reached out and grabbed her hand.

"It's true. Please listen to me, Lacy."

She didn't pull away, but she didn't relax, either. They stood, delicately balanced between the two forces—a momentary armed truce.

But it was something. It was time, which he needed desperately to plead his case.

"You have to believe me," he said, though he knew that was a lie. She didn't have to. She might well choose to jerk her arm away and disappear forever. "I love you, Lacy. I have always loved you. I will never forgive myself for abandoning you. Whatever hell you went through, you endured it alone. And that was my fault. *All* my fault."

She didn't speak. But she still hadn't pulled away, so he allowed himself to hope. The sun was gilding her hair, and catching on the soft folds of her sleeveless dress. Maybe it was a trick of the warm, golden light, but she didn't seem quite as cold now.

He couldn't quite remember his eloquent scripted arguments, and what he could remember didn't sound right. Perhaps, he thought, it would be better just to stumble through, letting the ebb and flow of her reactions guide him. Maybe however unpolished these unrehearsed pleas might be, maybe she could at least recognize that they were honest, and from his heart.

"I was a fool to leave you ten years ago. Worse. I was a selfish, egotistical bastard. I was so busy chasing my own personal dreams. I guess I thought you'd wait forever, if necessary, for me to catch that dream. I never once seriously considered the possibility that I might be destroying the bigger dream, the one we had shared together."

He had let his voice grow conspicuously impassioned. People were passing by, turning their heads curiously. But he didn't let it stop him. At least she was listening.

"But I'm not that big a fool anymore, Lacy. Yesterday, when I was getting ready to go to New York, I couldn't face it. Just the thought of leaving here without you nearly killed me. And it made me realize the truth."

"Which is?" She sounded guarded, determinedly unimpressed.

"The truth is that I don't care what happened before. It just doesn't matter. I don't need any details. I don't need any explanations. Because I *know* you, Lacy. I know that you are gentle, and loving, and full of more honor and courage than anyone I've ever met. Whatever you did, you did because you thought it was the only choice you had. The only choice I had left you."

She made a low, unhappy sound. Had he said the wrong thing? He searched frantically, looking for a new way to put it. Surely somewhere was the phrase that would convince her, that would thaw her....

"Lacy, can't we just find a way to forget the past? What you did, what I did—can't we—"

"I didn't do anything," she said suddenly.

He looked at her, worried. Her hand had begun to tremble slightly. Her eyes were gleaming in the sunset, as if she might weep melted-gold tears.

"Lacy." He could hardly bear the sight. Hadn't she cried enough for one lifetime? If she would only let him, he would devote his life to making sure she never cried again. "Lacy, it's all right. I swear to you. It doesn't matter."

"I didn't do anything," she repeated, as if she hadn't heard him. She suddenly looked so lost, her eyes so wide and vulnerable, as if she were caught in an endlessly repeating circle of the past. "I want to tell you. Can you bear to listen?"

"Of course," he said, hoping it was true. "Of course I can."

She put her take-out box carefully on the ground. Then, taking her hand slowly from his, she moved to sit against the edge of the window box, as if she didn't have the strength to tell her story and stand erect at the same time.

The box was filled with red and yellow snapdragons, which were beginning to fade to gray in the deepening twilight. She feathered her fingers across the small, rounded blossoms, obviously stalling. Finally she took a deep breath and began.

"I didn't choose to get rid of our child, Adam. It was just one of those horrible, unpredictable disasters." She inhaled sharply. "I was only about four months along. It was so early. And yet already the baby felt so real to me. I could imagine how it would look. Like you, I hoped. With your blue eyes."

She shook her head. "That's all I had asked for. I wanted someday to be able to look into your blue eyes again."

He moved closer to her, sharing the shadow of the alcove. He wasn't sure he could speak.

"They never could tell me what went wrong. They just didn't know. I simply began to…to bleed." She closed her eyes. "And there was this pain."

"Lacy." His blood began to run strangely slow and cold. "Lacy, no."

"Malcolm got me to the hospital as soon as he could. You have to give him credit for that, even though obviously he hadn't ever wanted the baby. He did try. But the doctors couldn't do anything. The pain just got worse, and worse."

She took another ragged breath. "And then it was over. Just like that. This little being, this little life that was the only thing I had left of you—"

He made a strangled sound, and he knelt in front of her, pulling her toward him roughly.

"Oh, my God," he said hoarsely. "Oh, my love."

She held herself stiffly for a few desperate seconds, and then, all at once, he felt the resistance flow out of her. She leaned down and touched his face.

"After that, I couldn't make myself care about much of anything. I offered to divorce Malcolm. He had married me to protect our child—and then, suddenly there was no child." Her hand trembled slightly.

"But he didn't want a divorce, did he?" Adam knew the answer to that one. Malcolm Morgan had wanted Lacy from the beginning. He had only been waiting for the brass ring to circle close enough that he could reach out and grab it. And Adam, fool that he was, had provided the opportunity by leaving town.

"No. He didn't want a divorce. He insisted that he deserved more thanks than that—after all, he had been willing to give another man's child a name, and a home, and security. And he was right. So I stayed. I entertained his friends, cared for his home, let him show me off like a trick pony. I went to school, and I became whatever he wanted me to be." She swallowed hard. "Except a mother. I refused him that."

Adam's mind flinched from the thought of those five wretched years she had spent serving time as Malcolm Morgan's trophy bride.

But if she could endure the reality, the least he could do it face the idea. He imagined her waking up, every day, knowing she was trapped. He thought of that beautiful home, that flawless wardrobe, that whole town full of people who envied Malcolm Morgan for having such a perfect wife.

She had played her role without missing a cue. Malcolm had persuaded her that he had "saved" her, and because her honor was without measure, Lacy had paid her debt a thousand times over.

"I'm sorry," he said again, his voice strangely thick, almost unrecognizable. "I'm sorry I left you here, with no one to turn to except a man who would exact such a terrible price for helping you."

She didn't speak. It was as if she had worn herself out telling the tragic story, and she could only fold herself limply against him, borrowing his strength until she could recover her own.

"You have every right to hate me. I can't ask for your forgiveness, Lacy, because I don't deserve it. But I want you to know that I love you. I have thought about you every minute of the past ten years, even after I knew you belonged to another man."

She turned her face into his neck, and her grip on his shoulders tightened. But still she didn't speak.

He touched her soft, dusky hair. "It isn't enough, I know that. Love can't bring back the ten years you lost. It can't bring back our child. But I want you to know this. I will always love you. Even if you tell me to go away, even if I never see you again, I—"

Finally she lifted her head, and the look in her eyes startled him. It looked like panic.

Could that mean…? He cupped his hands around her face. "I'll do whatever you say, Lacy. I'll go if you ask me to. Is that what you want?"

She didn't respond. He asked again. "Do you want me to go away?"

She seemed to be searching his face, as if she might find the answer written somewhere on his features. And it was, he thought. The answer was love. And it was written all over him—if only she could see it.

"I lost you once, and I survived," she said quietly. "And I'm stronger now. Perhaps I could survive it again."

He held his breath. He braced himself for the worst. He had promised that he would leave, if she said the word. But now that she seemed ready to ask him to do exactly that, he wondered whether he would be able to honor such an insanely noble vow.

"You are the strongest woman I've ever known," he said. "I don't think you need me, Lacy. The truth is that I am the one who needs you."

"I am strong," she agreed. "But even so—" She hesitated, and he thought he saw the first ghost of a smile beginning to play at her lips. "Even so, I'm not sure I'm strong enough to come right out and ask the man I love to leave me."

His body understood the words before his mind did. Relief spread like electricity through his veins. Then, as her message finally reached his brain, he exhaled the breath he'd been holding for what seemed like forever.

She didn't want him to go. He tightened his hands and pulled her in closer, until their lips were only inches apart. His whole body tightened, wanting her. Loving her.

"How strong are you, Lacy? Are you strong enough to come right out and ask me to *stay?*"

"I don't know," she said, and he recognized the gentle lilt of laughter in her voice. It took him back ten years, to when life was always soft with laughter, and with Lacy. "Am I?"

"Try." He brushed his lips over hers, deliberately building heat. "Try, Lacy. I want to hear you say it."

Slowly, she closed her eyes. She tilted toward him, bringing her lips even closer, so close he felt the sweet warmth of her breath mingling with his.

"Will you stay, Adam?" Her words moved against him like soft fire. "Will you stay forever this time?"

"Yes." In the brief moment before intoxicating joy claimed his senses, in the agonizing second before he claimed the promise of her lips, he found the clarity to answer. "I will stay with you forever. And forever. And a day."

EPILOGUE

GWEN WAS LATE, OF COURSE, so when Lacy and Adam arrived at the house they let themselves in, using Lacy's old key. Adam, who was carrying the suitcases, whistled as he stepped into the foyer. Lacy couldn't make it past the threshold, stunned by the transformation within.

Apparently the locks were the only things Gwen hadn't changed in this historical house. Gone were the antique furnishings, the bottled ships, the seascapes, the maroon flocked wallpaper.

Instead, the walls were colored in a marvelous, soothing shade of pale green with sparkling white woodwork. The paintings were bold and modern, the pine floors stripped to a simplicity that complemented the uncluttered wooden furnishings.

The new atmosphere was light, sophisticated and contemporary. Lacy loved it. She took a deep breath, as if testing the air. Yes. It was clean. Fresh. She could sense real happiness here.

Of course, in the year she and Adam had been married, she had found happiness just about everywhere she went. It had glittered on the canals of Italy, where they had honeymooned. It lit the walls of her new office, at the public television station. It gleamed from every room in their gorgeous new Boston town house.

Especially from the nursery. The little blue nursery with its pale wooden rocking chair and its white, lace-ruffled cradle. The nursery that would, in about six weeks or so, be welcoming home their son. Lacy put her hand on her stomach, sharing her joy with him now. He shifted sleepily, as if he understood.

Adam, who had been exploring the parlor, came back and smiled at her. "When Gwen decides to change something, she means business, doesn't she? I don't think she's left a single inch of this house untouched."

Lacy nodded. But he was wrong. She could see one small thing that remained from the old days. On the mantel, right in front of the colorful brushstrokes of a very expensive modern master, sat the tiny full-masted ship that had once fallen from a table and found its way to freedom.

Adam came up behind her and moving her hair out of the way, kissed her neck. "Do you mind, sweetheart? Do you regret letting her have the house?"

"Of course not," she said softly, reaching back to run her fingers through his hair. "I couldn't be happier."

He put his arms around her, smoothing his hands possessively over her stomach. "Good," he murmured, nibbling kisses against her ear. "The two of us consider it our mission in life to make sure you're always happy."

A booming roar broke the moment, as a noisy machine rumbled into the front drive. There was a small crunching sound, followed by a sputtering engine and a low curse from a feminine voice. Adam and Lacy looked out the window to see that Gwen had rammed her motorcycle into the back fender of their car.

Adam's kiss turned into a light chuckle. "The Hell's Angel Schoolmarm has arrived, I see."

Gwen pulled off her helmet, releasing curls everywhere. And then she dropped her kickstand and swung her long leg over the seat in a rather graceful dismount.

"Well, she's getting better," Lacy said, smiling. She knew Adam didn't care about the ding in his fender. He had grown to love this gawky, passionate young woman as much as she did.

Gwen came loping up to the house, swinging her backpack full of school assignments from one hand, her helmet from the other. She let out a whoop of delight at the sight of her visitors.

"Oh, my God, look how *big* you are!" She squeezed Lacy in an uninhibited hug, then patted her stomach. "It won't be long before Junior can ride behind me on the Harley!"

"Only about a hundred years," Adam commented dryly.

Gwen stuck out her tongue at him, but then she reached up and gave him a big hug, too. Lacy felt a strange lump in her throat, watching Gwen's easy affectionate nature. No wonder she had been so rebellious, she thought. All that love, and no one to shower it on.

Gwen peeked around the corner, into the kitchen. "Where's Travis?"

Adam shrugged. "Probably still out on the golf course. He arrived this morning, I think, and he said he was going to play a few holes until you got off work."

Gwen grimaced. "God. If he hasn't corrected that slice yet, a few holes could take him all day." She dropped her helmet on the foyer table. "I put you two in my old room. Is that okay?"

"Of course," Lacy said. "And actually, I think I could use a nap already. I'm such a slug these days. I sleep all the time."

"Well, that's perfectly natural," Gwen said firmly. "Your body is doing a lot of extra work here at the end. Are you taking your vitamin supplements? You know, the baby is just going to drain away everything he needs without even asking. And then you won't have enough for yourself." She paused, grinning. "Sorry. Can you tell I just took a class on this topic?"

"Never would have guessed," Lacy lied happily. Gwen never ceased to amaze her. Not only was she working full time for Tina Seville—who had miraculously ceased to dislike the suddenly wealthy, landed Morgan heiress. Gwen was also taking Internet classes to work toward her teaching certificate. She'd own her own school one day, Lacy was sure. And her wonderful, creative talents would run that snobby Tina right out of town.

"Oh, by the way, there's a card here somewhere for you. From Tilly. She says to tell you she'll definitely be back in time for the baby." Gwen eyed Lacy's stomach suspiciously. "Although she'd better hurry, that's all I can say."

"Don't you dare tell her that," Lacy ordered. "I want her to have all the time she can with Claire." A few months after Claire's baby had been born, Tilly and her granddaughter had traveled to Florida for a get-acquainted visit, and they hadn't come home yet. The comfortable intimacy the two had already established filled Lacy with a profound contentment.

"Besides," she assured Gwen, "I saw the doctor just yesterday, and he says it's definitely another month at least."

Adam wrapped his arms around her once again, resting his cheek against her hair. "But Gwen might be right, sweetheart. The doctor just might underestimate how eager our son is to meet his beautiful mother."

He kissed her collarbone, and then her neck. Lacy turned in his embrace, winding her arms around his neck, suddenly so filled with love for him that she could hardly breathe.

"I love you, Adam Kendall," she said, smiling into his sexy sapphire eyes.

"Not as much as I love you, Mrs. Kendall," he answered, leaning down, as she had known he would, to kiss her waiting lips.

"Oh, *please*," Gwen cried out in utter disgust. "Could you two possibly pull yourselves apart long enough to take this upstairs?"

Adam winked at her, then reached down and scooped Lacy into his arms. "It would be our pleasure," he said. "We thought you'd never ask."

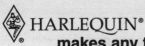